...and then along came Rudy!

For my wife Jill.

...and then along came Rudy!

A Novel by
Sam Schichter

LOON IN BALLOON

A LOON IN BALLOON BOOK

... AND THEN ALONG CAME RUDY!
© 2006 Sam Schichter

Library and Archives Canada Cataloguing in Publication
Schichter, Sam, 1949-
        --And then along came Rudy / Sam Schichter.
ISBN-13: 978-0-9737497-2-4
ISBN-10: 0-9737497-2-5
        I. Title.
PS8637.C434A54 2006   C813'.6   C2006-905423-1

Published by: Loon in Balloon Inc.
                     Suite #3-513
                     133 Weber Street North
                     Waterloo, Ontario
                     Canada
                     N2J 3G9

Cover and interior design by Steve Penner

Printed and bound in Canada by
Friesens Corporation
Altona, Manitoba, Canada

FIRST EDITION
987654321

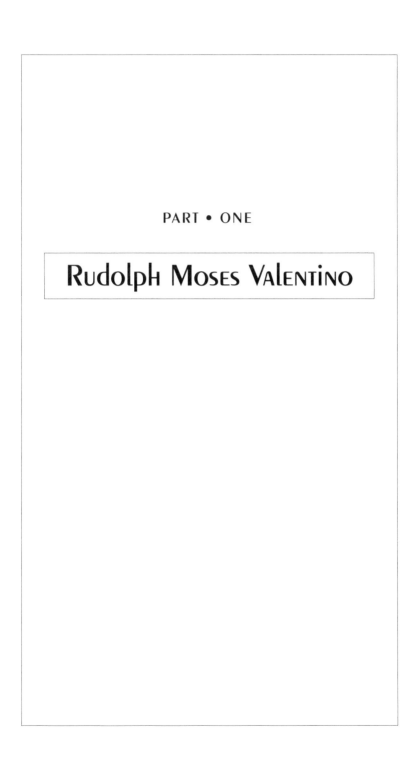

PART • ONE

Rudolph Moses Valentino

Chapter 1

I returned to my seat and heard the captain tell us that we'd be touching down in twenty minutes. The "Fasten Your Seat Belt" sign flashed. As I heard the sound of the buckle securing me in, I felt a tightness in my chest. Only twenty minutes of freedom left.

I'd come back and nothing had changed. The airport looked the same, the people looked the same and ... Ma! Ma? I looked at the woman who had been my mother for twenty-one years and was not at all surprised that she would meet me at Customs. She was squeezed into a lilac pantsuit that was one size too small, and her carefully teased jet-black hair was starting to frizz from her frantic attempts to find me.

"Rudy... Rudy, let me look at you. I think you've grown," she said in her whiny, high-pitched Polish-Yiddish-Brooklynese.

I tried to snap out of my bad mood.

"Ma, how did you manage to get in here?"

"What's the matter, Rudy? Nine months you've been gone and already you're ashamed of me?"

"It's just that... never mind. Where's Dad?"

I knew exactly where my father was. Standing against the glass partition, his face creased and turning red trying to catch a glimpse of us. He hadn't aged in twenty years. Slight, balding and dressed in his usual short-sleeve white shirt – impeccably pressed by Ma – grey flannel pants and nondescript tie, it was comforting to see his familiar presence. I picked up my knapsack and headed towards my father, my mother practically jogging behind me in her high heels. I reached the partition and smiled at Dad. He smiled back, his face lit up, and the three of us, my mother and I on one side of the glass wall, my father on the other side, walked towards the entrance.

"You must be tired, Rudy," my father said as we left Kennedy and headed out for Brooklyn. "Jet lag."

"Maybe," my mother cut in. "But what excuse, if any, can you give me for the once-in-a-while postcards?"

"Ma, come on. I didn't always feel like writing a letter."

"Always feel! One letter in nine months!"

"I sent you postcards from every country." I was beginning to feel trapped already.

"Pictures of museums I wasn't waiting for. They all look the same. And your father? Don't you think he worried?" Here we go again. Should I get myself involved in a futile argument, one I can't possibly win and one that will continue for the rest of my life every time my mother and I are in the same room and Europe is mentioned? No. I'll ignore it and create a diversion.

"So, Dad, how do the Giants look?"

"Pretty good, Rudy. All they need is a quarterback and we might have a winner."

"All I'm saying, Rudy, is that we worried plenty about you," my mother relentlessly continued.

I stuck to my strategy.

"Did you go to their first game?"

"Of course. I haven't missed a game in thirty years."

"Nine months away," Ma continued, "and all you two can talk about is football. What is happening to this world? What?"

"So, Ma, how's Julie and Leon?" I asked, but only to be polite. I couldn't have cared less about the two of them. They were only my self-centred sister and her pompous husband.

"Only after football does your sister appear in your mind? Only after!"

"Esther, he's tired. He didn't think."

"All right. Maybe." Her cheeks seemed flushed.

"So, Ma, tell me already." If she's talking about someone else, she's not attacking me.

"Your brother-in-law," she began proudly, "is doing so well that he now drives a fancy Jag-u-ar sportscar and they just bought a condominium in Manhattan and up till yesterday they were in the Catskills, swimming, if you don't mind, in the lake that comes right up to their summer home which they just bought four weeks ago."

"What happened? Julie win the lottery? Leon settle a lawsuit with a patient?"

"Leon's practice is doing well and all of his investments came through. He also had the good luck to find a bright accountant. In any case, your sister is living the life of Riley all because she had the good sense to marry a very enterprising young man who works hard and is not afraid to take chances in life." She gave my father a stern look.

We approached the driveway and I stared at the old house. The blinds were drawn in order to keep the sun from discolouring the red couch that sat just beneath the living room window. The lawn was being watered and the three of us ran up the walk to avoid getting wet. My father opened the door and declared, "Welcome home, Rudy! We missed you!" He hugged me and planted a kiss on my cheek.

I entered cautiously. This had been my home for twenty-one years but all I wanted to do was go back to the small hostel in the south of France.

"So, Rudy, you want to have a nap before supper?"

"May I remind you, Morris," Ma broke in, "that my brisket is timed and has to be eaten in twenty minutes, otherwise it gets dry."

"Maybe I'll just take a shower."

"Make it a short one. No daydreaming, just washing."

I walked towards the bathroom and opened the door. Everything was as it had been: my father's razor was still near the soap dish, my mother's hairbrush a few inches away from the toothpaste. Even the cologne I had left behind was still on the lower shelf of the medicine cabinet, in the right hand corner. I quickly looked in the mirror and took a quick inventory: 5' 8", slim, dark brown wavy hair, long sideburns, a carefully cultivated tan and perfectly straight teeth from four years of braces put on by my second cousin – Dr. Irving Mellman. All in all, I was ready to take on the world.

I undressed, stepped into the bathtub, closed the curtains and turned the shower spigot upwards. The water was hot and soothing. I closed my eyes and utterly lost myself. Paris... Nice... Marseilles...

That's it! Europe! What better place to write a novel? Hemingway did it. I, too – Rudolf Moses Valentino Petinsky – will become an expatriate and write in cafés overlooking the Left Bank. Roam the underground sewers of Paris looking for memories of a bygone day. Sip martinis on the Champs Elysées. Guzzle wine while watching girls do the can-can in Montmartre. Search through the Louvre for inspiration. Visit the countryside in pursuit of Balzacian heroines. It'll be terrific. Why didn't I think of this before? It just sounds perfect. The right move. Fate. Six months, maybe even a year. Maybe more? We'll see how things go. God, this is terrific. Fantastic! Ma, Dad, see you. Leaving for Europe. Of course I'll write. No, no, not just postcards. A letter every week? But Ma, there won't be that much to say. All right, all right, once a week. I promise. Like clockwork.

Paris was sensational; but I couldn't seem to meet anyone. At night I would hang around Place Pigalle, munching on Parisian hot-dogs, hoping to meet a hooker, yet knowing that I couldn't possibly afford it. Money was tight. I was existing on pickles, peppers, tomatoes, potatoes, cauliflower, lettuce, cabbage, huge amounts of baguette and cheese, and regular hand-outs from a great aunt.

My great-aunt saved my life. On her recommendation, I found a room in an old apartment building not too far from her place and right across the street from the Métro. I promised myself that, before I began to write my novel, I would set off in search of the Left Bank.

Trouble is, I couldn't find it. Believe me, I asked people. La Banque Gauche? La Bankee du Leftee? But my French was as pitiful as their English. Eventually I gave up and concentrated on my writing in my Parisian hovel.

At first I wrote quite a bit of poetry. My poems were not to be shown to the outside world. I was experimenting:

Oranges: Tangerine-flaked
People: Purple-hazed
Chipmunks: Blue-faked
Dandelions: Chartreuse-dazed

That sort of thing. I couldn't seem to sustain a thought long enough to form a sentence. Masturbating and dreaming took up most of my time. I imagined coming home with a complete portfolio of avante-garde poems, submitting them to the Guggenheim Foundation for a grant, and receiving the unexpected reply that I was to become the next Poet Laureate of the United States.

Eventually my writing habits matured. I was now composing carefully thought-out pieces. My search for the perfect word often consumed the better part of the day:

Just think of all the time you spend
upon a bed on which you depend — dreaming.
It helps you mend
the life you spend — dreaming.

After five months of writing poetry, I finally made an attempt at prose. After all, poetry would not make me a millionaire and, to be sure, I was after money. I wanted one of those chic, thin women – with amazing asses – who walked along the Champs Elysées. I instinctively knew that a poet would mean nothing to those Gucci-bagged, Pucci-shoed women. They would not Fucci a poet; they were after a novelist.

But I couldn't come up with a plot, or even a theme, or any of the one thousand and one ingredients that make up a genuine novel. The best I could do was short existentialist essays filled with brilliant hidden meaning. I had visions of communicating with Jean-Paul Sartre and being heralded as the Kierkegaard of our time:

Life is like a puzzle and we are the gigantic
pieces trying to fit into this maze and just
when we find the way to slip in, the design
changes. It's hard enough as it is: being
shoved around, pulled and pushed,
bullied and neglected, propelled and
pressurized. Must we suffer so much in
our continual search to fit in properly?
Must we always try to find the zig-zag
path? Are we never supposed to win
the game? Are we always to remain
failures? Are we always supposed to be
looking and seeking and inquiring and
pursuing? And what if you don't realise
that, in order to exist, you have to play the
game? And what if you don't realize that,
in order to play the game, you have to learn
the game? And what if you don't realize
that, in order to learn the game, you have
to master the rules? And what if you don't
realize that, in order to master the rules, you
have to have a sense of organization. A sense
of discipline. A sense of balance and rhythm.
Let's face it. Nobody extends you a formal
invitation. You instinctively know that you
must play, but what if your instincts let
you down? It happens, you know. Asylums are
full. Standing room only. And then what?
Back to a never-ending beginning? A never-
ending finale? A wasteland?

Mornings, I would walk up and down the alleyways, through
the grand avenue, past the impromptu marketplaces, searching
for colourful episodes to put in my novel. But I soon became

disillusioned, as well as bewildered. Disillusioned because I was not writing anything of value; bewildered because there were too many of my kind in Paris. Too many would-be Hemingways. I felt they were crowding me. Not letting me be an original. So I decided to push on. But where? Opening up my map of Europe, I skimmed through the countries. Belgium – only has waffles to offer. Holland – too many canals. Norway – too cold. Luxembourg – too small. Spain – too sunny. Italy – too much tutti-fruity art. Greece – too many ruins. Germany – too... too... German? Mozart Germany? Schiller Germany? Concentration camp Germany? No. I couldn't. My father wouldn't forgive me. My mother would think I had completely lost my mind.

"Go, go to Europe, Rudy. If you have to go, go. But for God's sake, NOT ONE FOOT inside that filthy country!"

"What country, Ma?"

"What country, he asks? Did I bring up an idiot? Or worse, a gentile?"

"Ma, can't you even say the name?"

"I don't ever want to say the name. Ask your father if he'd be happy with you inside that... that... country."

"Rudy," my father said, "Go to Europe. Explore, experience, but not in Germany. A Jew has no business being in Germany. Maybe your mother and I are old-fashioned, but we know what we're talking about."

"Dad, the war's been over for a long time."

"Rudy, time isn't a cure for everything. Not in this case."

"THEY STILL HAVE NAZIS IN THAT COUNTRY!" My mother shrieked, her chest heaving.

"Esther, calm down. You'll snap something."

"Ma, there are Nazis everywhere. In every country."

"Does that mean you have to go to where they have the most? Where's your sense, Rudolf Moses?"

Damn it. How much longer would I let my mother manipulate my life? I knew she meant well. I knew she didn't want me to suffer. But she overprotected me. Smothered me. I didn't even feel the air I breathed was the same as that which others breathed. I was sure my mother had gotten to it first and purified it – taken out all those polluted particles. It was high time I started living life my own way! If I wanted to see Germany, I'd see it. Damn it, I'd see it all. Ma had been running my life for too long. It had to stop. Right here. Right now. Otherwise I'd remain an insecure dreamer wandering around Europe.

I turned off the water and slowly parted the curtains in the shower window. The house directly beside ours blocked my view of the sunset but it didn't matter. Nothing mattered when I thought back to Germany…

As I stood outside Dachau, I wanted to scream. I had heard all the stories. They were nothing new to me. I had lost grandparents, uncles, aunts and cousins in these camps. I knew, as much as my father would permit himself to tell me, about his four years in Dachau. I knew from him about my mother hiding in someone's basement with her family – for two years. How she had fled one night, when the pounding at the door began. How she had run and run, following her brothers and father, who led the way to freedom. How she had turned around, for some inexplicable reason, and saw her mother in the clutches of the Gestapo. And then a blank followed by a nightmare and waking up in a death camp — disoriented, screaming, being beaten. Another blank. Another nightmare. Another two years. I knew the stories. I had heard them over and over again. Now I was standing on the land. The very land where the SS made their selections as to who would live and who would die.

Here was the fence, the wall, the barbed wire, the searchlights, the watchtowers, the machine guns, the dogs, the roll call area, the experimentation centres, the pits, the crematoria.

And at the very edge of the camp, beyond everything, lay the gas chambers. Inside, only a large room with fake shower nozzles. Nothing else. But on the ceilings, fingernail scratches. Millions of them.

I threw up.

Then I ran away.

I went back to my hotel in Munich, feeling hate and rage and wanting to kill every German alive. Just drop a bomb on the whole country. The whole goddamn country.

I packed my bags and took the first train out. Somehow I ended up in the south of France, in a daze. I rented a cheap room in a cheap hotel and locked myself in during the day. I wrote a letter home, a few postcards to friends and an outline of my long-awaited novel. My bestseller. This was it. Do or die. No more sightseeing, no more wandering, no more silly poetry or directionless existentialism. The kick in the rear end had finally come. It was time to put up or shut up.

I heard a pounding on the bathroom door and then my name being called. I saw the doorknob being twisted frantically. I shook myself from my reverie, wrapped a towel around me, and opened the door.

"Why is the door locked?" I was confronted by my mother. "Don't you know by now that you never lock a bathroom door when bathing? God forbid you should have an accident. How would I get in?"

"Call the firemen? Or Larry the Locksmith?"

"Funny. Always making jokes. And why, may I ask, are you not yet dressed?"

"I have a lot on my mind."

"Good. So you'll have plenty to say at supper."

I walked into the living room. My sister Julie rose from her chair, careful not to wrinkle her pale orange Bill Blass outfit. Her jewellery and her Farrah Fawcett hair sparkled in the glow of the matching red velvet lamps sitting on the new matching end tables. Unable to give me a welcoming smile because of the layers of foundation on her face (bad case of teenage acne), she settled for giving me a peck on the cheek.

I shook hands with her husband, Leon, amused as always by his outrageous fashion sense. His powder blue leisure suit looked ridiculous on his heavy-set frame. He obviously couldn't figure out which decade he preferred as he still wore Beatle boots and gold chains adorned with peace signs.

My mother ushered everyone to the dining room. The brisket sat in the middle of the table on a sterling silver platter, surrounded by vegetables. At each setting was a plate of chicken soup, steam rising upwards. I thought to myself how nice it must be to be steam: floating up and away, dissolving.

Leon plunged into his soup. My father interrupted him. The blessing hadn't been said yet. Leon protested. My father told him that after the meal, when his stomach was full, he'd argue with him. But first the blessing.

"So, Rudy," Julie began, "did Mom tell you about all our good fortune?"

"Yes."

"Everything?" She looked at Ma despondently, wanting to say, *you could have left something for me.* "Our new car? Our condominium? Our chalet in the Catskills?"

"Yes."

She pouted. Not knowing what else to say, she continued eating her soup.

"I see you redecorated, Ma. Looks nice."

"You know me, Rudy. I'm always busy with the house. Something gets old, I like to replace it. Your father, on the other hand, would keep everything. If it was up to him, we'd still have the furniture we had in Poland."

"And what was wrong with it? Your mother has no sentimental feelings. Furniture is memories."

"Memory," Leon said as chicken soup trickled into his wild and bushy beard, "is simply the reproduction of past impressions."

"That's nice, Leon," my father said. "Very nice."

"Take for example my latest patient. He has amnesia. Everything's repressed. Freud uses the term counter-cathexes..."

"Maybe later, Leon, after coffee. Then we'll all be more relaxed. Right now I'd like to hear about my son's voyage."

"Why do you always cut him off, Morris? Let the boy talk.

Maybe we'll learn something. Go ahead, Leon, tell us about Freud."

"Esther, all I said was that, for me, furniture has memories. That's all. I don't need to know the psychology behind it."

"So be a peasant. I would like, if you don't mind, to become educated. And with a psychiatrist…"

"That's psychoanalyst, Mom," Julie blurted out. "I told you last week, just as soon as Leon passed his exam.

"And what's the difference?"

"The difference is," I felt a need to say something, "that psychiatrists can go to psychoanalysts when they get sick, but when psychoanalysts have problems they have no one to turn to. They have to analyse themselves. Ergo, Leon now has no one to turn to when he goes over the deep end."

Leon looked up at me. "That's cute, Rudy. Everything wrapped up into one neat nutshell."

"All I was saying, with a doctor of the mind in the house, it's like having a free education."

"Nothing in life is free, Mom," Leon said.

"So, Leon, is this amnesia victim of yours loaded?"

"Take a look at your sister's jewellery. Julie, lift your arm up. See that bracelet, Rudy? Five grand."

Julie, now that the spotlight was back on her, told us all about her trip to the jeweller's. The brisket was eaten and, as coffee and tea were being served, Julie wrapped up her story by telling our mother that she should have her jewellery appraised.

"I have insurance. Who needs appraisals?" Ma answered back.

"Now, maybe," my father said as he put a cube of sugar in his mouth and took a sip from his glass of tea, "we can find out how my son spent nine months of his life?"

"I still can't figure out why you went to Europe," my mother said.

"I had to get something out of my system."

"Why couldn't you have cleaned out your system here?"

"I just couldn't."

"Why? Is Europe so special? You remember, Morris, the first week we were in this country and we went to the bank and the manager told us we could have our very own safety deposit box for our private papers? They even gave us our own key," she said as her voice rose in pitch. "Imagine that, Rudy, if you can! I'm talking about 1946 and already this country was great."

"Imagine," I said.

"Sure, what do you know? You didn't suffer like we did. What's a safety box to you? Well, let me tell you something, Mr. Around-the-World-Traveller who couldn't even take time from his busy vacation to write a letter. And when he did write, all we got was 'Hi, how's it going' on the back of a postcard. Well, let me tell you something. A safety box meant security to us!"

"In that respect, your mother is right," my father said as he loosened his tie.

"Our own private key!" she proclaimed. "In Poland the only key I ever had was for the front door. In this country I have more keys than I know what to do with!" Sweat started to form on her wide brow. "Let me ask you something: do banks in Europe give out keys?"

"Yes."

"Now, maybe. But then?" She sat down, looking fatigued. She plopped some marble cake into her mouth and let out a sigh. Looking me in the eye, she asked: "So, Rudy, what are your plans for the future?"

"For God's sake, Esther, he's just come home and already you're pushing. Let him relax. Let the boy get used to his home."

"And then what? Magic?"

"Your mother's right, Rudy," Leon said. "The sooner you decide what to do with your life, the sooner the pieces of the puzzle will fall into place."

"That's nice, Leon," I said. "Where did you steal that bit of philosophy? From Time magazine — the section on behaviour?"

"You're home two hours and already the hostility has set in.

That's not a good sign."

"Speaking of hostility," I casually said, "did you know that our country and Vietnam are having serious peace talks."

Leon choked on a mouthful of brisket and glazed carrots and turned to me, waving his fork wildly.

"It's not over. It'll never be over. Not until we completely overtake every nook and cranny of that godforsaken commie country," he bellowed.

"Leon, it's a disaster… a serious mistake," my father said. "We should never have gone in."

"What do you mean we shouldn't have gone in? We need to wring their necks. Wring and twist their red-bellied commie necks and when the war is over I'll volunteer my services and clean up anything the military has forgotten to clean up."

"Can I help you pack?" I asked.

"On this war, Rudy, we're winners. Big time winners." And as he yelled out "big time winners" one more time he stood up, saluted the picture on the wall of 16th century Venetian ships at port that my mother had won at a Hanukah bazaar and stood at attention for a full fifteen seconds all the while chanting "God Bless America."

My mother sternly told him to sit down and finish his meal. He was causing an unwelcome interruption. She hadn't finished with me and my future.

"Never mind all this," my mother cut in between us. "What's important is the future. Surely in nine months you must have thought of it?"

"Ma, I have plans. Don't push."

"Somebody has to push you. If it wasn't for me, you'd never have gone to college." Another sigh. "All right, so it wasn't Harvard."

"I graduated. You can stop pushing."

"When you get your Ph.D., that's when you'll be finished."

"You're going to nag me until I get my Ph.D.?"

"No, first I'm going to nag about you finding a girl and getting married."

"Mom, come on," Julie said. "Rudy's got plenty of time for that."

"I agree," Leon said.

"You agree?" my father asked, surprised that Leon would agree with a layman. When my mother heard Leon she backed off. If a psychiatrist decided that her twenty-one-year-old son was too young to get married, who was she to argue?

"In any case, will you please enlighten us all with these special plans you have."

"I wrote a novel."

"A novel!" Julie snorted derisively.

"A *book*!" Ma gasped, recoiling in shock. "You spent nine months in Europe writing a book and *that's* your special plan? Forgive me, but I'm missing something. What exactly is your plan?

"My plan is to get my novel published, sell a million copies, live on the Riviera and drink banana daiquiris for breakfast."

"Ba... banana what?! Rudy, what are you doing with your life? I thought your writing was in the past. I thought Europe would mature you. If I had known, I never would have let you go."

"If I may interfere," Leon said.

"Maybe later," my father answered.

"Let the boy speak. After all, on this subject, Leon should have a wealth of information. Isn't that correct, Leon?"

"Well, Mom, as you know, I did not specialise in maturity, but I do know that maturity is the process by which one advances towards ripeness."

"We're talking about my son, Leon. Not a nectarine," my father said.

"Bananas! Nectarines! What's everybody talking about?!" my mother shouted.

"Maybe I could say something?" I calmly lit up a cigarette.

"And since when do you smoke?"

"Ma, I'm not a kid anymore."

"Bigshot. In any case, I can't deal with two problems at the same time. We'll deal with your lungs later. Right now, all I can see is that plans you don't have. What you have are just dreams, and dreams will not put butter on the table."

"Maybe I only want margarine."

Ma's face turned red and she squashed the piece of cake she'd been holding in her hand. "Morris!" she screamed. "If you don't talk to your son once and for all, I'll... I'll... Jokes! You hear your son? Jokes. That's what he makes. The world is falling apart. Israel's in trouble. His future is hanging by a thread and all he can do is make jokes."

"A defence mechanism," Leon observed. "You remember when we had our last session and I explained to you about your defence mechanisms?"

"Not now, Leon. We're discussing Rudy," Ma stated, quietly and politely.

"Is that true, Ma? You're seeing Leon?"

"Whose future are we dealing with? Mine or yours?"

"Shame on you, Leon," I said. "I thought it was very unprofessional to talk about your patients. Perhaps the AMA would be interested in this."

"Well, Julie, I think perhaps we're in the way. It's getting late."

"You're leaving already?" my mother whined, really meaning to say, *you're deserting me. Now it'll be two against one.*

"Let the boy alone," my father said as he stood up to get Leon's jacket.

"Rudy," Leon turned to me, "come by first thing in the morning. I have to get my hair cut. We'll talk on the way."

The four of them went to the door to say their good-byes and I returned to the bathroom to smoke a cigarette in peace. For some reason, I didn't feel tense anymore. It was all out in the open — well, not quite all. I heard my name being shouted. "Rudy, Rudy! Where is that boy? Why is he always disappearing?" I returned to the living room and sat down. Round two was about to begin.

My mother was sitting on the sofa, staring out onto the street. Her hands fidgeted. My father came beside me and asked if I went to

Venice. I answered yes. He seemed pleased that we had something in common to talk about. As he began to tell me about the day he spent in Venice in 1936, my mother turned to us, enraged.

"Fun!"

We stopped talking about Venice and looked at her.

"That's all you want in life."

"Esther. Tomorrow's another day. We can continue then."

"That's okay, Dad. Let's clear it up now. What's troubling you, Ma?"

"Troubling me? Do you believe the *chutzpah* of this boy? Troubling ME?" She opened her mouth but decided against saying what she had planned to, and then shrieked out: "FUN!" The word exploded into the air like a firecracker. "Fun! Fun! Fun! That's all you think about. Wake up, Rudy, and face life. For your information, you're not supposed to have fun anymore. You're twenty-one years old. The fun is over. Now it's time for hard work."

"I agree," I said.

She paid no attention, and plowed ahead.

"You think your father has fun? You think I have fun? You think your father and I had fun when we were twenty-one? For your information, Mr. Graduate, your father began work at the age of twelve, when your grandfather, may he rest in peace, passed away. There were five boys and your grandmother to take care of. And as for me..."

"I know. At eight you began helping your mother with the washing and cleaning and, when your mother became ill, you took over the household."

"That's correct. So as you can plainly see, you've been very lucky — and spoiled, I might add. You've had more than your share of fun. Now you have to work. Or..."

"Or?"

"Or go back to school and work towards getting a Ph.D."

"I'm not going back to school and I'm not going to become a businessman, a lawyer, or, God forbid, President."

"You're breaking my heart. Do you know that? You are breaking my heart."

"I want to become a writer."

"You really seem determined," my father said.

"And how will you live?"

"I still have some Bar Mitzvah money left."

"Enough to live on?"

"For awhile."

"And then what?"

"And then," my father said, "we'll help. Put it this way, Esther. If he went back to school, wouldn't we pay? So what's the difference?"

"Ma, imagine. You could walk down the street and someone will point you out and say: 'There goes Mrs. Esther Petinsky, mother of Rudy Petinsky, the famous writer.'"

She said nothing, but in her mind the wheels were clicking. She seemed to like the sound of it. She was already thinking about the interviews she would grant the *New York Times*. "Sixty Minutes" would do an in-depth segment about the mother behind the son. She turned her back to us and silently stared out the window. I knew what she was thinking. On the one hand she was saying, "*All right, destroy your life. After all, it's yours to ruin. Lord knows, I did my best.*" And, on the other, she was telling herself, "*If Rose's son could become famous, why not mine?*"

"So, Rudy," my father said, "what's your book about?"

"Well, Dad, it's sort of a..."

"So, Rudy, what now?"

I looked at my mother. She still had her back to us.

"What do you mean, Ma?"

"What now? What's the first step?"

"I guess I have to submit my manuscript to a publisher."

"Do you know of one?" my father asked.

"Nope."

"Morris, didn't you once know someone at the B'nai B'rith? A writer?"

"Did I?"

"A distant cousin on your mother's side. What was his name?"

"Frank? Simon? Joey?"

"Who are these names you're throwing at me? What are you, a comedian?"

"I don't know who you're talking about. I don't know anyone in the B'nai B'rith. I don't even like that organisation. They don't really help like they should."

"Stop it, Morris! That's blasphemy. The goys can talk like that, but not you. The B'nai B'rith is a wonderful organisation. Without them, who knows where we'd be?"

"Esther, the B'nai B'rith is as helpful to the Jews as the Christian Science Monitor is to the Christians."

"Feh! Ptew!" my mother responded.

"Ma, Dad, cut it out. Who's this distant cousin who's a writer? I never heard of him."

"Your father has a cousin who writes articles or poems or essays or something like that for the B'nai B'rith."

"I do not."

"You do! Don't argue with me, Morris."

"Esther, I have a cousin, twice removed, who writes propaganda for the Jewish Anti-Defamation League."

"See, Rudy, I told you there was a writer in the family. I'll call him up and see if he can help you."

My mother, with a lot of persuasion, flattery, and a sob or two, eventually got through to Irving Goldman's detached heart. Yes, he did know of a publisher, by the name of Edwin Plaster, who was something of an anomaly. Plaster welcomed untried, never-before-published writers. I was on my way.

CHAPTER 2

The waiting began. For the first few days I was calm, knowing that my manuscript was still in the mail. After four days, I figured it had arrived and, after five days, I figured the publisher had read half the book. On the sixth day I began to chain-smoke and, on the seventh, developed a bad cough which turned into bronchitis. I wouldn't take any medicine because medicine would make me feel drowsy and I wouldn't stay in bed because I was afraid I would fall asleep and not hear the phone. On the eighth day I began to make life miserable for my mother. Every time the phone rang and it wasn't Edwin Plaster, I yelled at her. And the phone was ringing all right. If it wasn't the butcher, or my mother's canasta partner, or one of the neighbours, then it was Julie, needing some kind of marital advice. Today's problem was that she found some porno magazines tucked away in one of Leon's drawers and had become hysterical thinking that her body no longer pleased her husband. My mother's advice: "I'll have a word with him. He'll see the light." And off she went to Leon's downtown office. Unannounced, unexpected. Several hours later she returned.

"You know what he said, that future Nobel prize-winning psychiatrist son-in-law of mine? He said that looking at naked ladies and reading erotic literature is therapeutic."

"You'd think he'd be tired of reading after all those years of study," Julie answered my mother.

"Maybe he's not reading and just looking at the pictures?" I decided to put in my two cents.

"What for? He can look at me."

"Maybe you don't look like them."

"If I wanted to, I could pose just like them."

"Do you?"

"What do you know about sex? About marriage? About life?

You're still a kid with your head in the clouds. You think it's easy, don't you?"

"Sex, marriage or life?"

"Jokes, always jokes. Daddy, what should I do?"

"Have you spoken to Leon?"

"Of course I've spoken to him. I phoned him immediately after I discovered his filthy stash."

"And?"

"He gave me some mumbo-jumbo. Who can understand?"

"Well, Julie," my mother said as she placed a tureen of hot soup in front of us. "I'm surprised at you for not being able to understand your husband. His mumbo-jumbo, as you put it, makes a great deal of sense to me."

"That doesn't surprise me."

"Rudy, don't be rude to your mother."

"Morris, thank you but I don't need a lawyer. I have my own mouth, knock wood."

"Dad, it's a joke. Just kidding. Why is everyone so hot under the collar?"

"Because," Julie stared at me, "if you remember, my husband, Dr. Leon A. Carp, psychoanalyst, owner of a summer cottage in the Catskills, driver of a Jaguar XKE and a vice-president of the synagogue, looks at smut."

"Movies, too," my mother added.

"WHAT??!!" Julie screamed.

"I saw them. Very interesting."

"You're making a joke, right Esther?"

"No, Morris, no jokes. In his office. He showed me one."

"In his office?"

"Yes, Morris. You know something, we're old-fashioned, the two of us. Our bodies might be in America but our minds are still in Poland."

"Get to the point, Esther."

"The point is what I said before. Therapeutic. Leon shows these movies to all of his patients. He says movies such as these get rid of hostilities."

"They make you warm, that's all," my father blurted out.

"The word is hot, Dad."

"Don't interrupt, Rudy!"

"They give you a tingle, I won't deny it. But that's a small price to pay for getting well," my mother commented.

"The two of you were made for each other," my father said as he stormed out of the kitchen.

"And what about me, Mom? What about my marriage?"

"Do yourself a favour, Julie. Go home, take a good hard look at his magazines, watch a movie or two. You'll be a new person."

"And probably pregnant," I said as I quickly left the room.

The next morning, as he was leaving for work, my father found me hovering over the phone again, like a neurotic bumblebee.

"Rudy, maybe it won't be in the form of a call," my father said. "Maybe you'll receive a letter."

I hadn't thought of that. Now I became anxious when I heard the mailman bang the mail through the door slot. At 9:25, I would post myself at the door and peer through the seeing eye, waiting for my delivery which came promptly every morning at 9:30. With one eye looking out for my mail and one ear on standby for that ring, I became a nervous wreck.

I decided to go for a drive and ended up at my father's store: Petinsky's Women's Wear. It was a small dive, situated between a supermarket and a travel agency.

I was always surprised how my father could eke out a living from such a small store, but surprisingly he did well.

"Hi, Dad."

"Rudy? What brings you here?"

"Just thought I'd drop in."

"Are you hungry?"

"No. I just ate."

"Rudy, excuse me a minute... Madame, if you want quality, you'll pay $75. How much quality do you expect for $12.95?"

My father gave me a wink.

"Of course you can try it on. Here, let me help you. Very nice. What do you think?"

"A bit large," the woman said.

"Large?" my father replied, sounding surprised. "Large? Let me see. I don't think so. In my opinion, it fits like a dream. Made in heaven."

"You think so? You don't think it's too large?"

"No, Madame. Fits nice. Should I wrap it up for you? Rudy, do me a favour and wrap up this jacket. I have another customer."

"Sure, Dad."

My father had a big smile on his face. He always had a smile when I came to the store.

"No, I'm sorry, can't do. Under $32 I can't go. I'm sorry. No, I just can't. Impossible. It costs me $30. I have to make some profit. No, really, I'm sorry... $31? Okay, okay, take it. I'll be with you in a minute, Rudy. There you are. Enjoy and have a nice day... So Rudy, what's new?"

"Nothing much."

"No calls?"

"No calls, no letters."

"Why don't I close for an hour? We'll walk, have a coffee. Okay?"

"Great."

We walked up and down the avenue, my father pointing out the stores that had disappeared, the apartment buildings which had housed friends and relatives.

"You see this McDonald's, Rudy? Used to be an empty lot. You used to play there with your friends."

"I remember. Dad, you want to stop here for a coffee?"

"You know what, Rudy? Let's forget the coffee and go visit where we used to live. Unless you want a coffee?"

"No, no. That sounds good."

My father put out his arm in front of my body as we stepped off the curb and waited for the light to change.

"I haven't been there in... in years. I don't know why. I should, you know, close the store more often and walk. Especially now. On such a nice day."

"You should, Dad. It'll do you good to exercise. Stretch your legs."

"Yes. I should. Look, look Rudy. Your old school."

"Yeah." The school where that goddamn kindergarten teacher had told me to stop singing. *Rudy, just mouth the words, pretend you're singing. You're putting the rest of the class off-key.* Bitch. Pitch-bitch.

"Do you remember all your friends you had in school? You were always so busy with friends. Never time for homework."

"Yeah. I should have studied harder."

"You see, now you regret. Anyways, what does it matter? You'll become a famous writer, go to Hollywood, make movies... you'll see. It'll happen."

"*Fin dein maul in Gott's öihren.* From your mouth to God's ears."

My father laughed like he always did when I said something in Yiddish. He didn't laugh often enough.

"The building hasn't changed, eh Dad? It still looks good."

"The landlords always took good care of it. It was a classy apartment building when we lived here."

We sat on the front steps and pulled out our packs of cigarettes. My father never offered to light my cigarette. He considered it bad luck and I never offered to light his. I knew that he loved smoking and the ritual of lighting his own match added to his pleasure.

"What are you thinking, Rudy?"

"When I was a little boy, how life was so much easier then."

"Why do you say that?"

"Because I had no responsibilities. Everything was taken care of. By you and Ma. I don't know, it was just easier."

"And now? Life is so hard on you?"

"Not really. It was just easier then. No pressure."

"Rudy, your time will come. Be patient."

I put my arm around him and kissed him on the cheek. Something I had not done in a long time. Years. He smiled. So did I.

"Well, Rudy," my father said as he slapped my knee, "time to go back."

"I'll walk you."

On our way back we passed the lane near our old apartment building. I noticed two small boys playing Hide and Seek. Ten years ago that was me. Now I was a man waiting desperately for a phone call.

Chapter 3

My street, Franklin Crescent, always came alive in the spring. Flowers dotted the driveways, trees sprouted their leaves and fruits, and children played in backyards. The street was divided into three sections. The Lebanese lived to the north; the Italians to the south; and the Jews in the middle. There was never any looting, beating or desecration. I never once saw a swastika on my street. The reason for such perfect harmony was that the Italians kept to themselves, the Jews to themselves, and the Lebanese to themselves. It was perfect. And as long as there were no burning crosses or lepers to be seen, and no screaming babies to be heard, there was peace and quiet. It was really perfect except for the fact that when I turned twenty-one I realised that most of my friends had left the neighbourhood.

Gloria got married to an Israeli boy. Barry eloped. Michael left home with dignity. I say with dignity because a few years before Michael left home, his older brother Franky had run away from home. Mickey, my best friend in high school left, for "Inja, Polynizious and other erotic countries" as his mother would say in her broken Austro-Yiddish-English. Karl left out of necessity. He moved into a richer neighbourhood with his parents. Only Judy and I remained.

Judy was a very sweet girl with the largest pair of boobs any of us kids had ever seen. Everyone had a crush on her, but I used to be in love with her. In love!

She sat in front of me in my Philosophy class in college, and I tried to get up the nerve to ask her out for Saturday night.

No, she'll never go out with me. And, even if she does, what will I do? Where will I take her? Should I double date? Triple date? Should I take her to a discotheque? To a movie? Out to eat?

I'll take her to a discotheque, at least that way I can get close to her on the dance floor. Oh God, let's say she doesn't respond. I won't know what to do. I'll be so embarrassed. Here I'll be showing her my love and she'll probably be saying, "God, is this guy ever horny. I can hardly breathe." But what if she does respond? Then what'll I do? Should I kiss her? God, should I kiss her right on the dance floor? Maybe I'll say something real cool like, "Baby, pucker up 'cause you're driving me crazy" and say it the way Bogie would have said it. Or maybe I'll just stroke my fingers through her hair and stare into her eyes and hope that she makes the first move. But how will she see the love in my eyes with my glasses on? I can't take them off just before starting, then she'll know what I'm up to. I can always take them off, pretend to wipe the sweat off my face or say… that's it, I'll say I have something in my eye. Goddammit, I'll have something in my eye, and she'll come closer to help me with my problem and then I'll say... God, what'll I say? What'll I do? I must be crazy. She won't go out with me. And, even if she does, what'll I wear? Oh God, what'll I wear? I don't have anything to wear. All I have are jeans. Why must my Dad own a *women's* clothing store? I don't even have any money and, if I ask her out, I'll need a pair of pants and a sweater. That means at least fifty dollars and I'll have to ask my parents and they'll give it to me 'cause they like me to be dressed. But then when they see me all dressed up on Saturday night, my mother will say:

"Look at Rudy, all dressed up. Where are you going, Rudy?"

"Out, Ma."

"Go, go show your father how handsome you look, go. Morris, Morris, look at your son. Look how handsome he is."

"Very sharp. You need some money, Rudy?"

"A little, Dad. I'm going out."

"Where?"

"To a discotheque."

"With David?"

"No."

"Then with who?" my mother would ask.

"A girl."

"A girl? What girl?"

"No one special, Ma. Just a girl."

"Is she Jewish? What's her name?"

"Bye, Ma. Bye, Dad."

"Will you be home late, Rudy?"

"I don't know, Ma."

"Leave him alone, Esther. Always with your questions. He'll come home when he wants to."

"Big shot, at eighteen he'll come home when he wants to. As long as he lives here, he'll..."

"Good night, Rudy. Have a good time."

"Thanks, Dad. Bye, Ma."

Jesus, I'll have to put up with my parents. And they'll tell their friends that I had a date and my relatives will start asking all kinds of questions. Oh, God, what'll I do?

"He... he... llo, is Judy there, please?"

"Speaking."

Damn, why couldn't her mother have answered?

"Hello, Judy?"

"Yes."

"How are you?"

"Who is this?"

"Don't you know?" How could she know? I've never spoken to her.

"It's Rudy."

"Rudy who?"

"Rudy, in your Philosophy class. I sit behind you."

"Oh. That's right, you do. How are you?"

"Fine... uh... Judy, can I see you?"

"When? Tonight?"

"Uh, no. For the weekend."

"When on the weekend?"

"Saturday night?"

"Sure."

"Great." Oh God, she said sure. I thought my heart would

explode right out of my chest. "What would you like to do?"

"It doesn't matter."

"Uh, would you like to go dancing? I know you're a great dancer."

"Sure."

"Okay. I'll see you Saturday night, about eight. Bye."

"Rudy, aren't you coming to school tomorrow?"

"Yes."

"Then I'll see you tomorrow."

"Uh, oh yeah, that's right. Tomorrow. Okay. Bye."

"Bye, Rudy."

Oh God, what'll I do? What'll I say to her in school? I'll be sick tomorrow. I'll say I don't feel well. My stomach hurts. Sure. I'll be sick. Tomorrow. But what about Wednesday? I know. I'll be sick on Wednesday too. I can be sick two days in a row! And then on Thursday, when I come to school, she'll come over to me and say, "Hi, Rudy, how come you weren't in school? I missed you." And then what'll I say? What can I say? I'll have to say "I missed you, too" and then what?

I must be crazy to even think she would say such a thing. She'll probably just say "Hi" and run along. No, she won't! She said she would go out with me. She'll say something more. But what? Maybe I should go to school tomorrow after all. Oh God, what'll I do?

That year, Judy and I became a hot number.

At first I was surprised. Everyone had said that Judy was such a sweet girl, such a pure girl. No one could get past first base with her. So how come me? Because Judy was not quite as sweet and as innocent as everyone claimed. She had been through the wringer.

On one of our very first dates, we went to Truscades — the amusement park. After the Tunnel of Love, where I still couldn't get up the nerve to put my arm around her, we went to the Ferris wheel. When we climbed to the top, the wheel stopped. Well, I knew I had to do something then and there. So I pulled out a joint. Judy was neither appalled nor repelled. Seems it wasn't her first time.

"You know, Rudy, I usually get quite horny when I smoke."

I wasn't sure whether I had heard her right, so I said nothing. I just smiled. By the time we had finished the joint, not only had I managed to place my arm around her and gone through quite a few French kisses, but my hand also managed to hover over and finally conquer her right breast. Sweet stuff for an eighteen-year-old virgin.

Overlooking the park – for we were still stuck – Judy nestled close to me and her lips grazed my ear.

"Rudy, I want everything. In every way."

"What do you mean?"

"I want to be fucked in every possible position. In every corner of every room of my house. Under the stars, in a barn, on a bicycle, in a classroom, on a horse. I want to be fucked standing, sitting, and lying down. In a rowboat, in a museum, in a theatre, in a library. While swimming, while dancing, while exercising. Rudy, I want it all. Every which way."

"Oh wow!… Judy!… Oh God!"

"Rudy, I've never done it on a Ferris wheel. Rudy? Have you?"

"Oh, well ... uh ... no Judy. Never on a Ferris wheel."

I can even, to this day, remember my body tension screaming to be released. I was harder than a rock, no… a diamond! And when it was over, I just sat still, hardly breathing, talking to myself. Oh dear compassionate God. I've just been laid. Hallelujah! Yet, it wasn't all that wonderful. Maybe because the Ferris wheel swayed a bit too much for my liking, making me slightly queasy. Nevertheless, beggars can't be choosers. What the hell? Why make excuses? Be thankful. Thank God.

"Rudy, let's do it again."

"Again? Up here?"

"Yes Rudy, again. It wasn't long enough."

True. She did have a point. It had only lasted six seconds.

The second time we did it was better, but far from perfect. Making our way to the Tunnel of Horror, we quickly got into our car and entered the forbidding darkness. Judy quickly got into position – for time was of the essence – and straddled my diamond penis. I was concentrating hard on an old shopping list my mother had given me: toilet paper, apple juice, bread, milk, toilet paper, bananas, toilet paper, soap. I was completely taken aback when a skeleton shot up in front of me. I screamed and lost my concentration. At least I had beaten my old record by a full seven seconds.

The third time was a fiasco. I was sure Judy would never speak to me again. We were on the Salt and Pepper Shaker, a macabre device that sits two per compartment and spins, rolls over, twists, dives, and then shoots skyward at an alarming speed. During the best of circumstances, I throw up just watching the thing go through its gyrations. But no! Judy wanted to do it in there!

Lying on the floor, just below the seat into which we should have been strapped, I half-heartedly tried to convince her that we should stop. Unfortunately, Judy just wrapped her legs tighter around my waist, especially when the Shaker went into its tailspin. I tried to break free, but it was no use. Judy was exhilarated and I could no longer hold it in. So she orgasmed and I threw up.

When I wobbled off the Shaker, Judy apologized for making me do it.

"Are you okay, Rudy?"

"Yes... I'm sorry, Judy. Really sorry."

"Never mind. It was my fault. You warned me that you had a weak stomach. Let's go home. I think you've had enough for one day."

She was right.

After the amusement park episode, I realised that Judy had an insatiable appetite for sex. I simply could not keep up with her. I had to feign headaches, dizzy spells, stomach cramps, or nausea. And more often than not, I wasn't feigning because Judy actually seemed to have a Ferris wheel fetish. So I ended the relationship.

Shortly afterwards, Judy went to Italy to study Fine Arts. Three years later she returned from Italy with a pleasantly robust figure. She also returned with a two-year-old daughter, but no husband.

I now kept my distance because I didn't want her to see me.

I was embarrassed. Here she was, three years in Europe, married and divorced with a daughter, a promising future teaching Italian Rococo Art at Bruckner College and here I was still living at home with Mommy and Daddy. No marriage, not even a steady girlfriend. No children, no intriguing divorce, and certainly no prospects of anything remotely resembling a future.

Chapter 4

I tried to make myself as comfortable as possible while Edwin Plaster was reading my manuscript.

I looked out the window. It was raining. I stared at the floor, then at my shoes. I desperately needed a cigarette. I scanned Plaster's desk to see if there was an ashtray on it. There was, and in it a pipe was resting. I took out a cigarette, lit it, and inhaled deeply trying not to fidget as Plaster started to read.

THEN WAS FOREVER

by Rudy Petinsky

Chapter One

The seaside resort was filled with the happiness of holiday makers. Dainty women sat under the warmth of umbrellas while the sun produced delightful gleams on the young girls. Just in front of them, they could see the faint yellows and pinks of the sunbathers and just beyond them lay the black streamers and white sails of the regatta.

On the east side of the resort was the café where delicate men in tail coats and tall top hats enjoyed the flatness and brightness of playing-cards. The sky tingled, the waters mingled, and the clouds sparkled. It was to become a day that lingered in their memories for the next twenty years.

Henry Jaykins and Sal Doroni were sitting in the café, looking out towards the sea. They were young men and in good health. Surprisingly, for they had just come through a war. "The Great War" as it had been labelled by the newspapers. Both men had been friends since childhood and, when the United States declared war on Germany on April 6, 1917, Henry and Sal enlisted and were assigned to the 1st Infantry Division. They arrived in France on July 4 and paraded down the Champs Elysées, singing tunes from Irving Berlin. Six weeks later, Henry and Sal were entrenched in Ypres and, on October 1, their division was transferred to Argonne, near Verdun. After three months of gruelling warfare and squalid conditions, the Argonne offensive was over. Henry and Sal were given a five-day pass and they quickly returned to Paris where they met, one night at Madame Foch's (a first-rate bordello), an intriguing gentleman named Paul Kesselring — actor, magician and expatriate of Germany. He had also been in the Argonne but, after three weeks of fighting, Paul had decided he had enough and took matters into his own hands. War was not for him. He did not care about Archduke Ferdinand, had never wanted to fight for his country and the Argonne was not his idea of spending a few weeks in France.

Madame Foch's, on the outskirts of Paris, looks, when sunlight bathes it, like a whitewashed monastery. It is situated on a hill, shaded by a few trees with flowers springing up everywhere. Sweet-hissing peacocks with fans of half-transparent linen walk unmolested throughout the gardens. The trollops don't fare as well. On any given day, a passer-by would see children blowing bubbles, young girls clasping racquets, shuttlecocks flying through the air, wrinkled old men puffing on pipes.

At night, in the moonlit solitude of the woods, sweet mists of bright colours can be seen on the graceful costumes of the beautiful young sluts. Caviar, shimmering like jewels, is served and champagne — silver-lemon in colour — served from pewter vases is poured.

Mr. Plaster leaned back on his worn-out corduroy chair. He crossed his right leg over his left, pushed his horn-rimmed glasses closer towards his anaemic face and continued to stare at my manuscript for a full thirty seconds before he began to speak.

"I don't like it."

"I beg your pardon," I said, my heart sinking fast.

"I said it won't sell."

Plaster's voice was thin, almost effeminate and, when he spoke he had an annoying habit of sticking out his tongue. How he did this I'm not sure but it gave him the appearance of a peculiar jungle bird.

"You've read two pages and that's it? Two pages and the book won't sell!! Are you crazy?"

"Now, now, Mr. Petinsky, let's not get nasty. I've been in the publishing business for over thirty years and if I couldn't tell by now what sells and what doesn't, I would have been buried long ago. I won't say that your writing is bad, but sexually suggestive romanticism is out. Realism is in."

"The book is romantic in a realist way," I said petulantly. "Are you saying it should be realistic in a romantic way?"

"No. I think a rewrite is in order. Take your manuscript, read it a few times over, get to know it, study it, memorise it, correct it, take out the seeds, streamline it, condense it, toughen it up, make it more attractive, make it realistic. Forget romanticism. Doesn't sell. Tell you what, Mr. Petinsky... take half a year, a year to polish up your manuscript and present it to us again. We'll see what we can do. Right? Good."

What was I to do? Nine months of my life gone down the drain. Nine months of anguish, frustration, fatigue and wavering nerves. Nine months of dreams, hopes and prayers all washed away. Nine months from conception to birth, and now a last minute miscarriage. My baby was dead. How could this be possible? This was to be the all-time best seller. More sales than the Bible. One hundred weeks on the *New York Times* best-seller list. A Pulitzer prize. A movie. And then the Nobel Prize for Literature.

Why had I made all the sacrifices? For a jackass named Edwin

Plaster to tell me that romanticism doesn't sell? In ten minutes E.P. told me that nine months of my life had been spent on romantic bird dung. I just didn't understand. What should I do? Spend another six months rewriting and then be told by that rotten publisher that my book is unsellable? Damn you, Edwin Plaster. Damn you to hell and beyond.

After the shock died down, a severe depression took its place, and was in turn replaced by thoughts of suicide. In the end, I decided not to commit hari-kiri but, rather, to rewrite. What choice did I have? Make it more realistic, he said. Screw romanticism, he said. All right, all right. If he wants realism, I'll give it to him. Forget weathervanes flying over misty fields and winding roads cluttered with messengers on horseback. The hell with pale slender girls with dark eyes and wrinkled old men puffing on pipes. Screw rivers drenched in silver-lemon moonlight and women with faces the colour of raspberries. Fuck horsedrawn trams and yellow gravel paths. And grain harvests, church festivals, Christmas mornings, Sunday evening baths, childhood memories. If it's realism that he wants, that's what he'll get. From now on, no more coffee houses and dilapidated archways. All he'll get from me are all-night diners with empty stools. And a goddamn neon sign with an arrow pointing the way in!

Chapter 5

My first setback occurred the day I was born. My mother was overcome with joy because I was born partially circumcised. Supposedly Moses was born that way and it was considered a great honour. Some honour: I was twelve years old before Dr. Saxe decided it was time for the foreskin to go.

I can still remember the pain. And the embarrassment! Especially when my Uncle Sheldon visited me in the children's ward and boomed, "So, Rudy, they finally lopped it off! Now you're a man."

I had nightmares for months afterwards. Horrible dreams about an angry foreskin, bent on revenge, wandering through the streets, seeking its rightful owner.

My mother, the former Miss Esther Chelmno of Krappitz, Poland, thought she would give me a good head start in life by naming me after her favourite actor, Rudolph Valentino, and after my grandfather, Isaac, a revered Polish rabbi. She was convinced that with Rudolph, Isaac and Moses backing me I would become, at the very least, a brain surgeon. After a while, when she saw that this profession was a bit unrealistic, she pushed for paediatrician, then lawyer, then dentist, then pharmacist. All I wanted to do with my life was play with marbles.

"But Rudy, you have to think of your future. You won't be young for much longer."

For Christ's sake, I was ten years old and she was telling me to grow up!

"Rudy, you've got to decide what you want. You can't play with marbles the rest of your life. C'mon, Rudy, tell Mommy what you want to do."

"All right, I want to own a store."

"A store, Rudy? A businessman. My son, the business tycoon.

Yes, Rudy. It sounds good. And, after you've opened up one store, you can branch out and open up another and another and have franchises... my son, the business tycoon. I like it, Rudy. Tell me, have you thought about what type of store you'd like to operate?"

"Yes, Ma. A candy store."

"A candy store!"

"Yes. Like Benny's across the street. And I want the same kind of barrels that he has where he keeps millions and millions of candies in them."

"Out of the question, Rudy. You're not being realistic."

"But Ma, I want a candy store."

"No. And that's that. I'll think of something else for you."

I began to cry. Not because I couldn't get a candy store, but because Ma never agreed with me and, even worse, I was getting fed up with her not letting me do anything for myself. She would say: "Don't try and fix the wheels on your truck, Rudy, you'll only make it worse. Let Mommy do it." Or: "Don't hang those pictures in your room. You'll only make holes in the wall. Let Mommy do it."

It seemed as though Ma could do anything. She was an accomplished pianist, an excellent handyman and an avid reader, with an incredible thirst for knowledge and the drive to obtain it. It frustrated her that I stumbled over "Chopsticks" ("You know, Rudy, I won awards when I was your age") and that my reading was confined to *Mad* magazine ("This house is full of books. Good books. From now on you have to spend one hour reading every day") and that my brain short-circuited my hands when I performed tasks as simple as changing a lightbulb ("You're doing it all wrong. Here, let me show you").

One day, while in the midst of an inadequacy attack, I spotted a copy of *Life* magazine lying on the living room floor. I suddenly got an irresistible urge to write captions to the pictures. I became so engrossed that an hour passed before I looked up — to see my mother standing in front of me.

"Rudy, there you are. You've been so quiet. What's wrong?"

"Nothing, Ma."

"What are you doing with the magazine?"

"Nothing, Ma."

"Let me see." She started riffling through the pages. "You know, Rudy, this is very creative. There's a third cousin on your father's side who writes for the *Jerusalem Post* and my Aunt Leah, may she rest in peace, wrote poetry. It's probably in your genes. I'd love to be able to write but I guess my genes aren't good enough."

"You really think my writing is good?"

"Take your feet off the couch. Yes, it's good. But not great. In order to write great, you have to read and read and read. So instead of one hour a day reading, let's make it two."

A few years passed before I tried my hand at writing again. Unbeknownst to my mother, I had spent the two reading hours catching up on *Sports Illustrated* and *Mad* magazine, so any writing ability I had lay dormant. But in grade 9, one book changed the course of my life: *Catcher in the Rye*. Required reading. I can't remember why I decided to read the book — after all, it was only homework — but when I finished Holden Caulfield's tale, I knew then and there what I wanted to do with the rest of my life. God, to be able to write like Salinger! And why not? Ma said my writing was good, and at that time I wasn't even trying. Besides which, that particular talent seemed to run in my family and this was one thing Ma couldn't interfere with because she knew bugger-all about how to write. That's it! It was meant to be. I became an avid reader and started to dress and act the part of a writer. I wore the standard jacket with patches on the sleeves and retrieved my prescription glasses from the back of my drawer. I walked around school with a bemused expression on my face and I would have smoked a pipe too, but it was forbidden on school grounds. It also made me nauseous.

When my English teacher, Mr. Zenkowitz, from whom I had acquired an insignificant amount of knowledge, asked the class to write a composition over the weekend, I couldn't wait to get home and begin my artistic career. The title for the composition was "How To Do Something Correctly." Although the composition was not entirely my own (I stole the idea from *Bicycle World* magazine), it did show originality.

How To Butter Your Eggs - Rudy Petinsky
Eng. Room 265

To enjoy your screwing and become a good screwer, it is important that you should know and appreciate the rules of the road as they apply in your part of the world.

Before screwing, make sure that your partner is in good condition. Particularly check that your balls and penis are inflated to correct pressure; that the vagina operates satisfactorily with nice lubing; that the tits comply with the law; and that your screwing position is comfortable. When screwing, always hold on. Obey all regulations, give clear hand signals, and do not carry anything which may affect your balance. Do not carry a passenger unless your partner has been properly forewarned!

The best screwing position is the one which gives you, the screwer, the greatest comfort consistent with good balance. No two people fuck alike but the following hints should help you to find your most comfortable and efficient position. Correct height is most important. This can usually be determined by fully extending the leg and placing the heel at the foot of the bed with the toes at its lowest point. This allows for a slight bend at the knee when the ball of the foot is on the bed. Your weight should be so balanced that your hands rest lightly. This prevents strain on wrists and forearms when screwing. Remember that few things equal the thrill of fucking.

Take care of it and it will take care of you.

The End

My composition caused quite an uproar at the School Board. Mr. Zenkowitz called my parents. So did the principal and one of the school commissioners. All of them wondering what kind of a child my parents had brought into the world.

My mother's first words were: "Why? Why?"

Her second words were: "I don't understand. I just simply can't understand."

Her third words were: "You're crazy. Absolutely crazy, Rudy. A crazy pervert. They're going to take you away to a loony cell and put you in a white jacket. How can you do this to us? We'll be the laughingstock of the neighbourhood. How can you think of such things? You're crazy, Rudy. Maybe insane. God forgive me, I've given birth to a lunatic. I'm going to call Dr. Saxe and make an appointment for you."

"But Ma, I don't talk like that or always think like that. It's called literary licence."

"Literary licence! Big shot! You're fifteen years old. Who gives you the right to write whatever you want to? You have to be more responsible."

"Esther, maybe Rudy just didn't think when he was writing. That can happen. Haven't you ever made a mistake?"

"That's no mistake. That's deliberate filth. Admit it, Rudy. You deliberately tried to humiliate me. Didn't you? Didn't you? Answer me, Rudy!"

For a split second my brain cells didn't fire properly and I nearly lost my balance. I could only make out every third or fourth word coming out of my mother's mouth: "mistake... filth... deliberately... humiliate... answer... pervert."

I had to suppress a smile.

"That's enough, Esther. After all, he didn't commit a crime. He just wrote a composition."

"HE JUST WROTE A COMPOSITION! Thirty years ago, with a composition like that we would have had to move to another town."

"Well," I said, "see how lucky you are for being born thirty years later. You can still live in your house. You don't have to leave."

"Monster! Crazy person! Is that any way to talk to your mother? *Oy Gottenyu*, I can't cope anymore. I have to lie down. Morris, talk to your son."

I should have quit writing then and there. But at the time, I figured that I was simply a misunderstood genius. I daydreamed constantly, rewriting my Pulitzer Prize acceptance speech over and over in my mind.

I figure that instead of putting all the man-hours which I put into daydreaming during my high school career, I could have written three novels the size of *War and Peace*, painted the Sistine Chapel and still have had time to invent the lightbulb.

One of the courses I took in college was American History and, when I received an A+ on my first essay, my mother announced that she was sure I had finally found my niche in life. The perfect profession: *President of the United States.*

"If Rose's son could become the first Catholic, why can't my Rudy become the first Jew?"

"And do you know how much money it takes to become President?" my father asked.

"Did I say he should jump from college to the Oval Office? He'll work himself up."

Working myself up was a series of carefully calculated steps. N.Y.U. — Harvard — meeting a rich and influential girl from Arizona — moving to Arizona and setting up a law practice — running for local office — Congressman — Senator — President.

And why Arizona? Because my mother had once spent a week in Phoenix, visiting her sister, and had fallen in love with the desert.

"Esther, I don't understand you. For most Jews the desert means Israel."

"And what would I do with all those *greasies*?" *Greasies* is how she labelled the Arabs. "But Arizona has cowboys and Indians. Good people. Honest people. You know where you stand with a cowboy."

I had nothing to do with getting into NYU. It was entirely my mother's fault. What with the yelling and crying, the cajoling and pushing, the kvetching and lamenting, I think the Admissions Officer had no more strength left in him and so he accepted me as a partial, independent night student, on trial. My mother said that she would plant a tree in Israel for him. Maybe that convinced him.

During the second year I took my first and last course in psychology. Leon simply couldn't understand this. Now that he was a big shot psychiatrist and had just moved into new quarters on Park Avenue, he said that there was no profession in the world more satisfying than probing the mind.

"Leon," I said, "I don't care why rats go through mazes and I don't give a damn why dogs salivate, and I couldn't care less why guinea pigs push down on levers."

"You're an idiot, Rudy. A one hundred percent bona fide simpleton. Don't you understand that rats and dogs and pigs are only the beginning? Can't you ever see beyond your nose? Once you get through all that Skinner crap, then you'll advance to human beings. Don't you remember high school biology? There weren't any humans in formaldehyde — they gave you frogs. What's the matter with you? You have to start at the bottom, like I did. But no, Rudy Petinsky wants to attack the entire human psyche in PSYCH 101. Well, forget it, you have to pay your dues, like everyone else. And, as for rats, let me tell you..."

"Leon, please, we're eating," my father said.

"All I meant to say is that these big, beautiful rodents are the key."

"The key to what?" I asked.

"To what?" Leon said, jumping up from his seat. "To unlocking the lock!"

"What lock?" I asked.

"Your lock, my lock, your mother's lock. All our locks. The whole human race's lock. Our minds, Rudy. The locks of our minds."

"And with these keys, the locks are going to open up?"

"That's it. They'll open up as easy as abracadabra."

"And do you have one of these keys?"

"Well, no, not yet. I'm still working on it. These things take time."

"And when you're through, you'll have a key?"

"I most certainly will!"

Taking a psychology course, and listening to the pseudo-intellectual undergraduates (twenty-five Leon clones), reaffirmed the fact that I would never enter this profession, not to mention that I would never be able to stomach Leon as my colleague. Yet it was in PSYCH 101 where I figured out that daydreaming was the forerunner of thinking, and thinking was the forerunner of analysing, and analysing was the forerunner of stress, and stress was the forerunner of worrying, and worrying was the forerunner of neurosis, and neurosis was the forerunner of psychosis, and psychosis was the first step in trying to understand Leon. And since I'd never be able to figure him out, why bother to daydream in the first place? So I stopped daydreaming and applied myself to other studies. Three years later, I received my B.A. with a major in film aesthetics.

"And what kind of a job will you be able to get because you now know why a film director uses a close-up?" Leon asked.

"Maybe a job in Hollywood," I answered.

"Fool. Dreamer. Imbecile," he answered back.

CHAPTER 6

I began my assault on *Then Was Forever*. The main problem was how to make it realistic, considering I thought it already was. After two weeks of torment, I decided that it might be easier to begin a brand new novel. No sooner had I said "new novel," then ideas popped out of my mind. I decided that my protagonist would be a female. A bit neurotic, a little crazy, maybe retarded, even psychotic. And very ugly. This would give me ample material to talk about and I could base quite a bit of the character on Leon. She would be a sickly girl plagued by nightmares. She would be friendless and would have to make up imaginary friends. She would have a pet — an old canary, possibly dead. She would live in Chicago with her parents, in an apartment building. Her father would be the caretaker of the building and her mother could be an alcoholic, or a junkie, or an ex-hooker, or all three. The possibilities were endless. Halfway through the first chapter I realised that Susan was going nowhere. All I had was a miserable character with no direction. I tore chapter one out of my binder and threw the pages into the garbage can. Susan would not be born. I lit a cigarette, wrote "Chapter One" on a fresh piece of paper and tried again. I came up with a fantastic idea about this fun-loving couple: high on life, real party-goers with a combined weekly salary of two thousand dollars and then both lose their jobs. Their savings dwindle down to nothing and very soon they stop going to discotheques on Saturday nights. Instead, they end up at the local pharmacy looking for bargains: Q-tips, soap pads, hair conditioners. Disillusionment sets in.

A voice in my head told me: "*Black humour is not what you're looking for, Rudy.*"

Another voice told me: "*Your idea is ludicrous.*"

I abandoned my fun-loving couple. And before I knew it, I

abandoned any further attempts to write a brand new novel. I did not want three strikes on my first day at bat. So I went to the store, got the latest edition of *Creamy Butts* and jerked off.

The next morning, after a restless sleep, I sat down at my desk and started all over again. Nothing was working. No ideas, no inspirations, no thoughts. After four hours of imagining that I was the greatest writer of all time, and that I had written every important work that had ever been published, and that I was worth somewhere in the vicinity of two billion dollars, I turned on the T.V. and watched the last fifteen minutes of "The Price Is Right." As Johnny Olson was saying "Come on down" for the fifteen millionth time, my mother came home.

"This is what it all boils down to! A twenty-one-year-old watching a game show in the middle of the day!"

"I need a break."

"You need a job."

"I have a job."

"You have a dream. That's not a job!" she said in disgust as she marched to the kitchen, hauling her groceries.

"Ma," I yelled. "I'm stuck. Plaster wants me to rewrite and I figure I should start a new novel so I'm trying to find an idea."

"Oh, I see. That explains it. Writers get ideas while munching potato chips and watching T.V."

"Writers get ideas at all times of the day. The brain is always receptive."

"So be receptive at your desk."

When my father came home, my mother told him how she had found me in front of the T.V.

"Rudy," he said, "what you do with your life is your business, but watching T.V. in the middle of the day is not healthy. It's not being productive."

"Dad, I sat at my desk for four hours and nothing clicked. I needed a break, that's all."

"I wonder what Leon would have to say about all this?" my mother piped in.

"Esther, leave Leon out of this. We don't need a two-hour sermon from him."

"I can't understand the both of you. I turned on the T.V. to hear voices. It was quiet in the house. I could have just as well turned on the radio, or gone for a walk."

"Rudy," my father said, "I don't know anything about writing but I would think that writing is like any other kind of work. Even if you're stuck, you stick with it."

"I just turned on the T.V. for a few lousy minutes! Just to take a break. Call it a coffee break, if you will."

"You call it a coffee break. I call it goofing off!" My mother said, furiously slamming the pantry door closed.

That night, I set the alarm clock for 7 A.M. I wanted to begin the day with a healthy breakfast, then shower and shave, and then attack my new novel with a vengeance. I was determined to have a first draft by nightfall and at supper I would gloat as my parents would say: "Hmm, not bad. Not bad at all."

The alarm went off and I pushed the snooze button to give me an extra ten minutes of sleep. I woke up at 11 o'clock, never having heard the second alarm. I panicked. I quickly ran to the bathroom, splashed some water on my face, combed my hair and frantically shaved, nicking myself twice. I entered the kitchen with pieces of Kleenex stuck on my lip and chin. I was greeted by my mother, who glared at me. I plugged in the kettle and scrambled up a couple of eggs.

"All the time in the world to become famous, eh?" she said. "Just wait till your father hears the hours you keep."

"I slept in. I just slept in. It happens, you know. Why do you have to make such a big deal of it? And what do you mean you're going to tell Dad? Don't you think that's a bit childish? After all, I'm twenty-one. Why are you squealing on me?"

"Because maybe he'll come to his senses."

"What do you mean?"

"He really believes that you'll become a hotshot writer and get everything you want."

"And you don't?"

"Maybe I do and maybe I don't but at the rate you're going, it might take fifty years. I don't see why you can't get a job and write at night."

"At night! I'll be exhausted. I have to have an open mind to be creative. Not be inundated by petty things that go on during the day at work. Besides, I feel most creative in the morning."

"Where? In bed?"

"It was an accident. I overslept."

"Today you overslept, yesterday you watched T.V. What's on the menu for tomorrow?"

I thought that if this continued, I would have to move out. But there was a problem with moving out. I would need to find a job, and if I had a job, when would I write? For the time being, I would stick it out.

I took my coffee, toast and eggs to my room. As my frustration dimmed, an idea began to formulate. At first, all I could see was a salesman but, as I began putting pen to paper, the salesman took on a life of his own. My new novel was going to be about a man named Thomas Watson — aluminium siding salesman. He is frustrated because he can't seem to make a success of himself. All of his friends have made it. They live in big homes and drive expensive cars. Watson's problem is that he can't seem to shake loose the kid that lives inside him. He sees his friends turning into adults, attaining responsibilities and becoming rational, but he still likes to play with yo-yos and bolo bats. He is continually struggling to recapture his youth. The turmoil inside his head is devastating. So much so that he quits his job and leaves the city. He travels all over the world, finally settling in New Guinea and marrying the tribal chief's daughter, Orgul, who resembles a Sumo wrestler who has had one too many wrestling matches. What with her giant lips, bulbous nose, gargantuan breasts, massive behind, puffy thighs, swollen ankles and webbed toes, she is considered the prize catch of all of the tribal chief's twenty-seven daughters.

Tom and his new bride return to America. They buy an average bungalow in an average suburb and settle down to an average life.

They have children — the national average, 2.3. They buy cars — the national average, 1.8. They take vacations — the national average, 1.2. Everything seems fine for a while until Orgul develops a brain tumour which sets off a rash of irrational behaviour. She buys a shotgun and attacks the SPCA, telling her husband that the poodles were going to eat up her geraniums. Then she sets fire to the local barber shop and explains to Tom that "Gino's Hair Emporium" is really a front for the CIA and that Gino had bugged her telephone, listening to her while she had placed orders to the supermarket. Finally, half mad, she murders Tom and the kids. Then she reconsiders, has them stuffed and placed around the table, serving them pineapples and kumquats for dinner.

I was feeling alive and revitalised and renewed and fresh and good and burning with desire to finish at least one draft of the first chapter, until I read what I had written. An hour had passed while I wrote this frivolous piece of junk. I put down my pen and left the house. I walked around the block a few times and returned home, hoping to start again. As I opened the door I was confronted by my mother, who had just come in.

"I went for a walk. I was upset."

"Upset? Whatever for?"

"I thought I had the answer, but I didn't."

"The answer?"

"The plot for my new novel."

"Oh, the plot."

"Yes."

"It wasn't good?"

"No."

"So you went for a walk?"

"Yes."

"I see."

I was taken aback by my mother's calm attitude. I had expected fireworks.

"Who are you calling?" I asked.

"Leon. I think the two of you should have a private discussion."

I said nothing. I was sure I would hear more of this at supper. I was right. As soon as we sat down to eat, my mother said, in a very nonchalant voice, "Morris, guess what your son did today?"

"He wrote a book?"

"Not quite." Her voice took on a menacing tone.

"What?"

"He went for a walk."

"Fresh air is good for the mind."

"Absolutely. I'm the first to admit that fresh air is healthy. And so is sleep."

"I don't understand."

"You will, Dad. Ma's going to tell you."

And so she did. In the most shrilling and piercing tone she could come up with. And when she had finished, tears welling up in her eyes, my father looked at me and said, "Rudy, is everything your mother is telling me true?"

"Everything except the part about breakfast. I had scrambled eggs, not sunny-side up."

My parents were very disappointed in me. They thought that I was ruining my life. I tried to explain that coming up with ideas for a novel was no easy task. It wasn't like any other kind of job. They would have to put up with my unorthodox ways. What they simply couldn't understand was that I could not come up with an idea. After one week of beating this subject to death, my mother finally said, "Rudy, you're an idiot. You're looking for an idea, your father's looking for one for you, I'm looking for one too and all along it's right here, in this house."

"Where?" I asked.

"Here. With us. In this very room."

"Where?"

"Me. Your father. Even you."

"Where?"

"Don't you see?"

"No."

"Morris, do you?"

"What?"

"See the idea."

"No, Esther. I don't."

"I don't either, Ma."

"You're both idiots. Rudy, listen. You need something realistic, right?"

"Right."

"What's the most realistic thing you could write about?"

"What?"

"People. People you know. And who do you know better than your family? Me, your father, your sister. Yourself. Write about us."

"Us?"

"Why not?"

I thought about it. I mulled it over. I scribbled down some thoughts. A few sentences. A short outline. Why not indeed?

THE PETINSKY CHRONICLES

Chapter One

Both my parents were products of Hitlermania and persecutionitis. They survived, as did countless others, in order to begin my glorious generation. By the time they...

"Rudy, come over here."

"What do you want, Ma?" Dammit! I told her never to bother me when I'm writing.

"You forgot to get the toilet paper. Leon and Julie will be here soon and we have no toilet paper."

Jesus. Here I am, writing the definitive novel on the lost tribes of Poland and she's talking toilet paper. Was Camus plagued by his mother to get toilet paper? Was Tolstoy?

"Rudy!"

"Okay. Okay. I'm going."

"And don't get the plain white kind like you did last time. Look for green flowers."

CHAPTER 7

Leon pushed his chair away from his table, loosening his belt.

"That was some meal, Mom," he said, belching contentedly. Morris, you're a lucky man."

"And Mom has such a sense of style," Julie chimed in. "Why even her bathroom tissue is colour-coordinated."

Ma smiled at me triumphantly.

"So how's the writing going, Rudy?"

"Fine, Leon. Today I chose a pen name. Before you know it, I'll be sitting poolside surrounded by banana daiquiris."

"You spent a whole day choosing a pen name?" my mother said, as she gave me a curious look. "This is how you write?"

"I was writing. I was choosing a pen name. I decided on: 'Max Vocab.' Rudy Petinsky isn't exactly Book-of-the-Month Club material."

"Eight hours, Rudy? It took you eight hours to choose a lousy pen name?"

My mother decided that she wanted me to see Leon — professionally. She insisted I'd turn over a new leaf. Leon agreed and figured three hours a week for six months would do the trick.

Somehow I couldn't bring myself to trust someone who used to be a plumber — a plumber who suffered from low blood pressure, haemorrhoids, halitosis and acute acne. One day Leon got fed up with plumbing, joined the Armed Forces and discovered his vocation: psychology. According to Leon, he was vaguely considering becoming a rabbi (and had grown a beard, just in case) when the idea of psychology came by divine inspiration, while he was hitching a lift on a reconnaissance mission. "It was as if God put his finger on my beard and said: 'Cure thy anguish by curing the world's anguish. Psychology, Leon. Forget the Talmud. There are too many rabbis already and, besides, psychiatrists make more money.' "

That night, after dinner, I quietly pulled Leon into a corner of the room and asked, "What would we do in your office?"

"I don't know."

"There must be something. A cure? Therapy?"

"No. I'm sorry."

"Leon, let me ask you this. If a man with the same problems as me had walked into your office and you had diagnosed his problems, what treatment would you recommend?"

"None."

"What do you mean? Wouldn't you like to be able to help your patients by offering them a cure?"

"Rudy, there are no cures. We may be able to figure out the causes but there's just no point in trying to effect a cure. And I'll tell you why: A person who goes to a psychiatrist obviously has a problem. Big or small, it's not important. No matter what his problem is, I can cure it. But I won't. Know why?"

"No."

"Because if I did, two weeks later he'd be back with another problem and another. It would never stop. Know why?"

"Why?"

"Because people who go to psychiatrists are sickos. Deeply troubled people. So troubled in fact that, when all is going well, they create a problem. So what's the point in cures? I just sit there, listen to them, take a few notes, prescribe a couple of pills and tell them not to worry so much..."

Ma enjoyed seeing Leon. She believed that everyone should consult a psychiatrist, whether there was something wrong or not. She felt it cleansed the soul. Shortly after she became Leon's client she began to collect stamps from African nations. Maybe she just felt it was time to put some colour in her life. Or maybe she continued to see Leon because she felt he needed the money, otherwise he'd have to go back to plumbing and she would rather drop dead than have a daughter who was a plumber's wife.

I didn't want to see Leon professionally. Hell, I didn't even like to see him socially. There were only two things I had in common with him: vegetables and erotic literature. Once a week, on Friday nights, we would meet at my parents' house for supper. And after the meal Leon inevitably ate his paper table napkin for dessert. He discreetly snatched off a tiny corner, crumpled it, rolled it into a tiny ball and plopped it into his mouth. By the end of the evening, three-quarters of his napkin was resting safely in his stomach. Could you really expect me to have confidence in a man like this? From what I'd heard, all of his patients were buddies from his Army days. All of them had yet to be cured and all of them were on Endirol, Leon's trick pill. He felt that slowing down their heart rate would reduce the amount of blood rushing to their brains. Leon honestly believed that all psychiatric disorders were caused by too much blood accumulating in the brain. So he prescribed Endirol to all of his clients.

It was hard to believe my sister loved him.

And why did Julie love Leon? Because Julie didn't expect too much from life, and because Julie was realistic and practical. She simply understood that if she wanted to get married she'd have to settle for second best. With Leon, she got seventh.

After twelve years of marriage, Julie was still childless. The doctors felt that Leon's sperm weren't working properly. Maybe they weren't coming out fast enough, or maybe they were coming out too fast. But if you ask me, Leon wasn't putting it in the right place and Julie, who didn't expect too much from life, was content that Leon could at least ejaculate: never mind that it hit her in the armpit or between the toes. For Julie, it was enough that Leon tried. She didn't believe in miracles.

On the same day that I decided to abandon *The Petinsky Chronicles* (most of my characters got wiped out in concentration camps and I was too depressed to continue), we received a call from Julie telling us that Leon was in the hospital.

At first Julie thought Leon was having a nervous breakdown. Instead, he was having a heart attack and, as a result, Julie would no longer have sex with him. Leon pleaded and cajoled, whimpered and cried, screamed and threatened, to no avail. Julie wasn't giving in. Even in the blue paper given to him by his doctor (under heading #4 and just below item #3, <u>Do not eat schmaltz</u> <u>herring)</u> was the statement: <u>You can have a normal healthy and active sex life.</u>

Julie would not give in. She firmly believed that humping would be too much of a strain on the heart. "Too much pumping blood," she said authoritatively. Leon had only one alternative: *Playboy* magazine. Every so often he would shuffle off into the bedroom and give it the old college try. One for the old pippick. A forty-year-old man pumping sperm into a handful of Kleenex, praying that this secretive exertion would not land him back in Mt. Sinai.

Even after she caught him doing it one rainy afternoon, Julie still wouldn't budge. Her main concern was that, God forbid, Leon would collapse on top of her. God forbid! The humiliation of it all! Having to call an ambulance, and before its arrival, having to clean up, get dressed and composed. This was not her way. No, she would wait and so would Leon. I think it was the waiting that did it because, seven months after his heart attack, he finally got what I had all along thought he would get: a nervous breakdown.

Chapter 8

I felt I was on the verge of joining Leon with my own breakdown as I sat in front of Plaster's desk, awaiting his verdict on my new novel.

CLIMBING THE LADDER

by Rudy Petinsky

Chapter One

The bungalow was not exactly a bungalow in the typical sense. It wasn't exactly somebody's home and yet it was the home of Dalia Productions, an independent film unit belonging to Dale Needlemyer who rented it out from Paramount.

Once inside, the first thing that hit Mitch was the receptionist. A tall, striking blonde dressed in a white clinging dress that showed off a delicious body. Delicious like a Danish, which maybe she was. She came from behind her desk, which wasn't a desk at all but resembled a dining room table — smoked glass on four gold pillars — and greeted him with a very friendly smile. Mitch couldn't help noticing how her white shoes disappeared into the very white carpeting. Like they melted into a marshmallow sea. He sat down on the white corduroy couch and tried not to stare too much at her.

"Mr. Needlemyer must like the colour white," Mitch said to her.

"I'm sorry?" she said.

"I said that Mr. Needlemyer must like the colour white."

"No. Not particularly. I do."

"Oh."

"Mr. Vermeer, Mr. Needlemyer will see you now. Please come this way."

Mitch followed behind her only to realize that he would need every effort not to enter Needlemyer's office with a hard-on.

As they entered, Mitch was told to have a seat in front of the desk, which looked like a dining room table: a dark wood Colonial model. Needlemyer was on the phone talking to someone about someone else named Saul. His office was excessively large and had the look of a well-lived-in living-room: plush rust carpeting, live plants in every corner, a couch, two chairs and coffee table in one part of the room and dark wood panelling rising from the floor going one third of the way and meeting up with a dainty pale brown wallpaper. Very stylish. On the wallpaper were wood-framed posters of movies he had made. At the far end of the room was a fireplace and on the mantel stood four Oscars.

"Tell Saul that he can go to hell. And if he's in hell then I don't want to talk to him because, if he's in hell, then he's dead and I don't talk to dead people. Good-bye!"

"I'm sorry to have kept you waiting. I'm Dale Needlemyer. Please call me Dale."

Mitch got out of his chair and shook his hand. He hated shaking hands. He was always afraid of squeezing too hard. He was also never sure when it was the right time to let go.

"It's nice to meet you, Dale. I'm Mitch."

As Mitch was about to pull back, Dale reached over with his left hand to cover both their rights. With this manoeuvre, Dale had managed to bring the ball back to his court and he would have to be the one to pull back. Which he did, but not before Mitch had reached the count of six.

"How was your flight?"

"Good. No turbulence."

"Would you care for a coffee? Something stronger?"

"Coffee would be nice."

Dale walked over towards the fireplace. Next to it were bookshelves built into the wall panelling. At the touch of a button, a section of the wall rotated, and out came glass shelving with cups and saucers on one shelf, spoons on another and a pewter tea set on another. On the bottom shelf was a coffee urn busily brewing, unbothered to be in another room.

"If you had wanted something stronger, I would have pushed another button," Dale said in a pleasant voice with a smile on his face.

As coffee was being poured, Mitch admired the cut of Dale's chocolate brown suit and his stylish cream shirt. His tie was tucked behind a vest and straddling the two pockets of his vest was a gold chain. His shoes, a pair of brogues, told Mitch that even though he was modern in appearance, he still enjoyed the past. As for his age, it was hard to tell. His face was freshly shaven and tanned, no moustache or beard. His sideburns were thick and full and grey and just reached the tip of his earlobe. His hair was thinning but had not yet turned grey. He had a strong, firm jaw with a very pronounced cleft and brown eyes that were soft and welcoming. He must have been around sixty and, for sixty, he looked in good shape. Not too heavy, not too thin.

"Do you take milk and sugar?"

"Yes. One spoonful of sugar."

"I take three. I guess I like the good things in life."

"It doesn't show."

"No. I try to keep fit. I swim a lot, play tennis every day, golf, fish, but I can't say no to chocolate. Chocolate cake, sweets, that's my downfall. Anyway, at seventy-two, I don't think I look too bad.

"I would have given you sixty. Not a day older."

"Another compliment like that and I just might give you what you're asking for."

"And what's that?"

"According to your telegram, you want to write the script."

"That's right."

"What do you know about writing movies?"

"Nothing. But I didn't know anything about writing novels and I wrote one."

"Movies are different. Each word counts and each word has to be seen. There are no extra words in a movie like there are in a book."

"I can do it."

"By yourself?"

"No. I'd want to work with an experienced screenwriter."

"You're honest."

"Listen, Dale. I want to work in movies. I can write. Give me a chance."

"Will you be willing to sell the rights?"

"If the price is right."

"What did you have in mind?"

"You tell me."

"What I had in mind is not what I had in mind before you walked in, but I'm going to take a chance with you. You seem like you know what you want. How's the book selling?"

"It sort of fizzled. It was doing good business but, for some reason, it just sort of died."

"I can fix that."

"What do you mean?"

"The book can be reprinted with a new cover design. With the star of the movie on the front. A soon-to-be Paramount movie. That sort of thing. Was your book ever on the *Times'* best seller list?"

"No."

"That, too, can be arranged."

"How?"

"By placing a few strategic calls to bookstores, asking for it, buying the book in large quantities. There are ways."

"You'd do all that?"

"If it means higher grosses, yes."

"Great. You have my permission."

"That brings us back to the rights and what you had in mind as a price."

"Dale, I'll be honest with you. I have no idea. You make me an offer and I'll decide whether it's fair."

"What you need is an agent. Fair is not part of the movie business."

"Do you remember what it was like when you first started out in the business?"

"Yes. It was thirty-eight years ago. 1933. I started out as a writer for MGM. I was given a three-month contract at $100 a week. If my contract was picked up, it was at $125 for another three months, then $150 for another three months and $200 for another three months. At the end of the year, if I was still around, my salary would jump to $350 a week."

"Were you picked up?"

"I'm still here, aren't I?"

"Yes. When you were hired, did you have any experience in movies?"

"No. I was a reporter."

"Who gave you your first contract?"

"Irving Thalberg. He took a chance on... excuse me. Yes, Linda?

No. I'm busy now. No calls for the next little while... as I was saying, Mitch, Thalberg took a chance with me and I suppose that's what you want me to do with you."

"Yes."

"Okay. For the rights I'll pay you $20,000. I expect a working script to be completed in three months. For that I'll pay you $500 a week. You'll be working with John Washington..."

"I've heard of him."

"... yes, he's won two Oscars for his screenplays. John calls all the shots. You work with him but, most important, you learn from him. He'll show you how to write a film script. Once the working script is finished, and if I like it, then I'll give you another $500 a week to do revisions and the final shooting script."

"Where do I sign?"

"I'll have a contract drawn up. You can sign tomorrow."

"Thank you, Dale. I won't let you down."

"It won't be me, Mitch, that you let down."

"I know."

"Wait a minute, I just got an idea... Linda, get me John Washington on the phone... Mitch, I'll have you picked up at the hotel around 6:30. You'll have dinner with me and my wife tonight and I'll arrange for John to come, too. That way you can meet him and we'll talk about the movie. Is that all right with you?"

"Yes. Thank you."

"Fine. Just let Linda know where you're staying."

Mitch got out of his chair and said good-bye to Dale. As he walked past the receptionist, he couldn't help but think how far he had come in the last seven years...

Plaster fidgeted in his chair and looked up.

"I don't like it. As a matter of fact, it's boring. Horribly boring.

Incredibly boring. Mind-numbingly boring."

"Boring? A year ago you told me to make my novel more realistic. Realism, you bellowed. REALISM! What do you want from me? Blood?"

"Mr. Petinsky, control yourself. It's true that I said to make it more realistic, but I don't believe the word 'boredom' ever cropped up in the conversation."

"Cropped? No. I don't believe you did use the word 'boring'. You did mention that my writing was romantic tulipdung, and you did tell me to toughen it up and make it more realistic. So I did. This novel is not the one you read a year ago. I wrote a brand new story. A story about the past. A story about the future. A story about a man going through a nervous breakdown. A story about a man not realizing his goals. A story about a man who sold aluminium siding and ended up a writer."

"Mr. Petinsky, it's boring," Plaster repeated. "Perhaps another story line would be more appropriate. Give it another go. And remember to keep it realistic. Right? Realism, that's what people want today."

I wanted to scream. I mean, this just wasn't the way things were supposed to work out. After all, this was my second attempt. I had done what Plaster had asked me to do: write a realistic novel. What did this animal want from me?

"I really don't know what else to say to you, Mr. Petinsky. Would you like to give it another go?"

"Huh?"

"Another go, Mr. Petinsky. Would you consider writing a fresh novel?"

"Huh?"

I heard him. I might have been going mad but I was not deaf. I just couldn't respond in any intelligent manner. I was dazed. Confused. I had really not expected this. Why just the other day, I had eaten in a Chinese restaurant and my fortune cookie had said: "Fame will reach you before the end of the month." And I thought the Chinese were so clever. Another disappointment.

"Well, Mr. Petinsky, have you thought it over?"

"Yes, Mr. Plaster. Thank you for your time. I'll take your ideas into consideration."

"Fine. That's the spirit. By the by, if I may give you a bit of counsel?"

"Sure. Why not?"

"Relax for a bit. I think you've been overworking your writing. Stop for awhile. Give it a rest. Don't think. A couple of months. Take my advice, Rudy, if you permit me to call you by your first name..."

"Sure. Why not?"

"... stop writing for four, five months. You'll find that once you begin again, you'll be fresh and alive and simply exploding with ideas."

"Sure. Why not?"

It wasn't fair. It was no fuckin' fair. Working day and night just for the chance of immortality. For the chance of striking it rich and famous. A slight chance, but was it worth it? I just didn't know anymore. I just didn't know.

At least Plaster saw me and gave me three minutes of his time once a year. None of the other publishers did that.

After the meeting, I couldn't talk to anyone for weeks. Even my father couldn't get me out of my lethargy: "You'll see Rudy, one day all the pieces will come together."

My mother was no help at all: "The problem with you, Rudy, is that you're spoiled. Your father and I spoiled you. More your father than me, but it's my fault, too. For God's sake, Rudy, stop dreaming and grow up. You're not a little boy anymore. Go get yourself a job and start a family. You know, Rudy, your father is not getting any younger. He'd like to become a grandfather. Mind you, I'm not pushing. I'm just saying what's on my mind."

Even Julie, who rarely mixed into my business, offered me some advice: "Rudy, why don't you call Leon? Even though he's still not one hundred percent, I'm sure he could be of some help to you."

"Leon?"

"Yes?"

"It's Rudy. How are you feeling?"

"Fine. What do you want?"

"Julie suggested that I give you a call."

"Why?"

"I've got a problem."

"What now?"

"I need to know if I'm wasting my time."

"And your next question is: What does it all mean?"

"What are you talking about?"

"Rudy, I find you very exasperating. Let me ask the questions."

"Okay. Ask."

"I can't ask anything until you tell me your problem."

"My writing. Plaster says that I should take off a few months and stop writing. Experience, he says. Travel, he says. Explore, he tells me."

"You think you've got problems? Tomorrow's my birthday. I'll be forty. And instead of getting stronger and more beautiful, I'm going bald. And where I don't need any hair, that's where it's growing. On my knuckles, on my back, in my nostrils and in my ears. Forty! I can't believe it. Where have all the years gone? At the most, all I've got is another thirty years of productivity. Then I'll be seventy. Oh my God! Seventy! I can't believe it. I just can't believe it. Old age pension. Retirement. Shuffleboard. And when I'm seventy, your sister will be sixty. Yech! I'll be married to a sixty-year-old hag. Yech!"

"Happy birthday, Leon. May you live until one hundred and twenty."

It was good to hear that someone else had problems too and especially nice to find out that, after two months, Leon had made very little progress, if any at all. Julie had been right. I was feeling much better.

CHAPTER 9

"What? You're off again? Why did you bother to unpack?"

"Ma, it's been over a year. I need new experiences."

"The whole world comes to New York to experience. Am I right, Morris?"

"Yes, Esther," my father sighed as he took off his shoes and put on his slippers.

"Then why, Rudy, do you have to leave? Why do you have to be different?"

"I'm not being different. I just need to get away."

"For how long?"

"As long as it takes."

"Can you give me an exact time? A month? A year? Two years?"

"Esther, let the boy go. Now's the time for him to travel. When do you want him to go – when he's married? When he has children? Now, Rudy's got no responsibilities, so let him go. Let him have his fun."

"And where will he sleep? And eat? We have no relatives out there. If only I knew someone."

"Esther, let him go. You can't always hang on to him."

"If he was near home, I wouldn't have to."

"Ma, don't worry so much."

"You hear that, Morris? He tells me not to worry. Wait, Rudy, just you wait until you have children. I hope your son does to you what you're doing to me."

"Esther, relax... your blood pressure."

"One last word. I just want to say to you, Rudy, that this is a big mistake you're making. Now is the time to plant the seeds, to establish yourself for the future. Travelling to California just so you can get experiences for a book is very immature on your part... and naive."

"Thanks for your blessing, Ma."

"Rudy, Rudy, listen to me. Please listen to me."

"I'm listening."

"Hollywood," she said as she shook her head, "Hollywood isn't for real."

"Hollywood isn't for real?"

"No. Hollywood is dreaming and pretending and fun and games. This is real, Rudy. Right here. In New York. This is the real world."

"Ma, there's real people in Hollywood. Honest to goodness real people."

"Dreamers. Only dreamers in Hollywood. Dreamers and pretenders. No honest hard-working people live there. Only dreamers."

"Ma, you're crazy. I'm sorry, but you're crazy. How can you say such a thing? You think everyone in Hollywood works in the movies? Well, let me tell you, there's waiters and used car salesmen and teachers and businessmen and lawyers and doctors and bus drivers and construction workers..."

"... and they all want to be in the movies. Even the doctors."

"Ma, you're nuts."

"First crazy, now nuts. Very nice."

"Ma, I'm going to Hollywood. I need to go."

"What you *need* is a wife."

PART • TWO

Prince of the Bluestone

Chapter 10

Columbia to MGM to Paramount to Republic to RKO to Twentieth Century Fox to Warner Brothers to Universal to Disneyland to Bel Air to Beverly Hills to Forest Lawn to Griffith Park to MacArthur Park to Santa Barbara to San Diego to Santa Catalina to Burbank to Culver City to Glendale to Palm Springs to Marineland to Palos Verdes Estates to Rolling Hills Estates to Camp Pendleton to Camp Irwin to U.S. Naval Ordnance Test Station to Marine Corps Training Center to Vandenberg Air Force Base to Point Arguello Naval Missile Facilities to San Rafael Mountains to Sierra Madre Mountains to Greenhorn Mountains to Plute Mountains to Tehachapi Mountains to El Paso Mountains to Sidewinder Mountain to Big Bear Lake to White Water to Mission Creek Indian Reservation to Twentynine Palms Indian Reservation to Chuckwalla Mountains and to Little Chuckwalla Mountains all by the way of Van Nuys Freeway, Golden State Freeway, Ventura Freeway, Hollywood Freeway, Pasadena Freeway, Santa Monica Freeway, San Diego Freeway, San Bernardino Freeway and the Pacific Coast Highway.

And what was I thinking about while driving around L.A.?

"Rudy, your record in Hollywood is awesome. You have written and produced seventeen pictures and written, produced and directed twenty-three; winning the coveted Oscar a record sixty-eight times. In between all these movies, you have found time to write six best-selling novels — all Pulitzer Prize winners, as well as being last year's recipient of the Nobel Prize for Literature. You are a phenomenon."

"Why thank you, Johnny..."

And all of this dreaming left me back at point A: alone, bewildered, frightened, tired and depressed, as well as miserable, because it was only a matter of time before I would have to move out of my hotel with its free drink at the "happy hour" bar. And I was just beginning to acquire a taste for Pink Ladies…

And where was I going to live? Long Beach? Redondo Beach? Manhattan Beach? Will Rogers Beach? San Fernando? San Jacinto? San Bernardino? San Clemente?

The beaches were too expensive and "The San's" were either too far from Hollywood, too hard to pronounce, or just too cutesy. Imagine someone asking where I lived: "I live in San Juan Capistrano." I just wasn't ready for that; I wanted to bed beautiful women, not beautiful boys. Maybe after I made it, I'd be more secure with a "San."

I ended up at the Bluestone. My apartment was tiny but well preserved. One wall of the living room/bedroom was tastefully done in cork. Another wall had a huge fishing net on it. I was told that the previous occupant had been a retired Navy skipper. In the fishing net were clam shells, most of them opened and all of them brightly painted in reds, yellows and greens. In his retirement, the Navy skipper had taken up painting as a hobby.

The other two walls had mirrors on them. So did the ceiling. Very west coast. I was happy that I would not need to redecorate. I had one window with a splendid view of a used-car lot. I knew, at first glance, that I could never be bored in such a place. It was all about stimulation.

The kitchen was clean and well-lit and I was told when I signed the lease that the bathroom had had an interior decorator. I had noticed that immediately after my first leak. When I flushed, a chartreuse coloured liquid filled up the bowl and orange blossom petals cascaded gently onto the water as gracefully as Esther Williams performing a complicated underwater sequence. I wondered how Beverly Hills could possibly outdo my designer toilet bowl.

CHAPTER 11

The Bluestone, opened in 1922, was situated on Chocolate Avenue, five miles north of Hermosa Beach. Redecorated once too often, it now housed senior citizens at reasonable prices.

After my first day on the beach, I decided to sit on the porch with all the old people and just rake in the atmosphere. I couldn't do very much else as my body had turned a borscht red in the sun and was now aching. Covered in Noxema, I carefully sat down and slowly lifted my legs onto the railing. An old woman, plump but pleasant-looking, wearing a long sleeveless summer dress with large sunflowers printed on it, asked me who I was. I think she was surprised that I was staying at The Bluestone. Couldn't blame her. Besides me, the youngest resident was sixty-eight. I was later to find out that this woman, Bella, was the "yenta" of the group. She had been coming to The Bluestone for the last ten years, courtesy of her children, who lived in Seattle. It didn't take five minutes before I knew her life story; three husbands ("I outlived them all"); a gallstone operation; seven grandchildren; and two great-grandchildren. She had a mind like a fox.

"So Rudy, tell me, how come you're not staying at the shmancy hotels?"

"I want to save my money as much as possible."

"Save money? At your age? At your age you should be enjoying yourself. Saving money will come later. Now, you should enjoy yourself. Not here with all the old people. So tell me, Rudy, what's the rush to put money in the bank?"

And so I explained to her that I was a writer, and didn't want to spend too much money till I found myself a job, hopefully in a studio.

"A writer? Wait... wait. Nat... Nat. Come here. Nat..."

Nat turned out to be Nathan Bloomberger; irritable, cranky

and yet charming for someone who appeared to be one hundred and fifty.

"Nat, Nat sit down. I want you to meet Rudy Petinsky. Nat, Rudy's trying to make it in Hollywood. He's a writer."

"No shit," Nat said as he got up from his lawn chair smoothing down his full shock of white hair. His deeply tanned face, creased and wrinkled by years of California sun, came alive.

"Nat, stop with the toilet mouth. Is it gonna kill you to talk clean?"

"All right, all right, leave me alone. So you're a writer? Trying to make it, eh?"

"That's right," I said, embarrassed now that everyone on the veranda knew my business.

"Rudy, Nat knows about Hollywood. That's why I called him over. Used to be a bigshot or so he says. Used to know the big ones or so he says. Used to have a big shmancy home and three shmancy cars or so he says..."

"Bella, go blow someone. I can talk for myself."

"Always with the toilet mouth. Always..."

"So you're trying to make it, eh?"

"Yes. You know about the movie business?" I asked.

"Know it? Practically owned it! Years ago. Used to know all the big ones. Griffith, Chaplin, Fairbanks, Farnum, Bernhardt. All the big ones. Came out here in '05, or was that '06? No, 1905. Definitely. Could have owned it, if that fucker Laemmle hadn't've opened his big mouth. Could have been sitting pretty now. Could've, you know."

"1905. Jeez. That's before the silent movies."

"What's that you say? You'll have to speak louder."

"I said 1905, that's..."

"... that's right, 1905. It wasn't much of a town, Hollywood. More like a dust bowl. Just dust and lizards. Well, today, there's no more dust. Plenty of lizards left, though. You watch yourself out there. If you're not careful, they'll eat you alive. Movie lizards, that is. Movies took over and ruined everything."

"Oh, I thought you were in the movies."

"Movies!! Fucking speaking pieces of film. What kind of a business is that for a grown man? Fairytales, that's what it is. Playing with fairytales. No, no, I came out to California for gold. Gold, sonny. Not movies. Hmph!"

"Did you find gold?"

I knew there had been a gold rush in California in the 1850's, but what was this old coot doing looking for gold in 1905?

"Heard there was plenty left. Plenty of gold left for the picking. And all of it around a hole called Hollywood."

"Did you find any?"

"Find any? Sonny, I bought up 230 acres of it at a place called, what's that name? Sounds Spanish... ends in an o... San something or else..."

"San Fernando?" I offered.

"Yeah, that's it. Anyways, I bought up all the land. Used up all my money and borrowed as much as I could. Knew there was gold in that land. Was sure of it. Still sure of it. Worked the land, sonny, till 1914. Worked it for nine years. And then one day, along came a Mr. Carl Laemmle. Said he was in the moving-picture business. Said he had an offer for me. I took one look at him and knew I was looking at a fool. Offered me $165,000! Why, sonny, that was a fortune in those days. A man could live like a king for the rest of his life. Well, after nine years of eating sweat, I grabbed the money. Turned out this Laemmle fella was craftier than he looked. My land became one of those studios they talk about. Universal Studios..."

"Wow!" I said. I mean, this was history. Imagine talking to the man who had sold Universal Studios to Carl Laemmle. I couldn't believe it.

"... yep, Universal, big fucking studio too. Could have owned it myself. Should have made a deal with that fella. Should have taken a closer look into the moving-picture business. Shit, if a sawed-off pip-squeak like Laemmle could make a fortune, imagine what I could have done! Could have owned the whole kit-and-caboodle. The whole thing. The whole goddamn thing... the whole... Bella, lay off, go blow someone... leave me alone."

"Nat, don't get so excited."

"Buzz off, Bella," Nat muttered as he nodded off.

"He's not so bitter about losing out in the movies," Bella said. "It's more because of the way he lost all his money."

"How's that?" I asked.

"Booze, shmancy women, gambling, shady deals. Three years and he was broke. Completely."

"Too bad," I said.

"Yes, it's a shame. A good man even with his toilet mouth. Rudy, be careful in Hollywood. Keep your eyes open and your ears clean. And even then, get a doctor's opinion, if you know what I mean."

"Thanks, Bella. I think I'll go in now. Good night. See you tomorrow."

Chapter 12

Where to begin?
How to start?
Where to look?
Who to see?

I awoke, the next day, to these plaguing questions. I remember tossing and turning in my bed, my legs twitching like a newborn baby, and wondering what life had in store for me. Success or failure? It was that simple. Shoving a few California oranges, a Chiquita banana, a handful of raisins, a tablespoon of unspoiled yoghurt and a touch of Tabasco sauce into a blender, I prepared myself for my first assault on Cinderellaland. I was going to get myself a job: whether it was a floorsweeper at M.G.M., a guide at Universal, or a mailroom clerk at Paramount. I wasn't out for an Oscar my first day. I was willing to start at the bottom and work myself up to the top.

No one wanted me. Universal had a waiting list and the security guard at M.G.M. told me he wouldn't let me in to see Personnel. The security guard at Paramount didn't bother to talk to me at all. I called it a day. I ended up at the beach, trying to perfect my tan.

Days two, three, and four were not much better. Day five was a fiasco. Instead of beginning the day looking for a job, I first went to the beach, thinking it would be nice to relax for a while before becoming aggravated. I rented a surfboard, paddled out into the wild blue and fell asleep. I was woken up by a fog horn. Seems the U.S. Coastguard had spotted a floating object beyond territorial waters. Seems when they picked me up I was heading towards Japan.

Day six I stayed in bed.

After my first week on the job market, I added up my assets. Zilch! Not one lead. Not one interview. Not one appointment.

No one to see. No one to talk to. Times were tough, so everyone said. It was hard to land a job, they said. We were heading into a depression. We were coming out of a recession. Inflation was up. Hiring was down. Unemployment was rampant. But what the hell did all this have to do with the movies? They still needed writers. Writers were always in demand. How could movies run without scripts, and where were these scripts supposed to come from if not from writers? And how was I ever going to make it if I didn't even have a script to show these people? *What the hell's the matter with you, Rudy? You don't even have a script! All you have are two unpublished novels!*

Is that the answer? Stay in my room and write a script and peddle it to the studios? And what if it's not accepted? Another few months down the drain? Another rejection? I don't think I could take another rejection. Nope. That's not the answer. There must be another way. There's always another way.

I decided to meet the public. Talk to people who were in the same boat as I was. Aspiring this's or that's. Find out the best places to hang around. Where to be seen. Who was important. Who was on their way up. Who was on their way down and who was so far down that they didn't deserve a cigarette butt.

I met all kinds of people. Would-be actors, writers, producers, directors, musicians, singers, dancers, comedians... they were all over the place. They took courses at universities, drove taxis, worked in restaurants, baby-sat. Anything and everything, just to survive till their time came.

In time, they all became recognisable. They all looked like antelopes running in fright: from work to acting class to dance class to voice class and back to work. Most of them would eventually disappear into the sidewalks. Their claim to fame: "I used to room with Johnny A," or "I once shared a sandwich with Loretta B," or "Cliff and I worked in the same shoe store. Now look at him."

However, they did teach me a few things: "Try to be in the right place at the right time." Everywhere I now went, I wondered if I was in the right place. Maybe I should move to another spot. And with every calculated step I took, I glanced at my watch. Is it the right time? And if it's the right time, am I in the right place? Maybe I'm in the right place but the time is wrong? Or maybe the time is right but I'm in the wrong place? I became paranoid. I was afraid to take a step, afraid I would lose my place and someone else would jump in at just the right time. I considered cementing my own feet into the forecourt of Grauman's Chinese Theatre, ensuring I'd be there when destiny arrived.

Another thing the aspirants taught me was to look successful: "Pretend you've just received the Oscar." Look successful — Be successful. That was their motto. Easier said than done. How the hell can a person look successful when they get turned down for jobs on the average of twenty times a week? But I tried — I really tried. I thrust my shoulders back and slapped a big, self-confident grin on my face. After a week, I had a pinched nerve and a sore jaw. And no job.

The third thing the hopefuls taught me was: "Work. Keep trying the studios. Work as an extra. Get a part time job that leaves you flexible. And join an acting class."

"An acting class! But I'm not an actor. I'm a writer."

"So, what's the difference? An actor loses his inhibitions in front of an audience and a writer in front of a typewriter. Besides, it's the experience that you need and the contacts. That's where it's at. Experience and contacts."

I took their advice. And in the meantime, to survive, I became a cabby.

The Famous Pasadena Molding and Cultivating Actors School was located in a run-down old warehouse, on the seamier side of town. It looked like it had been put together with different colours of shoepolish and a lot of spit. Once inside, my eyes had trouble adjusting to the darkness.

"You must be Rudy," a voice called out, somewhere in the distance. I turned and saw an alarming figure in a dark cape whooshing down a rickety flight of stairs.

"I'm Bobby Shane!"

Shane appeared to have about three hundred pounds of fat

glued on his frame, two hundred and fifty pounds of which lay around his stomach. I couldn't take my eyes off him. Underneath his cape he wore purple leotards and a lime green tank top with a decal of a frog steamed into it.

"Are you going to be teaching...?"

"Yes, yes. Let's not waste any more time. Come upstairs and we'll begin our class."

I followed him upstairs, sneezing violently as the dust swirled around me. I was led into a large room with bits and pieces of mirror tacked onto the walls. In one corner lay a green gymnasium mat and beside it a dark brown piano stool.

"I suppose you want to know something about me," Bobby said. "Remember the movie 'Ticket to Glory'?"

I'd never heard of it. I later found out that it had never been shown in reputable theatres.

"I put the whole film together, you know. Wrote, produced, directed, edited. Wrote the music, chose the costumes, created the sets. Everything. This was too fine an enterprise to leave to backbiting, incompetent lackeys. Everything was done by me. Me! I only trust my cameraman, Rudy. In this business, only cameramen can be trusted, eh? Eh?! Well Rudy, why don't we begin?"

"Just me?"

"For now, yes. The rest will be along later. I like to spend personal, intense time alone with a new fellow to begin with. Sort of brings me into contact with your soul. Now, why don't you just sit on the mat and try to feel the room — get in touch with the air around you — feel your environment. Good."

Get in touch with the air! What kind of crap is that? Feel the environment! I paid $720 for this!

"Are you feeling your space, Rudy?"

Feeling my space? What does he mean? Is that actors' talk?

"Yes, yes. I'm feeling my space." Or at least filling it.

"Good. Good. You're doing fine. Just fine."

Why shouldn't I be? I know how to sit.

"Now, Rudy, let's begin to explore. First, let's commence by exploring with our fingers. Wiggle those five extensions of your hand into your space. Move them, explore, explore. Feel that air. Feel it. Good... good."

This is going to make me an actor? Wiggling my fingers? Is this how John Wayne began?

"Fine, Rudy, you're doing real fine. Nice natural technique. Now let's move those arms. Free flow them. Let them hang about you, limp... limp, feel the air, don't forget your fingers... explore, breathe in, breathe out, explore... feel... get in touch with your veins. Feel the blood surging through your arms. Feel those muscles. Explore, feel, breathe, get in touch..."

So many instructions, so little point.

"... all righty, very good, Rudy. Now relax and lie back. Good. No, not on your stomach, on your back. That's it. Now you've got it."

What's he going to do?

"Feeling relaxed, Rudy? Good. Now lift your legs slowly, very slowly, breathe in and breathe out... relax... feel the air..."

Again with the air.

"... try to get involved with the floor supporting your body. Concentrate on your back, concentrate on your legs, concentrate on the floor. Now get your arms going again. Good. Move those arms, slowly... slowly... and your legs, now your neck."

My neck? Jesus! What the hell does he think I am? A contortionist?

"Good, good, slowly, feel the air and relax."

Silence.

"Relax... relax... relax... you're drifting off... think of something pleasant. Think of a soft, juicy piece of tangerine just lingering over your mouth. Rudy, make me feel that you want that piece of tangerine more than you ever wanted your mother's milk."

Now my mother's involved. What next?

"Show me, Rudy. Show me you want that piece. Show me with your eyes, Rudy, with your eyes... now with your tongue, Rudy, with your tongue. Show me, Rudy... show me... ah... ah... with your tongue. Show me."

Jesus, this guy's getting turned on. I think I'd better end this now. How?

"Show me... show me... with your tongue... your tongue... ah... ah."

"Ah... ah... choo! Ah... ahchoo!" I hope that does the trick.

"Yes, well, uh... that'll be all for now, Rudy. You've shown me great promise in your expression. I particularly like the way you felt the air with your fingers. Shows great perception of things that aren't there. An actor's greatest tool, Rudy. Greatest tool."

"Is that it, Mr. Shane?"

"For today, Rudy. Tomorrow at four. Be prompt. Don't care for idlers. For that matter, I don't care for fools either. Talk long enough to a fool, end up one yourself. That's my motto, Rudy. Don't talk to cretins, eh? See you at four tomorrow. Be prompt and be sure to bring a scarf."

"A scarf, Mr. Shane?"

"Of course, Rudy. Can't always feel the air just with fingers. Have to extend yourself, move on, become flexible. Can't always rely on your fingers, Rudy. It's time to grow. Time to push on. Onwards and upwards. Any length will do. Do try and make it colourful, though. Colour always adds. Don't you like colour? Of course you do. Only dolts don't. Must always be colourful, Rudy. An actor's greatest tool, Rudy. Greatest tool."

"Okay. I'll be here."

"Fine boy, fine. Oh, by the way, a week from today I'd like you to bring in a small, home-made percussion instrument. Nothing extravagant, yet do try and be creative."

"A percussion instrument?"

"Yes, yes, a small iddy-biddy thing. It'll show me your true creativity and from there we'll be able to build. Well, I'm off now. Have a 5:30 appointment. Promptness, Rudy. A film depends for its very life on promptness. On budgets, as well, but that will come in time, eh?"

CHAPTER 13

"How's it going, Petinsky?"

"Good, Nat. Great."

"Feel great myself. Got fucked last night."

"Come on."

"Sure, whadd'ya think? Old folks don't do it? It's not something we forget, you know. God, what a piece. Had tits that sagged from here to Kalamazoo. And what an ass. Parted like the Red Sea. I don't have to tell you who played the part of Moses."

"Do you mind if I ask with who?"

"Sure. At her age, what's the point in being discreet? Name's Lucy. Juicy Lucy. Lives on the second floor. Room 214. Did it there."

"Are you and Lucy a number? Going steady?"

"Nope. Ran into her in the elevator last night after I left you. One thing led to another and, before you know it, we were sitting on the floor and drinking wine. I think she even lit a candle or two. So what are you up to today?"

"Well, I thought I'd go next door and get some breakfast, then go to the beach for a couple of hours. Maybe I'll get lucky and meet my own Juicy Lucy."

"Well, sonny, if you need any lessons just holler, ha ha."

"You want to join me for breakfast, Nat? My treat."

"Petinsky, I never pass up a free meal and besides, I like talking to ya. You listen, you know that? Most young'uns don't listen to old folks. Haven't got the time. The truth of the matter is that they just don't give a damn about us. Put us out to pasture and feed us cow manure. Hell, what am I complaining about — was the same way myself. Old people used to give me the creeps. I guess when you look at one it's like seeing yourself in the future — not a pretty sight, eh? But, Petinsky, you're different. I'd almost say, now correct me if I'm wrong, that you enjoy talking to us."

"You're not wrong, Nat. But it's more like listening than talking. What better place to learn history?"

"Atta boy. That's the spirit. Well, if it's history you want, I'll give you a spitoon full. Chew your ear off, sonny."

"Whadd'ya call these goddamn things?"

"Fried bananas," I said nonchalantly, tasting them for the first time.

"I'll be damned. First time for everything, even at my age."

"Nat, how old are you?"

"Ninety-eight."

"How do you do it? How do you keep yourself so fit?"

"You mean how come my feet ain't in the grave yet? Well, I'll tell you. I don't do anything. Never have. But the most important thing I don't do is I don't go to no city doctors. The only kind of doctor I listen to is a veterinarian. I figure if a doctor can cure a horse, well then, he can cure me. Only doctor I ever knew who was worth his weight in corn husks was Sigmund Freud. A Viennese boy. Now *he* was a doctor! Hey waiter, more of these bananas."

"Did you know Freud? *The* Sigmund Freud? C'mon…"

"Ziggy! Know him! You must be joking. Ziggy and I were like brothers. Like two peas in a pod. We did everything together. Introduced him to his wife. Did you know that?"

"No, I didn't."

"Yep. Had her first myself. Wasn't much in bed, so I gave her to Ziggy. What the hell, his mind was never much on sex anyways."

"But all his theories are related to sex!"

"Oh sure, in his books, but I'm talking about in bed."

"Oh."

"Yep. Ziggy and I go back a long time. What a guy. He never asked people, 'How are you doing?' Instead, he asked 'How am I doing?' He was very unsure of himself."

"Nat, what was he like?"

"Ziggy? What a guy. Prince of a fella. Know what he once said to me?"

"What?"

"We were sitting down at some café, enjoying a beer and he says, 'Nathan,' – he always called me that – 'Nathan, life's a bitch'."

"That's all he said? Sigmund Freud said, 'Life's a bitch'?!"

"Yep. That's it. Wasn't much of a talker but what a deep thinker."

"He must have said other things. What did the two of you talk about?"

"Sex, mostly. Loved the subject. Offered to do experiments for him, strictly on the up and up, but he was more interested in the aftermath than the actual doing."

"Is that all you discussed? I mean, there must have been other subjects?"

"Oh sure. Lots of 'em. Just can't remember. Ziggy was a nice fella. Couldn't get nicer — but dull, you know. Can't remember very much about him, but a classier guy or a cleaner guy... Jesus! Petinsky, you ain't never seen the likes of a man like Ziggy. He was like a cat. He was always cleaning himself. Brushing, scrubbing, even licking. Especially licking. Couldn't find a cleaner man in all of Vienna. Jesus, what a guy."

"Nat, who else have you met in your lifetime?"

"Lots. Knew 'em all. Knew everyone. All the big ones..."

Walking back to the hotel with Nat I asked him if he had any regrets. Anything he had wanted to do but never got around to doing.

"Nope. Seen it all, done it all. Knew all the big ones. Worked with Buffalo Bill in his Wild West Show for a summer. Toured all of Germany with Bill. Goddamn Germans. Laughing and applauding us and all the while preparing for two wars. Shows you just can't trust no one. Speaking of trust," Nat continued, "I once met Alvin Karpis."

"Who?"

"Alvin Karpis, the bank robber. Met him during the Depression years – '32 or '33. Saw him rob a bank in South Dakota. Good man, but too honest. Couldn't kill anyone."

"Why do you say that? I think that's admirable. Sort of like a Robin Hood."

"Killing's part of the game. If you're not willing to kill, shouldn't be in the business. He once told me that he was robbing some bank in Oklahoma and he held up a gun to the teller's head, and ordered the bank manager to open the vault otherwise he'd have to blow away all of those pretty blond curls off of her head. Know what the manager answered Karpis? Eh?"

"No."

"'She ain't nothing to me.'"

"You're kidding!"

"Nope. Well, Karpis just couldn't believe it. He wasn't an inhuman fella. He had too many feelings. Should never have gotten into the business."

"What did Karpis do?"

"He turned away from the girl and planted his gun into the manager's mouth. I don't think it took more'n five seconds to open the vault. Good man, that Karpis."

"Who else have you met, Nat?"

"Eleanor Roosevelt. Grand lady. Shook hands with her while she was campaigning for her husband. That was back in '35, just before the election. Ugly broad, but a hell of a lot of chutzpa. Good woman. Good kind to get hitched to. Did a lot for her man. Unselfish, you know. Not a mean bone in her body. Feisty little bitch, just like her uncle."

"Did you know her uncle?"

"Teddy? Bosom buddies. Why, at one time we were like two burrs on a mule's tail. Inseparable. Fought with him in the Spanish-American War. Was second in command in his unit — the Roughriders. Old Teddy's dead now nearly seventy years, but a finer man never put on a pair of spurs. Still ain't a politician to this day that can hold his own to old Teddy. Not even Eleanor's husband. Not even him. Did I ever tell you the story about San Juan Hill?"

"No. Tell me."

"Night before the big battle, Teddy and I found these two guys roaming around the camp — drunk as all hell. Well, to teach these fellas a thing or two about discipline, we undressed them right down to their skins and tied them up to the flagpole. The next day we left them tied up while we went to do battle. Before mounting, Teddy walked over to them and said: 'Men, I'm doing this because I don't want no stinking drunks riding behind me. No use to me if your heads are filled with liquor. Now, if we're back tonight, I'll untie you and, if we don't come back, well then, maybe the enemy will untie you. But don't count on it.' Well, two days went by and then we returned to camp just before daylight was coming to an end. Well, sonny, hee hee, you should have seen these two men sagging into the flagpole — redder than a liar caught in his own lie. Burnt through and through from the sun. The two of 'em were in mud packs for a week. And even after a week, they still couldn't have a peaceful leak without it stinging."

"God, what if the enemy had found them?"

"Couldn't have gotten worse punishment than they had. Anyways, we all had a good laugh about it, and Teddy, being the man he was, gave each man a bottle of his finest and a coupla cigars so as there'd be no hard feelings. What a man. Don't make 'em like that today."

"It must have been strange fighting a war back then."

"Strange? Nope. No stranger than it is today. A war's a war, whether you fight it on horseback, in canoes, or in the air. Result's the same."

"Do you think there will ever be another major war, like World War I or World War II?"

"Nope. Think the women this time are going to protest."

"What!!"

"Yep. Don't think the women this time will let their men go off to war. They can't handle it anymore. Get too horny without their men in bed. I don't think they'll allow it. They get itches they need us to scratch… if you know what I mean."

"Come on!"

"Nope. Ever think why we got so many lesbians in this

country? It results from the last war. Men were gone from '41-'45 and then came Korea and Vietnam. Men were gone for so long that the women got tired of waiting for them and so they started doing it with themselves. Ended up liking it so much, they never switched back. Anyways, that's my theory. Take it or leave it... here comes Bella. Hey, Bella, how come so many lesbians in these United States?"

"Always with the toilet mouth. Rudy, whatever this man tells you, don't believe it. All lies. He just likes to talk..."

"... aw go blow someone. Don't pay no never mind to that woman. She's just jealous 'cause I ain't never shown her my gorgeous body."

"... all lies, Rudy. Makes them all up. Did he tell you about Teddy Roosevelt?"

"Yes, he just finished telling me the story."

"Don't believe it."

Nat, by this time, had fallen asleep in his chair.

"Not one word of it," Bella continued. "Not Teddy, not Buffalo Bill, not the bank robber, not Vilma Banky..."

"He didn't tell me about her."

"... filthy. Dirtiest story I ever heard. She would have had to be an orangutan to do the things that Nat says she did. Not one word of it true. None of his stories."

"Sounded true to me."

"I'll admit he's a good storyteller. But he likes to make up things. Makes him feel important, I guess, and how are you going to check up on him? Everyone's dead."

"What about Carl Laemmle and the $165,000?"

"That part's true. Not exactly the way he says it, but the facts are true. He did get $165,000 for his land... did he tell you about his romance with Mary Pickford?"

"No."

"Ask him about it. Not one word of it true, but it's a funny story."

"Bella, how do you know his stories aren't true?"

"I know, believe me, I know. Even though he's ninety-eight,

he would have had to be one hundred and sixty by the time you've heard all of his stories. He forgets himself. One day he was General Grant's stable boy, mind you, that would have been twenty-two years before he was born; another day he practically flew with Lindbergh but at the last moment Lindbergh told him that he didn't think the extra weight would be good; another time he personally trained John Glenn for his flight to outer who-knows-where, mind you, at the time he was eighty-three and he says: 'Showed John the proper way to bench-press.'"

"Are you sure Bella? I mean, can you honestly say that Nat makes up all these stories?"

"Who are you going to believe? Me or him? You know what that crazy man said to me... how old are you Rudy?... twenty-two? Okay, you're old enough. He says to me: 'Bella, let's go to bed. You don't have to worry about nothing. I'll be gentle as a lamb and besides I've been impotent for the last three years. So what've you got to worry about? Pregnant you won't get!' Crazy man. I tell you, Rudy, I love him even with his toilet mouth and all his lies. 'Pregnant you won't get, Bella,' he says... ha ha. I'm seventy-seven, Rudy. Do I have to worry about getting pregnant? I'll leave that for the younger girls. Crazy man! "Rudy, if you want a real laugh, go ask him about Rockefeller. Go. It's the funniest story you ever heard. Zelda... Zelda, over here. I'm coming. I'll see you later, Rudy. I'm going shopping with Zelda. Eat something. You're so thin, Rudy. Go, have something to eat. You're much too skinny."

"... aw go blow someone..."

"Nat, Bella's gone. You fell asleep. It's just you and me."

"That right? Well, what'd that silly woman have to say for herself?"

"Nothing much."

"Never has, you know. Never says anything worthwhile. All she can do is pick on people. Boss them around. See that guy over there?"

"Which one?"

"That guy. The one in the orange chair."

"Yeah, I see him."

"Bella's got him wrapped around her fat thumb. He does anything for her. Matter of fact, so do most of the folks around here. Considers herself Queen of the Bluestone. Well, not this here fella. No sir. No woman ever bossed me around and lived to tell about it. Nope."

"I kinda like Bella."

"It's her charming ways, I know. Almost fell for it myself. But I got keen eyes. Spotted her evil ways just in time.

"Now, I ain't gonna tell you how to live, sonny, nope, don't see the point to it. A man's gotta make his own mistakes, but as I sit here today, I'm telling ya — watch that woman. Evil as a rattlesnake. You be here as long as I have and you'll see for yourself.

"But I guess you won't be staying much longer, eh? Got things to do in life, eh? Itching to get started, I bet? Well, don't rush it none. Hollywood ain't moving. It'll still be there when you're ready to go after her. That's a promise, Petinsky. It's a sly, wily town. Nobody's ever conquered her. Some think they have — especially when they've made it. But then they realise that making it is when the battle only begins. It's hard to reach the top, Rudy, and it takes a long time and a lot of hard work, but let me tell you, it don't take more'n half a second to lose your grip. That top is slipperier than a woman's bottom covered in Vaseline. I know. Been there."

Chapter 14

"I can't find my dress. Where's my damn dress?"

"Over here, Stephanie. By the lights."

A young man, wearing a black cape and white Stetson, was saying: "The belt, is the belt right or should I wear another colour?"

"No, no, Graham, it's fine, just fine."

"How about my shoes? Do they match what I'm wearing?"

"Fine, Graham. They're fine," said Mr. Shane, the acting guru.

Shane was running around: checking, stooping, laughing, praising, sweating. Adjusting the lights, listening to his actors, and telling the cameramen where to set up. Mr. Shane had forgotten to tell me that there was going to be a taping of a play by his troupe. And here I was with a red and white polka-dot scarf waving from my hand.

"Sit, Rudy, sit down. Sorry about not mentioning this. An oversight on my part. Sorry again. But do make yourself comfortable. Have a seat in the back and begin to absorb. Isn't it marvellous: the lights, the colour, the smell of it all. What an atmosphere. There's nothing like it. Nothing."

"It's very exciting," I said.

"Yes, exciting indeed. And soon, Rudy, very soon, I'm sure you'll be experiencing opening night butterflies yourself. Oh yes, very soon. Next production. I'm sure. We're thinking of doing a parody of that great flick "Wee Willie Winkie", depending on how Ihor is coming along with the script. If not, something else will pop up. Auditions will be held day after tomorrow. You'll join us, won't you."

It wasn't put to me as an invitation, not even as a question. It was an order. No mistake about it. A command.

"Yes, of course."

"Good, good. Never turn down an audition, Rudy. Not in this business. Never can tell who will be in the audience. Never can."

"No, I guess not."

"You'll have to excuse me for now, Rudy. I must get back to the production. I'm the overseer, so to speak. Without me, there would be utter pandemonium. Just have a seat and absorb. An actor's greatest tool, Rudy. Absorption. Nice talking to you."

"Yes," I said.

Pandemonium reigned. There was yelling, and shuffling, and moving about, and frantic conversation: "Move this here"; "Get rid of this, will you"; "That goes over there"; "I don't give a shit if..."; "Not me. I won't do it"; and on and on. One voice on top of another. Delirious cacophony.

And then a short, pudgy guy with glasses, rumpled clothes and a dirty complexion began shouting above the hoopla: "Quiet, quiet, quiet, everyone!"

What authority in his fat voice. What conviction. What silence! And then the director spoke: "Camera and... action."

Lights began to filter through the darkness, moving every which way, creating a circus atmosphere. Very impressive. And then the actors' faces were completely visible, their shadows behind them, mimicking their every move. Stephanie and Graham. The ones who had been shouting for their clothes not thirty minutes before. As the dialogue wore on and more actors appeared on the stage, I realised that this production was not of the highest quality.

Stephanie and Graham were mispronouncing their lines, falling off their cues, and trying so damn hard not to screw up. The other actors were even worse. They, too, mispronounced their lines, but they were also saying them at the wrong time or simply forgetting them and having to be nudged by the nearest person. Thirty minutes later it was all over.

So this was it. This was what I was going to do for the next several months: act in pre-puberty amateur productions. I wondered if I could forget about making a percussion instrument; after all if I was going to audition in two days...

"Well, Rudy, how did you enjoy that? I realise that it still needs a bit of work but, on the whole, it was rather splendid, eh?"

"Yes, very good. But why did you shoot it if it still needs a bit of work?"

"Shoot it, shoot... oh, you mean the cameras. No film, Rudy. They're dummy cameras and the technicians are all actors attending the school. This way everyone gets a job to do and everyone pretends they're someone else."

"Good idea."

"Yes, I thought so too when the idea hit me. Splendid idea, B.S., I said to myself. Sort of adds to the magic of it all. Being magical — that's the key, Rudy. An actor's greatest tool. Greatest tool."

"In any event, I did enjoy it, Mr. Shane."

"Glad to hear it, Rudy. Glad to hear... by the by, would you like to join us? We're going over to grab a bite and celebrate. Hard work deserves nourishment, eh?"

"Sure, I'd be glad to."

"Fine, come along then. Everyone, meet Rudy Petinsky, our latest acquisition."

I was now an acquisition. No longer a person or a body or a boy or a being — an acquisition. Pretty heady stuff.

Sitting down at the table, I was formally introduced to everyone —Stephanie, Graham, Isabella, Paul, Doriana, Guilliame, Christine, Mustakim, Lorena, etc., etc., etc. Munching on some cottage cheese, I asked Stephanie how long she'd been at it.

"Two years now."

"I've been at it all my life. Did commercials as a baby. Pampers, pablum, you know?" This was Sherryl – with two 'R's, she insisted – talking. An ego as fat as her body. She was the "actress" of the troupe. Had more experience than anyone else and wanted to "make it" at any cost. She wasn't much liked, I later found out.

"How about you, Rudy?" joined in Graham. "How long?"

"Not long. A few weeks. Been here only a few weeks."

"Where you from?"

"New York."

"Oh, really," said Stephanie. "I know someone who lives there on, now wait a minute, let me think of the street. It's a tree name. Elm? Maple? Birch? Birch Bark. That's it. Birch Bark Drive. Ellen Ogilvie. We used to go to school together and she had to move to New York because her father was transferred — business. Do you know her?"

"No."

"Oh," Stephanie said, a bit disappointed in me. However, I was not at all disappointed with her. How could I be? She was the spitting image of a young Elizabeth Taylor. I couldn't take my eyes off her violet eyes or her lush breasts.

"I heard it's a nice city. Very cultural," Sherryl offered.

"Yeah, it's all right," I said.

"So," Graham said, "you're trying to make it."

"Yeah," I answered. "Just like everybody else."

"How come in movies?" Graham and Stephanie asked in unison. I think they were a team.

And so I told them. I explained that I love movies: "I'm fascinated by Hollywood and my ultimate goal is to become a writer-director-producer."

They were all very impressed.

Graham and Stephanie insisted that I meet Ihor Faloney.

"You'll love talking to him, Rudy. He's also a writer. Writes all our scripts. You must have so much in common."

I don't know why they thought we would have a common bond, yet, regardless, I met Ihor – a short, stocky Russian who looked like he was a direct descendant of peasant farmers, which in fact, he was. It was hard to imagine his thick, stubby fingers pecking away at a typewriter instead of planting beets. We said our hellos and talked very briefly about writing.

I said: "Did you write tonight's script?"

He said: "Yes."

I said: "I liked it." (Lies, all lies, but you have to be cordial. These people are a family. They could turn on me).

He said: "I'm glad. Worked hard on it."

I said: "Yeah. Writing is hard work. Not as glamorous as people think."

He said: "Yeah, know what you mean."

The rest of the evening was as exciting as my conversation with Ihor. I desperately had to get out of there. But how? What excuse could I give these people? I thought of one: "Excuse me, will you, I've just come up with a smashing idea for a book and I've got to rush home and write it all down. I'm sorry, truly sorry to have to leave the party, but you know how it is — when the ideas come, must abandon all. The muse is a cruel mistress. See you folks."

As it turned out, I didn't have to give any excuses. I was just about to plead a headache when Stephanie got up to say goodnight. Graham followed immediately. Before I knew it, only B.S. himself and I remained at the table. He gave me a wink, put his arm around my shoulder and offered to buy me a drink. I declined, feigning fatigue, and told him I would see him in two days.

"By the way," I asked, "what's the audition for?"

Again with the wink he replied, "We're putting on a period play. Costumes and all. Big, very big, production."

"I see. What's it called?"

"'The Selling of Manhattan.' You should fit in quite nicely, Rudy, coming from New York, eh? Fit in nicely."

"The only thing I know about Manhattan," I said, "is that it's filled with retail outlets, porno outlets and stock market outlets."

"Retail... porn... Well, perhaps, but I know nothing about that sort of business. No, no, what I mean is the original Manhattan, you know. Forests and forts and Indians and Radisson – you do know Radisson?"

"Of course. He used to have a T.V. show."

"Yes, television. But this will be a production. A magnificent production. Full of earthy people, of compromised morals, of independence, of liberty, a stupendous production. Perhaps, Rudy, what with you coming from New York, you could test for the part of Radisson. Eh? You'd already be starting off on second base, what with your background."

"Sure," I said. "But is Radisson the lead?"

"Yes, well, yes indeed. Radisson is certainly the central character, the indomitable force that keeps everything together. Yes, I could certainly say that Radisson is like glue to a woodcutter. Yes, indeed. He *is* the play!"

"Well then, Mr. Shane, I don't think that I have the experience yet. Maybe I could test for a smaller role."

"Popscork! I saw the way you moved your fingers, saw the way you were at ease with the air — felt it, Rudy. Felt a tingle of magic when I was interpreting your body. You have what it takes."

"Thank you, Mr. Shane, but could I think about it?"

"Drumcrackers, Rudy. When I cast a role, it's cast. I see big things on the horizon for you. Big things, Rudy. Just don't screw up."

"Okay, Mr. Shane. I'll try it."

"There's the spirit, Rudy. Now you've got it. Take it easy until audition time. You may want to absorb some of the local colour for the play. Research, Rudy. That's what it's called. Research. Absorb your part. Feel it. Go, get in among the trees. Find yourself a park and move in and out of nature. Absorb, Rudy. Get the feel of what it must have been like living in a forest and eating berries, killing animals for your daily survival. Absorb, Rudy. Absorb."

"Do you think I could have a script, Mr. Shane?"

"Not ready yet. Ihor's still tidying it up. He assured me it would be ready by audition time. Perhaps you would like to collaborate with him, being a writer yourself? On second thought, maybe that's not such a titan idea — temperamental, that boy is. Extremely temperamental. But all writers are, eh?"

"I suppose, to some degree."

"To some degree. I do enjoy the way you put things, Rudy. You must show me your writing some time. See you at the audition. Come prepared."

Chapter 15

Having finished my percussion instrument for school — an empty margarine tin filled with uncooked rice — I decided to go to the beach for a quick swim and a bit of sun. I wanted to work on my tan. I wanted to look prosperous. I didn't want to show anyone that I was down and out. Besides, maybe I'd get lucky. Maybe I'd meet a nice girl. Maybe she'd be an actress. Maybe she'd have connections. Maybe she'd help me. Maybe I'd get a part. Maybe I'd become famous.

I grabbed a towel and my suntan lotion and drove off to the beach. Spreading out my towel, I lay down and picked up my copy of "Variety". The first section I read was the classified ads. Auditions and castings. Usually there wasn't anything in it for me. Everyone wanted experience. Nevertheless, I faithfully continued to check it out. All it takes is one part.

> The director and casting agent
> for the movie "Wheeling Summer",
> which starts shooting August 26,
> will be auditioning actors and
> actresses today from 10 A.M. until
> 4 P.M. at 6493 Sunset Boulevard.

I reread the ad. No mention of experience. Great, I'd give it a try. The ad said "from 10 A.M. to 4 P.M.". Hell, it was only 11:00 now. Two hours at the beach should do it. I'd be at the casting office by 1-1:30, at the latest — looking healthy. Appearances make a difference, especially in this town.

I put down the paper and began dreaming of getting the lead role and making love to the gorgeous actress who was to play my girlfriend in the movie...

... I must have fallen asleep. Damn! Now it was 1:30. Don't panic, Rudy. No need to panic. You've got till 4 P.M. Plenty of time to shower. Be there by 2-2:30 at the latest.

Jesus Christ! Will you look at all those cars! "Get off the road, where'd you learn to drive? In an amusement park? Jesus Christ!" Must be an accident. Damn, it's already 2:30. God, I've never seen so many cars. I'll be here for hours. Serves you right. Had to get a tan, eh? Had to look healthy, eh? Well, now you've got your tan. Gee, your parents will be proud of you. Ex-New Yorker makes good in Hollywood. People around town saying that Rudy Petinsky has the nicest tan they've ever seen.

Shit, it's already three o'clock.

Goddamnit, where is this place??!! Says 6493 Sunset. But where? It's 3:15 already and I can't even find the place.

Damn, if I don't keep cool, I'll blow a gasket. I wonder how that happens? If your blood pressure skyrockets, do you literally explode? Poof! Blood everywhere. Coming out of your skin? Sockets? Fingernails?... ah... what's that... no wonder I couldn't find the address. Couldn't see the sign with the arrow pointing to 6493. Must be around the back over the... Jesus Christ! People, people, where'd you all come from? Looks like everyone in North America read this morning's paper and decided to become a hopeful. Jesus! It's 3:40. Got twenty minutes to "make it", but if I stand in line, I'll get to see the next crucifixion before I ever get to see the director.

"Excuse me, how long you been here?"

"Since 5 A.M. Some have been here since last night. You just arrive?"

"Yeah. Just heard about it this morning."

"... got yourself a nice tan. I heard they're looking for people who look summery."

"Really?" I said, my heart pounding.

"Yeah. Movie's about summer vacations and college students enjoying themselves. Takes place in Fort Lauderdale. I heard they're looking for people who look athletic, have tans, rosy complexions, you know. Lots of blondes, muscular guys. Strictly for the drive-in crowd."

"Yeah, but it's too late," I said. "Got held up in traffic," I said. "Couldn't find the address," I said. However, I did not say that I was relaxing at the beach when I damn well knew that I should have immediately rushed over here as soon as I read the ad. Shouldn't have even brushed my teeth. Just rushed over. I don't know what it is in my character that makes me think that the world is waiting for me. I must ask Leon about that. *"You're lazy, Rudy. Just plain lazy."*

"So you think it's too late? I heard they're only auditioning till 4 P.M. You think they'll extend it?" I asked.

"Never know. Funny people, these show biz folks. Never can tell what they'll do next. Anyways, I don't know why I'm hanging around. You wouldn't exactly call me a sunny-looking guy. I'm more wispyish. I figure maybe they need a waiter or something. I've played that before. Been a waiter in "Sunset Strikes At Dawn." Did you see it?"

"Nope, missed it."

"Yeah, I was a waiter in that. Wore a red vest. Served a drink to the lead. Quite a thrill. It was my first acting job."

"Did you have a lot of lines?"

"No, as a matter of fact, they cut out my face. Bastards. You were supposed to see my face, but all you ever saw were my hands. Just my hands. The bastards cut out my face."

"You got nice hands. Anyways, you got the part. Can't start at the top. Maybe you'll get in this one and get a bigger part."

"I don't think so. I'm just going through the motions."

"How long have you been at it?"

"Fifteen years. And all I got to show for it is a three second clip of my hands serving a drink to the star of the movie."

I couldn't believe it. Fifteen years! Fifteen years of going through the motions and only getting one acting job — if you want to call three seconds of film acting.

"What makes you stick with it?" I asked.

"Don't know what else to do and besides, I love the business. I'd rather be a flop in Hollywood than be successful in Iowa."

"How do you live? I mean, fifteen years of this, without jobs, how do you survive?"

"Oh that. Well, for the first seven years I was out here, did a lot of porno work."

"Really!!??" I think my blood pressure was up again. I had seen some of these skin flicks and thought it might be fun… hell, at one point I was even envious of these guys having so many different girls to bang.

"Yeah. Good money in it. Lots of nooky but after a while, well, they're always looking for new faces."

"What for? I mean, what's so important in the face?"

"Oh, it's not the face. But after you've been around for some time, you begin to demand more money. It's only natural and let's face it, they don't have to dish out the money. They can get as many new faces as they want. They've got a waiting list."

"You're kidding!"

"Oh yeah. Lots of guys will do it even without pay. Just for the sex. Gives the business a bad name and makes it harder on guys like me, who need the money."

Should I ask him for an address? Who to see about getting a porno job? Should I? And what would be my porno name? Captain Cock? Harry Hardon? Billy Bob Boner?

"You know, if you're ever tight for a dollar, you might be interested in giving it a shot. You look like you've got a good body and can hang in there."

"Yeah? You think so? Well, what have I got to lose?"

"That's right. Let me tell you something. After fifteen years in the business, I've learned one thing."

"What's that?"

"Never turn down an offer."

"Sounds good to me."

"Here, got a pen? I'll write down who to see about an audition."

"You mean I'll have to audition? Like, with my dick?"

"Sure, got to."

"All right. Sounds good to me."

"Here, give this guy a call and give it a shot. Worse comes to worse, you'll have an audition with a good looking girl. A free fuck anyway."

"Yeah. But what if she's ugly? I mean, I've seen some skin flicks before and some of the broads are really filthy looking. And some of the things you've got to do with them!"

"Well, all jobs have their drawbacks. Pay's good and, like I said before, all the free sex you can dish out."

"Well, I'll think about it."

"You got the time?"

"Yeah... shit, it's 4:30. Well, I guess that's that."

"Not necessarily. They usually let the line know that they're finished auditioning for the day and then tell you if they're finished for good or if they'll continue tomorrow."

"AUDITIONS ARE FINISHED FOR TODAY," boomed a voice from a megaphone. "Auditions are finished for today. It's a wrap-up. No more auditions will be held."

"Well, nice talking to you and thanks for the information."

"Pleasure. Good luck to you."

"Yeah, thanks. Take it easy."

Should I go? Should I give it a try? Porno? What would Ma say? Can you imagine what my friends would say? Len? Karl? They wouldn't believe it. Jesus! Me in a porno movie! Rudy Petinsky sucking pussy on the silver screen! What if my father saw me? I'm sure he goes to the movies. What if it gets around town that I'm a porno star?

Chapter 16

"Yes?"

It took me a moment to answer the "receptionist" who, with his long scraggly hair, missing tooth, black eye patch and bandana festooned with skull and crossbones, looked like he was a biker-pirate.

"Hi, I got your address from a friend of mine. He told me that you're always looking for new faces and I'm here to audition."

"Come in."

Jeez, it's dark in here and quiet.

"This way, just follow me."

"Okay."

"Hi, Harry's the name. What can I do for you?"

"I'm here to audition."

"Good, good. Always on the lookout for fresh material. Just step into that room and take off your clothes."

"That room?"

"Yes. And take off your clothes. John, go in with, hey what's your name?"

"Jack." Hell, I'm not giving them my real name. I'm not a putz.

"Okay, Jack. Go in that room with John. He'll show you what to do."

So quiet. So dark. I didn't think it would be like this. Then again, what do I know from porno movies? Only see the end result.

"You can put your clothes on this bench. I'll just turn on the lights and get the cameras warmed up."

"Quiet tonight, eh?"

"Yeah. Most of the girls are tired. Was a hectic day."

"Yeah. Right."

"Okay, Jack. You ready?"

"Sure. What do I have to do?"

"Nothing much. Just lie down on the mat. I'll go get Rip."

"Okay."

So far so good. Seems like a respectable business. Nothing shady going on. Looks professional. Nice equipment. Plenty of lights.

"Jack, this is Rip." I craned my neck. Rip oozed sexuality from every pore of his 6´ 5" muscular black frame.

"Hi, Jack."

"Hello."

Why is Rip taking off his clothes?!! Is this going to be a threesome? A foursome? This is my first time, guys. Give me a break, will you?

"Rip, I want to get in a two-shot with you and Jack doing some preliminaries. So get close to each other, lie on your sides, face to face. Jack, all you got to do is follow Rip's lead. He'll show you what to do."

"Excuse me, John... hey, take it easy, Rip. One minute... do you mind?... Excuse me, John... isn't a girl coming in?"

"No, Jack. Girls are tired. Been working overtime. Told them to take the evening off. You'll be working on this one alone with Rip."

WHAT!!!!

"Where are you going, Jack?"

"I think there's been a mistake. No offence, but I'm not that sort of... I mean I don't do that sort of... I'm just not that...."

Jesus Christ! Got to get out of here. Where's my clothes? Where the fuck are my clothes?

"I thought you wanted an audition, Jack?"

"I did, but with a girl!"

"What's the difference? Sex is sex. Right?" Rip asked.

"Not to me. Sex is only with a girl. No offence, Rip. Well, good-by. It's been nice. See you."

I ran out of there half-naked and found myself on the street. I dressed in an abandoned parking lot. I lit a cigarette. It didn't do the trick. I needed a stronger stimulant. I quickly walked down the street, looking for a bar. There was one waiting for me on the corner of Hawthorne and Candelaria.

"What'll it be?" the bartender asked.

"Double vodka. Straight. No ice."

I downed it in one gulp and asked for another. This time with ice. I gulped that one down too. After my first vodka, I felt my heart was settling down to its regular beat. With the second drink, the bar no longer looked seedy. As I was sipping my third double vodka, this time with ice and orange juice, I realised that I was drunk. I knew it as soon as I tried to sit down. I didn't even care when the bartender asked me to get off the floor.

"I'm very cumberbul where I am, thank you."

"I'm sorry, but you can't sit on the floor."

"Why not?" I shouted.

I felt hands all around me. I was being taken somewhere. To a table, I think. Yes. It was a table. I was placed in a chair and left there. As soon as I sat down, I felt the room move. It was spinning. Faster and faster. I needed air. But first, I needed to get up. I couldn't. I tried to hang onto the table for support but it was moving too quickly. I lost my balance and fell down. I was now under the table once again, on the floor. I closed my eyes. Closing my eyes was not a good idea. It made me nauseous. I saw shoes walking towards me. It was the barkeep. He grabbed my leg and pulled me out from under the table. I wanted to puke. I did. All over myself.

Chapter 17

I hadn't prepared myself. I had not moved in and out of the woods as Bobby – the wizard of woeful acting – had suggested and I certainly had not killed any animals for nourishment. Nevertheless, I reluctantly agreed to test for the part of Radisson. I was about to go over to Ihor and ask him how Radisson and Prince Rupert fit into the story of "The Selling of Manhattan", knowing full well that the two had not yet been born when the Indians had sold Manhattan to the Europeans, when Bobby called me over and asked if I could read one of Radisson's speeches. Bobby handed me the script, fresh off the press and I quickly read it to him.

> Radisson: Everybody's so tired. So very tired.
> My father, my mother-in-law, my wife.
> All tired. So very tired. Even my mother.
> She's the most tired.

"Rudy, could you read that again. One more time and stress the word 'tired'. It's not coming over enough. And then try the next few lines with Prince Rupert. From the beginning of Scene III."

"Sure, Mr. Shane."

> Scene III

> P. Rupert: Welcome Mr. Radisson. Glad you could
> come see me. What is it that you want
> of me?
> Radisson: I, sir?
> P. Rupert: Yes. You called on me and now what is it
> that you want of me?

<u>Radisson</u>:	I came because I had heard that you wanted something of me.
<u>P. Rupert</u>:	Rubbish. Where did you hear that?
<u>Radisson</u>:	Indians, up on the lake, by the two narrow streams, beyond the ridge.
<u>P. Rupert</u>:	No. I never told anyone that I wanted to see you.
<u>Radisson</u>:	Then I'll be leaving.
<u>P. Rupert</u>:	Good. Come back anytime you need me. I'll be glad to help.
<u>Radisson</u>:	Good. Thank you.
<u>P. Rupert</u>:	You're welcome.
<u>Radisson</u>:	Good-bye.
<u>P. Rupert</u>:	And to you.

Graham eventually got the part of Radisson. B.S. decided that coming from New York would not give me enough room to "move around inside the role." Graham also threatened to quit if he didn't get it.

Later, I asked Ihor what he was trying to do with his characters. What were they saying? But he wouldn't answer me. He thought I was after his job and he wanted no collaborators. He wanted all the credit. Temperamental fruit-fly. But I persisted. I persuaded him that I was definitely not interested in changing one word around. I was just interested in why his characters did this, or that.

"Ihor, what are you trying to do with your characters?"

"Nothing. Why is it that they have to do anything?"

"Because, Ihor, they're characters that have to come to life and life is animated and so your characters have to live."

"Nonsense, the words speak for themselves. All the actors have to do is memorise the words and you'll see — there'll be life."

"How can the characters come to life, Ihor, if there's so much confusion?"

"Confusion?? Confusion! But Rudy, that's the theme, the

essence of the play. I want it to be confusing otherwise it'll be dull."

"Oh."

What else can you say? The author realises that his play is confusing because he did it on purpose and that justifies it. For him. But let me tell you, no one else in the troupe understood the play, yet no one said so too loudly. Seems B.S. liked to pamper Ihor. Seems it was Ihor's mother who kept the playhouse in the black.

CHAPTER 18

Hollywood. Babylon-on-the-Pacific. Glossy cars, luxurious homes, swimming pools, beautiful people, success, fame, power.

I was in the middle of all this. My two feet stuck in quicksand.

After five months of driving a taxi and pretending to act with Shane's troubadours, things were not working out. I had begun to feel listless, dejected, gloomy. Even Stephanie, whom I had stolen from Graham, was beginning to leave me cold. Her habits were becoming more and more annoying. The way she clicked her fingernails. The way she pushed her tongue underneath her sanitary bridge and produced wet, clucking sounds. The way she peeled an orange: making sure that no part of the rind was left on the membrane and no part of the membrane was left on the orange.

"What the hell difference does it make, Steph, if one itsy-bitsy piece of membrane gets into your mouth?"

"Membranes and heroin don't mix."

That, too, bothered me. Not so much that she was addicted. Hell, one out of two people in L.A. was addicted to something or another. What bothered me was that she expected me to shoot up with her.

"C'mon Rudy. Do it for me. Graham used to."

Two months with Stephanie was two months too long. I broke up with her, tried to find someone less exotic, and wondered what to do with the remainder of my life.

It didn't take long to find someone less exotic. More often than not, while driving people to and fro, I had fantasies – many of them – of attractive blonde bombshells arriving at the airport, flagging me down and giving me by-the-sea motel addresses in remote areas and, of course, coming on to me. In my daydreams I never had to do any of the talking. All I had to do was keep it up for three whole days so Miss Blonde Bombshell could be satisfied in her remote by-the-sea motel. Sometimes I even fantasized about two blonde bombshells – a sister pair – walking into my taxi and wanting me to do them. For three whole days. I never wavered. I thought three days of fun and stimulation would totally satisfy even me and my hardcore hallucinations.

My exotic and erotic fantasy came to be.

Polly, the former Paulina Marriacio, a stunning blonde with long silky hair and fish-net nylons and high heels and a short skirt and a tight cashmere sweater, entered my cab one bright, sunny morning at LAX. She had baggage to put in the trunk and, as I leaped out of my cab to handle her baggage, I became delirious with joy that such a beautiful babe would be sitting behind me for, I hoped, a long, lengthy journey. Perhaps as far as San Francisco.

I inadvertently bumped into her thigh as I proceeded to put her luggage into the trunk. Sparks shot out of every single spore I owned and I prayed that my T-shirt concealed my erection which by now was growing as fast as Pinocchio's nose when he told a lie.

I couldn't believe my ears when Polly gave me the address. It certainly sounded remote and desolate. I had never even heard of the district. When she explained how to get there, my erection was throbbing. She had given me the most isolated, the most inaccessible, the most secluded motel by-the-sea on the coastal highway. Was my taxi mirage entering reality land? Was this really possible? Could this really be happening?

"Are you in the movies and that's why you're doing this... driving a cab?" she asked as we left LAX.

Wow! I thought. She started the conversation. She was interested in me. In what I was doing with my life.

"Uh huh. Well, not exactly in the movies. Writing for them. I mean, writing them. Writing movies for other people to talk in them... those movies."

I was babbling. I had not expected her to ask me anything. At the time of her question I had just finished disrobing her and was nibbling on her right leg.

"You write movies. Wowee! That's so cool."

Wowee! She said 'wowee'. That's good. I'm far better with girls who say 'wowee' than the ones who intellectualize. 'Wowee' is a very positive sign.

I now felt relaxed and so told her all about my life and she told me that she had done one commercial, had been a stand-in for an off-off-off Broadway production and was now trying her luck in L.A.

"If you want L.A.," I said, "how come you're going to such an out-of-the-way place?"

"Well, Rudy, it's like this. I want to spend three days holed up in a quiet place with no distractions so I can write a novel."

A novel! Three days! She wants to live my fantasy, three days in a remote motel by-the-sea, writing a novel? I could help with that. I could very much help her with that. I could hold her hand while she's writing. I most certainly could do that for Polly. It would be my pleasure.

"I'm just like you, Rudy. I also want to write. I want to write the wowiest, zowiest novel of all time. Lots of love. Lots of fun. Lots of heat."

Holy Moly! Love! Heat!

"Lust, too?" I quietly asked.

"Wowee, Rudy. Yes. Lots of lust."

Could this get any better?

We arrived at the Golden Goose motel which was situated on a cliff overlooking the Pacific ocean and was the spitting image of the motel that Hitchcock had used in his film: "Psycho".

I liked it. It had a somewhat rundown, prostitute-kind-of-look. I also liked the fact that I was taking Polly's luggage out of my cab and placing it in her room and, when I had finished placing her luggage in her room, Polly asked me if I would like to stay for a while.

Was I dreaming? Had I just arrived in heaven? Could this... was this... I mean... Holy Moly! Yes! Yes! Of course I could stay. I could stay for years with you, dear wowee, zowee Polly.

"Great," she said. "In that case, if you're staying, perhaps we could exchange favours."

"I'm sorry," I responded as I stared at her, not understanding where she was going with that request.

"Exchange favours, Rudy. That was a very long taxi ride and a very expensive taxi ride."

"True. Long and expensive. This motel isn't exactly anywhere near L.A."

"True, Rudy. And what I have in mind is an exchange of favours," she said as she came really close to me and brushed her fabulous breasts into my chest.

I gulped.

I gulped harder when she placed her right hand on my thigh.

"Favour, Rudy. Tit for tat. An exchange," she seductively whispered in my ear.

Tit for tat? I liked that. It had a ring to it. A tit for a tat. I was really enjoying the way Polly used the English language.

"Polly, are you suggesting I waive the cab fare for a night of debauchery?"

"Not a night, Rudy. An hour."

"An hour?!"

"Just an hour. That's standard, Rudy."

"Standard?"

"Yes, Rudy. Standard."

Her left hand grabbed my right arm and placed it on her breast. Oh dear God! What to do? Waive the fare? But I need the money. But I need this too. But I don't want to pay for a fantasy. But I have such a hard-on. But this would be so not right. But she's already got hold of me but I need...

"Rudy. It's not just waiving the fare. You would have to throw in an extra fifty."

All of a sudden her hands released their grip on my body as she moved towards the bed, positioning herself suggestively. My loins were screaming with knotted tension.

"You're not really a novelist, are you Polly?"

"Yes, Rudy. I am. I'm writing my memoirs."

"You really didn't work as a stand-in in an off-off-off Broadway play, did you?"

"Yes I did, Rudy. For a few hours. The producer was a very nice man."

"You did a commercial?"

"The director."

"I see. Well, it's like this, Polly. The fare with an extra fifty is very... how should I say... excuse me... will you... for a moment."

I rushed to the washroom, locked the door behind me, pulled out my wowee-zowee, grabbed a towel and proceeded to relieve myself, vowing that I would have to stop fantasizing while escorting gorgeous "working girls" to windswept motels by-the-sea. Perhaps it was time to concentrate more on what I was going to do with the rest of my life.

More and more, I was bothered by the fact that I had yet to accomplish anything of lasting value. So many others had reached the top at such an early age. Orson Wells. Charlie Chaplin. Alexander the Great. My only consolation was that Alexander had died in his early thirties. At least I would probably outlive him.

What was I doing here anyway? I was ready to leave but I wasn't ready to go home. I could not envision going home empty-handed. It would be too humiliating. I never should have told everyone back home my plans: "*Yeah, I'm going to Hollywood. I'm gonna try it. Give it my best shot... yeah, that's right. I want to become a writer. It's not easy? Sure, I know that, but I've got to try, right?*"

Never should have told anyone. I put too much pressure on myself. Should have just left: "*So long, going on vacation. See you.*"

Plaster had told me to take a couple of months off before starting another novel. This I did. Now it was time to stop fooling around. No more acting, no more wandering the streets looking for inspiration, no more trying to make contacts or appearing to look successful. Hollywood was just not meant to be. Not yet. What lay in the future was to write a novel, have it published and then be invited to Hollywood to write the screenplay. That was the way the cards were to be played. Definitely. I could see it so clearly.

No more having to hustle around town or meet with Shane's troupe of rainbow-chasers. All I needed was about six months to write a first draft and then I could go home. Half a day of driving a cab and half a day of writing. Six months should do it. Maybe seven.

I was euphoric — until I began to write. All I could come up with were opening pages. My page ones were terrific. Funny, poignant — even hilarious — but page two eluded me. I drew a blank every time I put the second sheet of paper into the typewriter. I tried humour. I tried drama. Nothing worked — including the air-conditioning. The heat was unbearable and the tiny fan that Nat had loaned me seemed to be as old as he was. It whirred "whack-ke-whack" with every revolution. The fan was getting on my nerves, the heat was getting on my nerves and, every time I had an idea for a theme or a plot for my novel, I would end up reading about some other author using it, or seeing it on television. I was losing my touch. I was out of sync.

I experimented with marijuana. I bought a couple of joints and figured I would get stupendous ideas for a book. And I did. Immediately. It was fantastic. The best idea I ever had. I put a sheet of paper in the typewriter and began typing feverishly.

Number One on the Planet Earth

by Rudy Petinsky

"Jeffrey, Jeffrey. Wakey, wakey. Matthew's on the phone."
"All right, all right."
For God's sake, I'm twenty-five and she still says 'wakey, wakey'. 'Wakey, wakey, Jeffrey, it's time to go to work', or 'it's time to go to school', or 'it's time for this' or 'it's time for that'.

With her it's always time, time, time. Always saying there's a time and a place for everything. If she ever caught me playing with myself she'd probably say, "Jeffrey, it's not the time to do that."

Wow! If she ever caught me doing it! Can you imagine?

EXTRA! EXTRA! READ ALL ABOUT IT!
Twenty-five-year-old gets caught while doing it!

God! If my mother caught me in the act!

"Jeffrey, I would like to have a word with you. Now, I realise that a young man like yourself has to, from time to time, let out his emotions, sexually, that is. Now, if you enjoy doing such a thing, why don't you find yourself a nice Jewish girl and settle down. That way, you won't have to settle for second best, you'll be able to do the real thing. Am I right, Jeffrey?"

"Sure, Ma, sure. You're right."

"Is that all you're going to say?"

"What would you like me to say?"

"I'd like you to say that you're sorry."

"Sorry! Sorry! Are you crazy? What have I got to be sorry for?"

"But Jeffrey, it's no good for you."

"What do you mean it's no good for me? If I have to suppress that, I'll definitely go insane."

"Jeffrey, listen to me. Listen to your mother. I know what's best. The next time you get the urge, go take a shower or do some exercises."

"Okay. I'll do that if you promise me just one thing."

"What?"

"The next time Dad wants to make love with you, tell him to go take a shower."

"I'll do better than that. I'll take the shower."

"That's quite a sacrifice you're making for me."

"That's what a mother's for."

"Great. In a few short months you'll become the wife of a man who got an ulcer from taking too many showers. You'll be famous. Your name will be in all the medical journals. And, as for your son, well, he'll have a nervous breakdown because he promised his mother not to play with himself and, rather than break his word, he'd be willing to lose his mind. And what about the water taxes? Yeah, think of the water taxes. They'll rise to astronomical heights, what with so much shower-taking going on. What will you tell the neighbours? How will you explain the sudden increase in your water taxes? And let's not forget your daughter. She too, at her age, has normal sex drives. Don't exclude her from the family. She too will have to quit playing with herself. I think we should build another bathroom in the house. Two, perhaps. Goddamnit, are we ever going to be clean. The cleanest family in the neighbourhood. And then we can preach the good word to our neighbours and, before you know it, our whole street will be clean. In due time, we'll have reached the entire neighbourhood and then we'll infiltrate into outlying suburbs and, once we have the support of all the suburbs, we'll attack the downtown area and we'll keep pushing onwards, in all directions: north, east, south, west. And before you know it, before you know it, Ma, we'll have cleaned up the world. And you, Ma, yes, my mother, Mrs. Sonia Rabinovitch will be the person who wiped out masturbation in the world. But Ma, try to realise that some people, oh yes, some people will not listen, because there are always troublemakers around. And these troublemakers won't put up with your anti-masturbation laws and they'll revolt. Yes, Ma, they'll revolt and there'll be a revolution and what will you say to these frustrated people? Remember that some people can't be spoken to. Some people have to be hit over the head in order to understand. Will you set up a police state to take care of these troublemakers, and will there be informers watching people in their showers making sure that they don't play with themselves while trying to get clean? Ma, be careful. You're taking on the whole world and that's a big responsibility..."

Oh for God's sake, will you listen to me. Listen to what I'm saying. Here I am having a conversation with myself while Matthew's waiting on the phone. Damn, I wonder if she ever did see me doing it...?

I pulled the sheet of paper out of the typewriter and read the whole thing. I couldn't believe it. It was brilliant. Original. Scintillating. I was impressed with myself. Three pages. I had written three whole pages!

One month later I found myself with the beginnings of a sure-to-be best-seller. No longer writing with the aid of grass, I was now holding my own. Everything flowed. I had found my rhythm. I would still need a chorus, but the melody was there. Every studio would be dying to buy the rights and Plaster would look at me from his corduroy chair and say: "Well done, Rudy. I knew all the time you had it in you."

CHAPTER 19

My day was now relatively simple. Drive the cab in the mornings, write in the afternoons, do a few push-ups and still have an hour left to go to the beach, where I would unwind. "Number One on the Planet Earth" was developing rapidly. Three or four more weeks and the novel would be finished. Nights, I managed to pick up a few extra bucks by working as a busboy. Everything was going to be fine. In no time I'd be back in New York, sell my book and eventually be back in L.A. This time, though, I'd be a guest of Paramount or M.G.M. and have a suite at the Beverly Hills Hotel.

"So Rudy, what's new? You've become a ghost. We don't see you anymore."

"Busy, Bella. I'm just busy."

"So be busy a little less and come and talk to us once in a while. We miss you."

"How's Nat? I haven't seen him around lately."

"He doesn't come out of his room very much. He looks pale and old."

"Bella, he's ninety-eight. What do you expect?"

"I know Nat. There's something wrong."

"Where is he now?"

"In his room, I guess."

"Let's go visit him. I have a few minutes."

We took the elevator up to the third floor and proceeded down the corridor. Nat's room was at the end and, by the time we reached his door, Bella was out of breath.

"Can you believe, Rudy, that once upon a time I used to be quite an athlete. Swimming, running, even tennis. Now look at me. I walk a few steps and I have to catch my breath. Don't get old, Rudy. It's not worth it."

"Not much choice I have, Bella."

I knocked on the door. There was no answer. I knocked again. Still no answer.

"Nathan, Nathan," Bella screamed. "Are you in there?"

"Maybe he went out."

"No. I would have seen him. There's something wrong. I can feel it."

"Take it easy, Bella. I'll go get the superintendent. He'll open the door for us."

As the super let us in, we immediately noticed Nat. He was sprawled on the couch, his left leg dangling over the side. I was sure he was dead. The super checked his pulse. Nothing.

Funeral services were held two days later. It was a simple and quiet affair. After the burial, I decided against writing and went to the beach. I felt drained. I wanted to go home. I had had enough disappointing experiences to fill up three books. I had not expected death to be one of them. I thought about leaving the next day and finishing my novel in New York. But then I'd be a quitter. I'd also have to put up with my mother and her nagging might prolong the book by months.

I came out of the water and sat on the sand. The seagulls were beginning to arrive. I thought of Nat: how, when I first met him, he called the movies fairytales. *"Not responsible work for grown-ups to be in. That's why everyone who works in movies is a child. No grown-ups working there. Are you a child?"*

Was I? If being a grown-up meant letting go of your dreams, then I *was* still a child.

I left the beach and drove around aimlessly. I recalled the advice Nat once gave me when I was frustrated, depressed, and homesick.

"Listen, Petinsky, five hundred years ago, if Columbus had felt the same way you do, you wouldn't be having no problem right now. There wouldn't be a North America. But Columbus' mother pushed him to go, told him to stop being a cry-baby and for once in his life be a mensch. So, Petinsky, your mother ain't here, and as you came to me for advice, I'll give it to you. Stop being a baby.

"One of two things is gonna happen. Either you'll make it

or you won't. Simple as that. But if you go back home, one thing for sure is gonna happen to you. Ten years from now, when you're married and have kids, one day, you'll wake up, look in the mirror and realise that you once had a chance, an opportunity, but were too much of a coward to even try."

"Nat, I'm a writer. I can write anywhere."

"But you chose here. Why?"

Why indeed? Because Hollywood was where I wanted to make a living... because Hollywood was the town where children drank banana daiquiris.

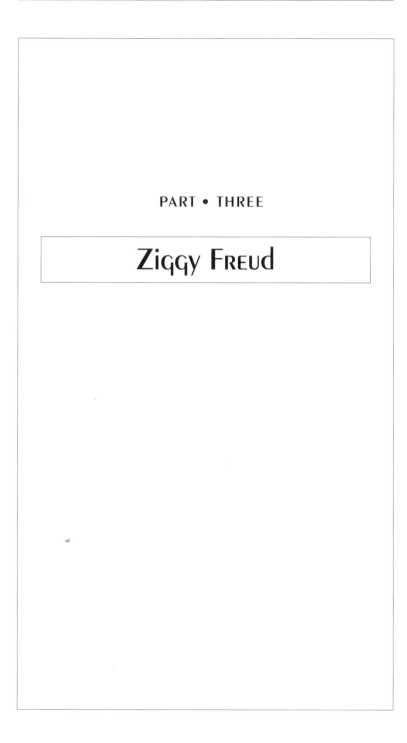

PART • THREE

Ziggy Freud

Chapter 20

"Kings Publishing. Good morning."

"Is Mr. Plaster in, please?"

"Who's calling, please?"

"Rudy Petinsky."

"One minute, please. I'll see if he's in..."

"Mr. Petinsky. How nice to hear from you. How have you been keeping?"

"Fine, thank you. Yourself?"

"Just dandy. How's your writing moving along?"

"That's why I'm calling. I'd like you to take a look at it."

"I hope I've been helpful in the past and I will try to continue to be of help in the future. How about some time next week. Let me take a look at my calendar... mmm... no, I'll be out of town, and then my wife and I are going on vacation. Mr. Petinsky, why don't you pass by the office, leave the manuscript with my secretary and as soon as I get back I'll have a look."

"That's fine. Have a nice trip."

Well, it was good to be back home. It felt secure. And right now, security was the best remedy. Hollywood had been a fiasco. It was not what I had imagined. What had I imagined? Nickelodeons, the big studios, Carole Lombard walking down the boulevard, L.B. Mayer wielding power... I know, all dead. Yet, to me, all of that was Hollywood. Now my dreams of making it in the movie business were put on hold. And, surprisingly, it didn't bother me as much as I thought it would. All I wanted to do was relax for the remainder of the summer, while waiting for Plaster's decision on when we'd go to press. No tension, no pressure, no...

"So Rudy, you've been back three weeks now. What's in the future?"

"Ma, stop pushing. I don't want to do anything till September."

"And then what? The Blue Fairy will pay you a visit?"

"Maybe."

"Don't talk in riddles. Explain yourself."

"Maybe my book will be published."

"And if it isn't?"

"Then I'll look for a job."

"What kind of a job?"

"I don't know."

"I do. What you'll get is a *bubkas* job. A nothing job."

"Thanks for having so much confidence in me."

"Confidence has nothing to do with anything. Look at your father. Sweating away all day in a store. Six days a week. That's what you want? That's how you want to end your days? In aggravation?"

"What do you want me to do?"

"Finish your education."

"I'm through with school."

"Very soon, Rudy, you'll see what this world is all about. You'll look for a job and, believe you me, you'll be very disappointed."

"Me or you?"

Throughout the conversation my mother was steadily raising her voice and I could sense that she would not be able to control herself much longer. I was right.

"YOU HAVE NOTHING IN YOUR HANDS!" she screamed. "Nothing. What's a B.A. today? I see children in the streets, five, six, years old who are as bright as..."

"Me?"

"Brighter. Even at their young age, they know not to worry their parents. Mark my words, Rudy. In five years, their kindergarten degree will have as much meaning as your college degree."

"I don't follow you."

"Think, Rudy. For once in your life, listen to me. Stop making mistakes. Go back to school. Be like Leon."

"How is the neurotic mushroom? Any news?"

"Nothing. They've both locked themselves up in their hideaway country cottage. You'd think a phone call once in a while wouldn't be asking so much. I have half a mind to drive up there and see what's doing."

"Go. The country air would do you good. Dad too."

"Sure. And the minute my back is turned, you'll be off to Honolulu."

"Not that far."

"What does that mean?"

"I think I'm going to move out. Get a place of my own."

"Did you meet a girl in Hollywood? Anyone serious?"

"What?"

"Is she Jewish?"

"Who?"

"The girl you met in Hollywood."

"I didn't meet a girl in Hollywood."

"Then why are you looking for an apartment?"

"Because I want to live alone."

"You'll hurt your father, Rudy. You'll hurt him very much."

If my father was hurt, he didn't show it.

"Let him go, Esther. Let him get his feet wet," my father said.

"Wet feet gets you colds! Rudy, don't go. Why do you have to go? You have everything here. What is it that you want? Tell me."

"Ma, what I want is freedom. To be on my own."

"At least wait until you get married," my mother pleaded.

"Ma, I'm leaving. As a matter of fact, I've already rented a place."

"Morris, talk to your son."

"Dad, it's a terrific place."

"I'm sure it is. Be happy, Rudy. It'll work out."

"Rudy, you won't survive. You'll be back," Ma said knowingly.

CHAPTER 21

It was three days before I settled in. The two biggest jobs were giving the bathroom a thorough going-over with Lysol and deciding how to arrange my books. I couldn't figure out whether to arrange them according to subject matter or in alphabetical order. I eventually decided to arrange them by colour. One shelf white. Another red. Another blue. Etcetera.

For the first few nights, I ate at my parents' but the conversation was always the same: "Rudy, come back home, I'll remodel your room. The sky's the limit..." Or, "Rudy, stop this nonsense. If you come back tomorrow, I'll buy you a new car."

I decided to cut the umbilical cord once and for all. They would have me for supper only on Friday nights.

At first I ordered in: pizza, Chinese, barbecued chicken. But this soon became costly. I decided that it was time to learn how to cook. Against my better judgement, I phoned my mother for a few simple recipes.

"I told you so, Rudy. I knew you wouldn't survive."

"Ma, I want some recipes, not a sermon."

"Rudy, why don't we compromise. Come have your meals at home and I won't bother you about sleeping here. How about it?"

"Ma, if you don't teach me how to cook, I'm going to start drinking Coke for breakfast and eating hot-dogs for lunch and for supper I'll go one night to McDonald's, another night to Burger King and once a week I'll open up a can of Spam."

"Over my dead body! All right, we'll start with chicken soup," she said bitterly.

My first official visitor, to my surprise, was my sister Julie. She entered my apartment and immediately began rearranging my furniture.

"This should go by the window, Rudy. That way the light will hit it just so. Like a Rembrandt painting."

"I like it the way it is."

"Suit yourself. Be common."

Fifteen minutes later, after I had vetoed every one of Julie's suggestions, she uttered, "Has Mom seen this mess?"

"Not yet."

"Wait till I tell her."

Once Ma saw my apartment, she decided to temporarily abandon her attempts to lure me home. Instead she vented her maternal frustrations on my furniture.

"People should be able to leave your apartment and say, 'What good taste he has.' Instead they'll say, 'Where did he get all this junk?' Incidentally, where did you get all this junk?"

"My old bedroom set isn't junk. When I fix the legs on the dresser, it won't tilt anymore. The desk I found in the unfinished basement. Don't you remember it, Ma? You bought it for me when I started public school. It'll look real nice when I paint over the ducks. The chairs and table are from Aunt Miriam."

"I might have known," Ma sniffed. "Your aunt wouldn't give anything away unless she was about to throw it away. She was probably going to pay someone to take it off her hands."

"So I did her a favour."

"Well, she didn't do you one. What about a couch, Rudy? Where are your guests supposed to sit?"

"Nobody has couches anymore, Ma. People sit on pillows these days."

"Pillows are for sleeping, not for sitting. You want people should laugh at you? You want they should get sore backs when they come to visit?"

I gave up. The next day we hit the factory circuit. A few of the owners owed my mother favours, so she called in her markers.

"Mr. Finklestein, my son needs a couch. Do something for him."

"What kind of a couch are you looking for, young man?"

"Something long, in sections, and in black."

"Black!" my mother yelled. "Black! What are you Rudy, the Gestapo? Mr. Finklestein, show him something in a beige or an off-white. Something light and airy."

"Ma, I don't want something light and airy. I want a dark couch. Maybe not black. How about navy blue or dark brown?"

"Mr. Finklestein doesn't make those colours," my mother stated with authority.

"Mrs. Petinsky, let me show you what I have. It'll be easier that way."

Six hours later, I ended up with a light pine coffee table with matching end tables, two lamps and two cream-coloured hide-a-beds — "Buy two, Rudy. This way, if your father and I are visiting and there's a snow storm, we won't have to drive."

On our way home, we made two stops. The first stop was the "Linen Cupboard". It wasn't my idea to spend a fortune on sheets and towels but my mother insisted that I buy the best: "Rudy, you never know when you might have... a visitor," she blushed. The second stop was the bank. I needed a loan.

Now that I had my furniture, sheets and towels, pots and pans (borrowed from my mother), wine glasses (a present from Julie), I was fully installed. Everything looked just right. It seemed the perfect place to have an orgy.

There was only one thing missing. Where were all the hot-blooded females? Why weren't they lining up in front of my door?

I stayed inside for the first few days, hoping that one of the housewives would knock on my door — a sugar bowl in her hand, a devilish look in her eye.

No such luck.

In desperation, I turned to the laundry room, hoping for a lusty encounter. I began to visit the laundry room ten times a day. Each load consisted of one towel, one jersey and a pair of socks. Out of ten trips, I met a pregnant woman with three kids in tow, two eighty-year-old spinsters, and — four times — the security guard, who eyed me suspiciously. The laundry room was a wash-out. I now had no recourse but to cruise the clubs downtown.

Discotheques aren't for everyone. It takes a special character, a certain flaw in one's chemical composition, to be able to enjoy the loud music, the bimbo personalities and the banal conversations. But I was willing to accept all that in hopes of attracting a Marilyn Monroe look-alike and persuading her to help me break in my new apartment.

It just wasn't meant to be.

Out of the fifty girls I asked to dance in fourteen different discos, forty-nine declined. They probably could tell that I wasn't the type to have a Corvette. The one that did accept me was very sweet and pleasant. Very bubbly and very talkative. She told me that she was a cashier at Montgomery Ward and that today had been her last day at work. She was leaving for Hollywood. She wanted to pursue her artistic career. She was an actress. She was also waiting for her boyfriend to come out of the bathroom and hated to sit around and watch everyone else have a good time.

I gave up on discos.

I began cruising the red-light district at 4:00 in the morning hoping to run into a whore who was having a slow night and willing to give a bargain fuck. Instead of running into a whore, I ran into my parents' neighbours who were out on the town, raking in the atmosphere. Asking me what I was doing out so late at night, I explained that I was doing research for my new novel. Embarrassed and thoroughly ashamed, I now had to prepare for an upcoming battle between my mother and myself. The barrage of questions would be endless, as well as humiliating and vicious.

"Are you crazy?"

"Have you gone insane?"

"Disease! These girls are like water rats. They're filthy. They're disease ridden!"

"How dare you?"

And on and on and on.

And how would I defend myself?

"But Ma, I only wanted to talk to one of them. Only talk."

"Do you take me for a fool? I wasn't born yesterday."

True. She wasn't. I'd have to think of a better excuse. Maybe the Handlemyers wouldn't say anything. Maybe they weren't just soaking up the atmosphere but were out having a good time. I mean a *really* good time. Maybe they were more embarrassed being seen by me than the other way around. Maybe there was still time to have fun?

I tried bargaining with the hookers. I couldn't pay full price. I had spent too much money on re-decorating and needed a discount. When bargaining proved futile, I tried pleading and, when that proved ineffective, I begged. No way, they said. Get lost, they said. Up yours, they said. What could I do? I happened to have picked a night when business was booming.

I eventually turned to my friend, Peter, for help.

"Peter, it's Rudy. I need help."

"What kind of help?"

"Girl help."

"Have I got a number for you! Cheap too."

Charlene was far from the full-bodied, good-looking woman that I had expected to satisfy all of my pent-up urges. To my dismay I was staring at an overly rouged, overly perfumed, bosomless, bored redhead of indeterminate age. When she appeared at my door, I debated whether I should call the whole thing off, but I instantly rejected the idea. She might have underworld connections. I wasn't prepared to spend the next fifty years in traction.

"What's your pleasure, Louie?"

"That's Rudy. Rudy... not Louie."

I was going to need help with this one. I poured two stiff drinks and offered one to her. She declined. I gulped mine down. And then gulped hers. Even with the whiskey in me, I couldn't look at her. I lay down on the couch, closed my eyes, unzipped my fly and pretended that Sophia Loren and I were on our honeymoon night.

Not even Sophia could help me. I lay there. Unexcited. Unmoved. Unfeeling. Charlene tried everything: posing, acrobatics, cream, sleazy photos, and a vibrator which only gave me the giggles.

"You've got to relax, Louie."

She was right. I lit up a joint and we tried again. I lay back on the couch and began smoking. I drifted off. Another world... another time... I was Razoff, commander of the planet Trux! All the inhabitants on Trux were female. Six million women and me! I opened my eyes and looked at Charlene. She was busy, oblivious to everything. What was going on in her mind? Did I really want to know? I knew one thing. I would never allow her to immigrate to Trux.

I took another puff, kept the smoke inside of me for as long as I could and slowly exhaled. My eyelids closed. I tried to lose myself in another erotic vision...

"Louie, I'm getting tired. Maybe if we tried something else?"

"Excuse me?"

"Do you have any Jell-o? That usually works."

Jell-o! Had it really come to that?

"Tell you what, Charlene. Let's call it a night."

"Okey-dokey," she said, a relieved look on her face.

I slowly zipped myself up and got off the couch. I felt sluggish. Charlene was already at the door, her hand on the lock.

"Here Charlene, let me help you with the lock. It gets stuck sometimes. There."

JESUS CHRIST AND FUCK!

"Uh... Ma?... Dad? What are you doing here?"

"Aren't you going to introduce us to your friend?"

"Ahhhh... Charlene... these are my parents."

"Pleased to make your acquaintance," Charlene said.

"Ma, Charlene was just leaving. Thanks again, Charlene, for clarifying Orwell's politics. I think I really understand him now."

"Huh??"

"Charlene," my mother said, "do you really have to go? I have some fresh-baked cookies we just picked up. Stay. Have some coffee with us."

"No Ma, Charlene really has to go. Besides, it's late."

"What late? It's Saturday night. The evening's still young. Charlene, do you have any place to go?"

"Well, I do have a bit of time before my next appointment."

"I beg your pardon?" my mother said.

Before I knew it, the four of us were sitting around the coffee table.

"Ma, Dad, how come you're here? I mean, it's almost 11:30."

"We went to the movies. We thought we'd surprise you on our way home."

"You succeeded. I'm surprised."

As I was talking to my mother, I noticed out of the corner of my eye that Charlene and my father were busily engaged in conversation. I wouldn't swear to it, but I think Charlene was trying to recruit my father.

My mother would not talk to Charlene once she noticed the cross around her neck. Twenty minutes later, Charlene left. Having polished off half the cookies, she no longer felt the need to be sociable. When I returned to my apartment after walking her to the elevator and apologising for the embarrassing episode, I blasted my parents. For the first time in my life I swore at them. My parents were shocked. But I didn't give a damn. They were never going to embarrass me again. I laid down the law. They were never, ever to drop by unexpectedly again. Never! They would have to get used to phoning beforehand. Period.

"A mother shouldn't have to make an appointment to see her son," my mother snivelled.

"Ma, if this ever happens again, I'm going to move out of the country without telling you. I swear it. I'll find biblical lepers like the ones in 'Ben-Hur' and move into their caves."

I think she believed me because she didn't argue. She thanked me for my hospitality and slunk out the door. As I walked them to the elevator my father whispered: "Rudy, this wasn't my idea, but I simply got tired of arguing with your mother. I'm sorry."

"That's okay, Dad. I know it wasn't your fault."

As the elevator doors closed, my mother couldn't resist a parting shot: "She's not the right girl for you, Rudy."

Chapter 22

I was surprised when a week went by and my mother hadn't called. It wasn't like her. Maybe she had finally gotten the message. Maybe she had finally accepted the fact that I could manage on my own without her meddling. Maybe the bawling out that I had given her had worked. I was about to give her a call when the phone rang.

"Hello."

"How are you, Mr. Rudy?"

"Hi, Ma. What's doing?"

"We don't see you any more. Why don't you ever come over? You know, Rudy, you don't need an invitation. This is still your home and your room is still there if you want it..."

"Ma, cut it out. I have my own apartment and I love it. It's terrific."

"Listen, Rudy, yesterday afternoon your father and I were at Stella's."

"Stella who?"

"Stella Zadulka. Brian's wife."

"Brian who?"

"You know. Those nice people we met a few weeks ago at Charlie's house. I told you about them. Don't you remember?"

"No."

"Well anyways, around suppertime, their daughter came home. A beauty, Rudy, a..."

"Forget it."

"Let me finish. How do you know what I'm going to say?"

"Forget it, Ma, no blind dates."

"Anyways, I was talking with her. Such an intelligent girl. She's at Columbia getting her Master's degree in some kind of therapy. A beauty, Rudy. An honest-to-goodness beauty."

"Did you say something? Did you mention me?"

"Mention? I told her I had a son, is that so bad?"

"What else?"

"What else? Let me try to remember. Let's see. I mentioned that you loved to travel, that you had written a novel and that you were going on in your studies; that you wanted a Ph.D."

"You got it wrong, Ma. It's you who wants the Ph.D. Not me. Why did you have to start? You just can't leave my life alone, can you! Ma, believe it or not, I can find girls on my own."

"So bring them home. Let me see."

"There's no one special yet."

"All right, so in the meantime, would it be so terrible if you called this beauty?"

"I'm not going to call her. I hate blind dates."

"Rudy, listen to me. It wouldn't be the end of the world. You call her up, take her out, get to know her and then we'll see. What could be easier?"

"Ma, I said I will not call her. I'm not interested."

"Rudy, don't embarrass me. I told her that I would give you her phone number and that you would give her a call. Don't make me out to be a liar."

"What!!!" One day I'm going to put out a contract on that woman. "I suppose she's waiting by the phone?"

"Beauties don't wait by the phone. And believe me, Rudy, she's a beauty and also intelligent. What more could you want?"

Not even in my own apartment am I safe from her. The next step is to move out of the country. Europe is out of the question; she still has connections there. It would have to be Asia or Africa. Maybe Ghana.

"Okay. Give me her number. What's her name?"

"Her name is Ellie."

"Great. Ellie Zadulka. Okay Ma, you win. I'll call her."

"When?"

"I'll call! I'll call! Maybe you'd like to be on the extension when I do?"

"That's not necessary. If you say you'll call, you will. I didn't bring up a liar. So what time will you be here for supper?"

"Ma, I'm not coming over for supper."

"Why not? Rudy, you've got to eat."

"I'll eat something here."

"Why aren't you coming over? Is it something I said? Your father will be disappointed, he was looking forward to seeing you."

"All right! All right! I'll be there... I'll be there."

Throughout the meal, my mother kept raving about this new girl she had found for me. I ate, listened dutifully to my mother, spoke enthusiastically to my father about the New York Rangers and ran home. I had done my duty. By the time I returned, my stomach was upset – not because of my mother's cooking, but because I was now forced to make a phone call.

"Hello. Is Ellie there, please."

"One minute, please. Who's calling?"

"Rudy Petinsky. Esther's son."

"Oh yes, of course. One minute, please."

Oh yes! Of course! Her mother is also in on the conspiracy. Jesus!

"Hello. Ellie?"

"Yes."

"Hi, I'm Rudy... Rudy Petinsky."

"Yes?"

Why is she questioning me? She knows about this. Why isn't she helping me out?

"Uh... I... you met my mother the other day. She told me that she spoke with you. She told me that you're doing a Master's greedee, I mean a dethree in grerapy."

Shit. Be cool, Rudy. Be cool. Hell, you're a world traveller. You've been to Barcelona and back. You've been around. This shouldn't be hard.

"Not exactly."

"What not exactly?" This isn't going the way I had planned.

"Not therapy. Social counselling."

"Oh. My mother must have misunderstood. To my mother it's all the same. Therapy, counselling, to her you're helping people."

"Oh."

Silence. Shit. I knew this would happen. Come on Ellie, say something. Help me out.

"I was wondering, Ellie, if you were busy this Saturday night?"

"No, I'm not."

"Oh. Well then, there you go." I don't believe I just said that. *Well then, there you go? There you go!* How did that come out? "I mean, would you like to go out with me..." – shit, Ma, look what you're doing to your son – "... this Saturday night?"

"Sure."

Sure! So easy she says it. No big deal for her. Sure! One word. Four letters. Here I am sweating bullets. I got to admit it, she's got a sexy voice. Should I tell her? Do girls like to be told that they have sexy voices? I know I'd like it if a girl told me I had a sexy voice. Maybe once I meet her, I'll use it as an opening. I wonder if she's hot stuff?

"Great. Do you like to dance?"

"Yes. Do you, Rudy?"

I hate dancing.

"I love dancing. Maybe we could have supper before. What if I pick you up around 7:30. Is that all right?"

"Sure. That would be nice."

"Okay..."

You better be worth it. You're already costing me a fortune. At times like this I hate myself. Equating a possible fuck with the amount of money I spend on her. It's my mother's fault. She brought me up this way: "*Always get your money's worth, Rudy. Bargain if you have to.*"

"... I'll see you Saturday... oh... could you give me your address? My mother only gave me your phone number."

I'm surprised at you, Ma. You must be slipping.

Chapter 23

Call me presumptuous. Call me irresponsible, but God, I want you. For the rest of my life. I don't care if you spit on old people, I don't care if you're into witchcraft — just marry me. Let me go to bed with you. Please. Please God let her like me. Please. I'll do anything. Please, do this one thing for me and I'll never ask for anything else. Please... please... God, she's gorgeous. Beauty isn't the word for it! Stunning is more like it. Long brown hair, deep green eyes, and five feet, six inches of the sexiest figure I've ever seen. God, I want to marry you.

"Hi, I'm Rudy."

"I'm Ellie."

"Are you ready?"

"Yes."

"I hope you like seafood. I forgot to ask you on the phone, but... I forgot to ask you... but they have meat, too," I babbled.

Oh please like me! Maybe I'm only 5'8", and I wear glasses and my hair is starting to thin, but I have a great body, I really do. I was almost a porn star. Damnit! Why couldn't our first date have been on the beach.

"Your mother told me that you've been to Europe."

"Yes."

"What made you decide to go?"

"I thought I'd have more freedom there."

"Freedom to do what?"

"To write a book. It's been a dream of mine for a long time."

"And did you write a book?"

"Yes. It was easier to do it in Europe. Nobody was breathing down my neck or pilfering my rough material to show the neighbours. That's what my mother used to do."

"God, that's awful. Did she really do that?"

"Uh huh. Can you imagine my mother going to the neighbours with bits of her son's writing and making them read it?"

"How embarrassing."

"Yeah. It was embarrassing when I ran into one of them and of course they would politely tell me how talented I was and I would politely smile and thank them, thinking strangulation was too good for my mother."

"I don't blame you. If my mother did that, not that she ever would, I don't know what I'd do. I'd move out, I suppose."

"Well, I did, a few months ago. Yet somehow, I still don't feel safe."

Ellie laughed.

We pulled into the restaurant's parking lot and I handed the attendant my keys. I desperately wanted to hold Ellie's hand as we walked the few steps to the main entrance but I thought that would be too pushy. Once inside, we waited for the maître d' to seat us.

"It's beautiful," Ellie said. "Do you come here often?"

"First time. I heard the food is excellent."

"I'm starving."

"Me too."

The waiter came over with the menus. I knew that lobster was out of the question. You don't wear bibs on a first date. Something simple was definitely called for.

"What did you decide on?" I asked.

"I think I'll have the scampi. How about you?"

"Salmon steak."

We placed our orders and I asked for a carafe of wine. When the waiter left I took out my cigarettes and offered Ellie one. She didn't smoke. I asked her if she minded. "Not at all," she said. I lit my cigarette and took a long puff, making sure that I exhaled the smoke away from her. I watched her. She was looking around the restaurant, admiring the decor. I was admiring her. She was very pretty in her stylish black pantsuit and white silk blouse with just the right amount of buttons unbuttoned.

During the meal I discovered that Ellie was as pleasant to listen to as she was to look at. She was also a superb listener. By the time the cheque arrived, I couldn't help but think how easy and effortless talking to Ellie was. I felt completely at ease with her. For once, my mother had done the right thing.

"Well, did you enjoy the meal?"

"Yes. Thank you very much, Rudy. It was delicious."

"Would you like to go to a club? I know one that's not too far from here. We could walk."

"Rudy, would you mind very much if we make it another time? All of a sudden I'm really tired and I feel a headache coming on."

"You know, Ellie, you could be a little bit more original."

"No, seriously Rudy, I really do have a headache..."

"Ellie, you don't have to lie to me. It's obvious what you're saying. I've been around, I know. Listen, it was a blind date, it didn't work out and I'll take you home. No sweat. Just do me a favour and don't lie. Be honest."

"I'm sorry. I really am. It's... well... it's that I just broke up with my boyfriend after three..."

"Ellie, spare me. Save the soap opera for someone else. I'd rather not hear about it."

"I was only trying to explain. You told me to be honest, so I was."

"Forget it. Don't explain. Come on, I'll drive you home."

Goddamn wasted evening.

Chapter 24

Goddamn disastrous evening.

It was a simple accident. An innocent misunderstanding. So my hand got caught in Ellie's blouse, ripped off her bra and her boobs nearly popped out. Big deal. I wasn't trying to seduce her. I was merely trying to reach for the box of Kleenex, because Ellie had started to cry. But I forgot that the car was still in gear and, as I turned around, I let my foot off the clutch and the car jerked. I panicked and my hand, by pure mischance, got stuck in her blouse and, unfortunately, the blouse tore. She screamed. I struggled to get my hand out as quickly as possible. She panicked. Her bra came undone and then she slapped me. And cursed me. And bolted out of the car, crying and vowing she would press charges.

The only reason I called Ellie the next day was to keep peace in the family. My mother threatened to tell the whole family, up to sixth cousins, what an uncouth, unpolished animal I was on a date.

"Rudy, what did you do to that girl? Her mother just phoned me. Stella said that Ellie was in tears and her mascara was all over her face and her dress was rearranged. What are you, Rudy? Some kind of animal?"

"Ma... Ma... stop it. I didn't do anything to her. I didn't even try."

"With a beauty like that? You didn't try? Rudy, are you... I mean, do you have..."

"Ma, I'm perfectly normal. The reason I didn't try is because the whole evening she was crying about her ex-boyfriend who she's still in love with. She was crying... ah, Ma, do me a favour and go back to sleep."

"Who can sleep?"

"I can. Good-bye."

"When will you call to apologise?"

"When I'm awake."

I had to call. It was the right thing to do. Maybe I was callous. Unfeeling. Maybe she really was upset about her boyfriend and couldn't help crying. I suppose our blind date was as difficult for her as for me.

I dialled her number. She was still sleeping. I ended up apologising to her mother and asked her to give Ellie the message. About two hours later, the phone rang. It was Ellie.

"Hello. Rudy?"

"Yes. Hi, Ellie. How are you?"

"Still in one piece."

"I'm sorry about last night," I said.

"So am I. I was very insensitive. I had no right spilling tears about someone else. I'm sorry."

She's sorry? She's apologising to me? Quite a girl.

"Forget it. Hey, I've got an idea, that is if you're not busy this afternoon."

"I'm not."

"How about Central Park? It's a beautiful day."

"In an hour?"

"I'll pick you up."

It was the perfect date. I could tell that Ellie was enjoying it as much as I was. By the time I drove her home I felt it was time to tell her that I was ready for a serious relationship.

"I'm not, Rudy. I'm just not ready. I still don't know if I'm over Stanley. It wouldn't be fair to you."

At first I was stunned. After our ideal afternoon, I thought she would go for the idea. I was even going to give her my high school ring. I tried to keep calm. My brain went into overdrive trying to select the right words to say.

"I understand, Ellie. At least we've made progress."

I walked her to the door. We both had a lot on our minds. I was wondering what to do. Should I kiss her? She was probably thinking: "Is he going to kiss me? Should I let him?" We reached the door and she turned around to face me.

"I had a lovely time today," Ellie said.

"So did I, Ellie. I'd like very much to do it again. I know you're mixed up about Stanley but I'm going to call you tomorrow and ask you out and if I'm pushing things, please tell me and I'll put the call on hold."

"You're not."

I put my arms around her waist and gave her a kiss on the cheek. She looked at me.

"We're not cousins, Rudy." So I pulled her closer and kissed her deeply.

I felt terrific.

I felt terrific till Ellie, on our fourth or fifth date, said: "Rudy, I wouldn't mind if you dated other girls."

"I can't understand you, Ellie. We have something going. I know you still think about Stanley but, when we're together, you seem to be with me."

"I am."

"So what's your problem?"

"I'm just not ready for another involvement."

"Fair enough. But can't you understand that I'm not interested in anyone else?"

"I just don't want to lead you on."

"I'm a big boy. I'll take my chances."

Our relationship continued like this for the entire summer. I couldn't eat or sleep and, to top it all off, Plaster didn't have the time of day for me. His secretary always had the same pat answer: "Mr. Plaster is tied up right now. If you could leave your name and number, I'm sure he'll get back to you." And all the while I was boasting to Ellie how great my new novel was. I wanted her to realise that if she chose me she'd be married to a world-famous author with twenty-four carat gold-plated faucets in his bathtub, in Beverly Hills, California. This would be a far cry from living with Stanley, who was only an insurance salesman.

Was Ellie impressed?

"Rudy, I... I just don't know. I mean, I believe in you. I'm sure one day you'll become a famous author. I... I just don't know if I want to get married."

"Ever?" I asked incredulously.

"That's not what I meant."

"Then explain it to me. Tell me what you mean. It's Stanley, isn't it?"

"No, Rudy, it's not Stanley. And it's not you. It's independence. Can you understand that?"

"Do you love Stanley?"

"No."

"You just love me?"

"Yes. And my independence. Give me time, Rudy."

Time for Ellie meant leaving. She was taking off for Europe — alone. I begged her to take me along. Told her she could have her independence. We would stay in separate hotels. She wasn't buying. She needed time to think — by herself. And if all this wasn't enough, I discovered that if I didn't get a job soon, I would be forcibly evicted from my apartment.

That's all Ma had to hear. She was busy night and day putting out feelers. She kept a journal. On one page she listed people with connections. On another page, potential employers. Within forty-eight hours, she had three prospects for me.

I rejected the first one — I did not want to work the graveyard shift as a trainee dispatcher for my Uncle Sheldon's trucking firm. And I also eliminated Mr. Finklestein. I did not want to learn the upholstery business.

"You never know, Rudy. Mr. Finklestein has no children. You just never know."

I should have been furious with her for meddling in my affairs, but all the stops had to be pulled out. It was a question of priorities. I needed to keep my apartment.

CHAPTER 25

The third lead paid off. Ma had placed a call to one of our cousins, a teacher, and was told that there might be an opening in her school. Something about a special class, something about art. That's all my mother could get out of her.

I called the principal and asked for an interview. It was arranged for the following day at 2 P.M.

"Mr. Petinsky," Mr. Paul said. "Have you any teaching experience?"

"Yes, I do. Three summers ago I worked in a children's camp and taught arts and crafts."

This was not altogether a lie. Yes, I had worked in a children's camp, but as the athletic director.

"Good," Mr. Paul said. "You must be creative."

"Yes, I think I am," I answered.

I was hoping Mr. Paul wouldn't give me an art test to prove my creativity. If he had, he would have received the same picture kindergarten children produce: a house, a sun, a tree, a Mommy, a Daddy, a child.

"Well, Mr. Petinsky, I'll tell you what we are looking for. By the way, are you certified?"

"No, I'm not. But I'd be willing to take night courses in order to get certification."

"Good. We have a class of special children. Fifty-seven students with learning disabilities and severe behavioural problems."

"Behavioural problems? Severe ones?!"

"Yes. What we are looking for is someone to teach these students art. For now, it's a one-year position. In May, the School Board will do an evaluation and see if it's feasible to continue the program for the following year. Is that clear?"

"Yes. No problem."

"Are you interested?"

"Yes. Very much."

"I'll level with you, Mr. Petinsky. We're a bit stuck and we need someone right now. School started last week and the position is still unfilled."

"I can fill it."

Mr. Paul stared at me. I stared back. Then he scribbled something down on his note pad and pushed his intercom button. His secretary arrived immediately.

"Mrs. Harmon, this is Rudy Petinsky, our new art teacher. Please give him the forms to fill out. Mr. Petinsky, in the meantime, I'll round up the head of the Art Department and she'll show you where you'll be teaching."

"Thank you, Mr. Paul."

"An art teacher?" my mother asked.

"That's right, Ma. I'm an art teacher. Says something about the educational system, eh?"

"What do you care? You have a job, a paycheque and now you can keep your apartment."

"I'm not complaining, Ma."

"You see, Rudy, it always works out," my father added.

Chapter 26

I hated teaching. I came home every day both exhausted and irritable. My desk had disappeared during my first week and, a few days later, I received a verbal reprimand from the head of the Art Department because my students had somehow managed to cover the ceiling with purple paint. I had no idea how I would survive till June with my motley crew, substituting for real children.

Patrick barked like a dog because he was afflicted with Tourettes; Alex, a seventeen year-old, was still having problems subtracting double digits when it involved borrowing and felt a constant need to touch me and, when he wasn't touching me, was racing around the room at devilish speeds, touching anyone and anything; and Pistola, a new immigrant from Portugal who hardly spoke two words of English, was amassing an odd assortment of knives, bullets and shards of glass in her locker. There was also a handful of autistic kids who needed to repeat everything they said three times as well as repeat anything anybody in the class said, three times. And lastly, there were the identical Thornsen triplets who were neurotic, anxious and worried about every little bit and piece of life and who couldn't get along with each other or anyone else in the school.

By the middle of the third week, I was ready to resign. My art room no longer resembled an art room. There were no desks, no stools, no jars or cans or paintbrushes or paint or paper. All had been used or destroyed. My students were bored.

"Serves you right," I shouted at them.

The kids didn't seem to care. They just sat on the floor, leaning nonchalantly against the bare walls.

A few of the teachers in the staff room had told me that music might be able to soothe my little beasts. I innocently asked the class if they liked music. The next day I had twelve "ghetto blasters" in my room.

Little did I know that music would cause such an enormous problem.

It began innocently enough. Two camps: Black Sabbath and AC/DC. Half the class loved one group and the other half, the other group. They continually argued about which group was more talented and whose lyrics were more meaningful. From day to day the arguing escalated and before too long these child aficionados of heavy metal music began coming to class dressed in combat boots and chrome-studded, black leather jackets with either a Black Sabbath patch stitched onto the back or an AC/DC one.

It didn't take long before one of the addicted AC/DC experts decided to end it all by smashing a Black Sabbath "ghetto blaster" to smithereens with a hammer that he had borrowed from the woodworking shop, starting an all-out war in my classroom and ending only when Ozzie Osborne could no longer sing.

Demolishing their music boxes got them so revved up that they all joined forces and paraded through the school, lighting firecrackers in all the garbage cans.

Fire extinguisher in hand, I quickly followed behind, shrieking for them to stop. And right behind me was Patrick – yelping and yowling. Seems, with all the commotion, Tourettes had kicked in full force.

For my heroic efforts I received a stern letter of warning from the principal as well as one from the school board.

So went the year. Ellie was still in Europe. My mother began preserving pickles. My father was preparing himself for a new football season. Leon and Julie were still in hiding and, when June rolled around, I found myself unemployed. My contract had not been renewed.

Chapter 27

It had been nearly a year since I had last spoken to Plaster and, even if no news is good news, I was becoming anxious. I had to know one way or another what was going on.

"King's Publishing. Good morning."

"Is Mr. Plaster in, please?"

"Who's calling, please?"

"Rudy Petinsky."

"One minute, please. I'll see if Mr. Plaster is in."

"Yes... but... wait." On hold.

"Mr. Petinsky, you must excuse me but it's been extremely hectic around here. As for your manuscript, I haven't had much time to give it my undivided attention. How about if we set up an appointment two weeks from today — say at two o'clock?"

Two weeks later I was in Plaster's office having an anxiety attack.

"Mr. Petinsky, I have always been polite with you, correct?"

"Yes. You've been very decent."

Jerk.

"Yes. My British background, I suppose. Very austere. Never let the one across the table know what you're thinking. Be polite at all times. Never lose control of the situation..."

What the fuck is Plaster talking about? I don't give a shit about his British background. I just want to hear one thing: "Mr. Petinsky, I like it." I'll even settle for: "It's rough, Mr. Petinsky, very rough. An uncut diamond but the possibilities are there. Let's get an editor to work out the rough spots."

"... be proper at all times. However, in this case, Mr. Petinsky, I am going to forsake my heritage and tell you point blank what I think of your latest manuscript."

This is it. This is really it! The moment has come. This could be big. This could really be something. I do believe I've finally done it! Congratulations, Mr. Petinsky. Well done, Mr. P.

"In three simple words, it is shit. Mr. Petinsky, I am tired of taking time out of my busy schedule to read your drivel. I've thought this over quite carefully but I feel it is in your best interests to tell you that you do not have any talent for writing. At best, your writing is secondary school material. Do you honestly believe that you have something to say? Something poignant to tell? Do you really believe that people will actually want to read your uninspired words?"

I tried to answer him but I couldn't unglue my lips.

"Mr. Petinsky, writing is not a job, not a career, not a hobby or a passing fancy. Writing is destroying oneself bit by bit. Writing is being able to pluck the roots out of your brain, so to speak. You must be capable of striking at that root with fire and with sword. Writing, Mr. Petinsky, in one word, is annihilation. I am very sorry but you do not have what it takes."

I think I passed out. I wasn't sure. All I know is that Plaster and his secretary were trying to revive me. They were trying to get some whiskey past my lips. I felt like vomiting and so I did. Some of it landed on Plaster's jacket. I know, because I heard him shriek in disgust and, just as I was about to crawl over to the couch, I saw a pair of legs enter the room. What the hell was *he* doing in Plaster's office? Was I hallucinating? Was the acid that I had tried two years ago just starting to take effect? What the hell was going on?

"Hello, Rudy."

I let out a small gasp.

"Cat got your tongue?"

I whispered, "Leon?"

"Yes, of course it's me. What's wrong with you, Rudy? You look pale. For God's sake, get off the floor and clean yourself up."

"What are you doing here?"

"I'm here for the same reason that you're here. Only difference is that I've succeeded."

"What are you talking about? And where's your nervous breakdown? You don't look sick to me."

"One hundred percent cured. While you were gallivanting around Hollywood, I was busy working. Seven days a week, ten hours a day. Edwin was kind enough to have a look at the book I wrote."

"Book?"

"Mr. Petinsky, your brother-in-law has written an extraordinary piece of non-fiction. That is the reason I've been so busy these last few months."

"You wrote a book, Leon?"

"Yes."

"You're going to be published?"

"Yes."

This was too fucking much to bear. Leon, the writer. In my family. With my mother. Oh God! Why?

"What's it about?"

"This and that."

"This and that?"

"Yes."

"I see." I got off the floor and found a chair to sit in. "And what is this masterpiece of yours called?"

"*Psychosexual Infantilism — The Beast In Us.*"

"Catchy title."

"Don't be snippy, Rudy. I can see right through you. It's not my fault that I've been blessed with an abundant amount of talent and you can't write diddly-spit."

"How would you know?"

"Edwin and I thoroughly examined your manuscript."

I couldn't believe my ears. Plaster had let my bimbo brother-in-law read my novel!

"I needed a second opinion, Mr. Petinsky. I wanted to make absolutely sure I was right in my appraisal."

"Rudy... Rudy... Rudy... how could you? How could you have your protagonist relieve himself on a golf course? That was a new low in taste. Might I add that your novel has zero interest, zero credibility, zero drama, zero conflict, zero characterisation, zero observation. Rudy, forget it. Go in with your father in ladies' clothing. At least you'll make a living. I really don't see any other possibilities for you."

I am not a violent person by nature. I had never used force to settle an argument. But, in this case, I made an exception. As my fist made contact with Leon's head, I heard his jaw bone crunch. Blood came gushing out of his nose, staining Plaster's expensive carpet. I was sure he would have to be hospitalised. I was right. Seems I broke his face.

CHAPTER 28

You have no talent. Your writing is shit. You can't write diddly-spit. Was it true? Could Plaster be right? Could Leon be right? Should I give it up and settle down? Get myself a decent job, a decent car, a decent place to live, a decent girl who wants all these decent things and some decent children to be followed by decent doctors, decent braces for decent teeth, decent clothes, a decent school and decent friends for a decent family?

Damnit! Was it all over? All my dreams? Desires? Ambitions? Hopes? Would I, too, become one of the millions settling down in a secure niche with a secure bank account — living a secure life? Was my writing really that bad? Was I fooling myself? And if I was, would I go on fooling myself for the rest of my life? What kind of life would that be? Would I end up in the gutter clutching a bottle of rubbing alcohol, singing "Hooray for Hollywood" and wishing it were all over?

Maybe I'm not as good as I think I am? Maybe it's just that I haven't developed my own style? Maybe I'm trying to copy another writer's style and it's just not working?

Maybe. Maybe. Maybe.

But Ellie told me that one day I would become a successful author. Was she lying just to be nice? Have I wasted all this time just to be told: "*Your writing is shit. You have no talent.*"

Should I stop believing in myself?

For three months, I brooded and sulked. I stopped writing. I walked the streets — directionless and alone. I refused to see my friends and avoided my parents. I took long drives on the open highways. I could barely eat or sleep. I began having nightmares. I stopped shaving and grew a beard. I let my hair grow long and unmanageable. I didn't care any more about my appearance. I just didn't give a fuck about anything or anyone. Life had become a tremendous struggle.

I spent many days sitting on my couch, staring at the walls. A day would pass. Another day. And another. Who knows how many days passed while I just sat on the couch staring at the walls? I was beginning to think that I had crossed the threshold — that fine line which separates reality from fantasy. I even thought I had gone mad. I began writing suicide notes.

> Dear Ma and Dad,
>   I can't take it.

> Dear Ma and Dad,
>   I still can't take it. I just can't take it!

> Dear Ma and Dad,
>   That's it! I really, really can't go on anymore.

> Dear Ma and Dad,
>   Sorry.

And how would I end it? Knives? Guns? Definitely out — I didn't like pain. Slash my wrists? Too messy. Pills? I'd have to mash them up in a spoon and dilute them with orange juice and cookie crumbs because I couldn't swallow pills. So what was I to do? Throw myself in front of a car? That couldn't be done because a friend of mine had already thought of that a couple of years ago. If I was going to take my own life, the least I could do was be original.

Some time during the third month of my isolation, the phone rang. I wasn't going to answer it. But the phone was so persistent that on the fiftieth or sixtieth or maybe the eightieth ring, I picked it up. I couldn't take the ringing. Even hiding in the bathroom and running the water wouldn't deaden the sound.

"Hello, Rudy."

God. It was Ellie. My mother must've called her in a panic: "Please, Ellie, help us. We don't know who to turn to anymore. Rudy's gone crazy. He's locked himself in and won't come out. Help us, Ellie. He'll listen to you."

"Hi, Ellie. How are you?"

"Fine, Rudy."

"When did you get back?"

"Oh... about three, four days ago. I've been trying to reach you."

"Really?"

What for? To be told by Miss Independence that she's through with independence and is now engaged?

"I'd like to see you, Rudy. I really would."

"Ummmmmm... well, Ellie... I'd like to see you, too."

"Great. Can I come up?"

"Sure."

"Okay. It'll take me about half an hour."

"Ellie, on second thought, let's meet at the park. I think I could use some fresh air. In about an hour and a half?"

"Which park?"

"The one with the white bridge."

"Okay. In an hour and a half."

Jesus. I couldn't let her see the apartment in such a mess. Or me, for that matter. Christ, I've got to get myself together. Clean myself up. Shower and shave and get a fast hair cut.

"Hello, Ellie." God, she's still beautiful. And so damn sexy in those tight jeans and high-heeled sandals. Damn you. Why don't you marry me?

"Rudy! Hi."

"How are you, Ellie?"

"I'm fine. I hear, though, that you've been having problems."

Frank. I like that. Frankness. No phoniness — just "I hear that you've been having problems." Cut to the chase. You haven't changed, Ellie.

"Why do you say that, Ellie?"

"Well, Rudy, hiding in your apartment for three months isn't exactly coping with life."

"Has it been that long? Really? I hadn't noticed."

"Rudy, cut the crap. It's me — remember?"

"Yeah, Ellie, I remember."

"You're still mad because I turned you down."

"Are you happy with your independence?"

"I can't understand why you hold that against me. Jesus Christ, Rudy! You had your independence. You had some freedom. Why couldn't you understand that I needed some too?"

"Have you had it?"

"Yes."

"Good."

God, how beautiful you are. Why don't we forget everything and get married?

"Rudy, what happened?"

"Not much."

"So why are you depressed? Why have you locked yourself up?"

"Plaster turned down my novel."

"That's all?"

"He also told me that I had no talent as a writer."

"And you believed him?"

"Why shouldn't I believe him? He's an experienced publisher."

"Because you should believe in yourself."

"I did. But this is my third rejection and, what with teaching not working out and, well... Ellie, what can I say? There's only so much rejection a guy can take. Maybe he's right. Maybe I should stop writing and look towards the future. Settle down."

"You're full of it."

"Thanks."

"No, Rudy, I mean it. Who the hell is this guy Plaster anyway?"

"A publisher."

"Publishers make mistakes. Do you have any idea how many

times Hemingway was turned down before he made it? Damnit, Rudy, don't give up. Believe in yourself. I believe in you. I know you've got it. You're rough. Your writing has to be developed and maybe you've yet to find your own style, but Rudy, from what I read of your writing, you shouldn't give up. Ever."

"Thank you, Ellie."

"Rudy, have you ever thought of taking a creative writing course?"

"Yeah. I don't know."

"Why not give it a go? See what it's like."

"Maybe."

"And as for losing your job, maybe the School Board has other positions. Call them up. What have you got to lose?"

"You make it sound so easy, Ellie."

"It is, Rudy. All you have to do is think positive."

"Maybe you're right. Maybe I will take a creative writing course. Couldn't hurt, eh? And tomorrow I'll call the School Board and see what's going on. Yeah!"

"That's the spirit."

"Say, Ellie, want to have supper with me? I mean, if you're not busy."

"No, I'm not busy."

"You still seeing Stanley?"

"Stanley got married."

"Ellie, are... are you seeing anybody special?"

"No one special, Rudy."

"Are you seeing anyone at all?"

"I had a few dates in Europe. Nothing to write home about. How about you?"

"Nope. Hard to date when you won't come out of your apartment."

"You're funny, Rudy."

"I'm also ready to date again."

"You are?"

"Yes."

"Anyone special?"

"No one special. Just a girl I met about a year ago. I just happened to have run into her today."

"You did."

"Yes."

"And how did she look to you?"

"As beautiful as ever."

"Did you tell her?"

"Not yet."

"What are you waiting for?"

Ellie smiled and put her arms around me. It felt great being close to her again. I smiled. We kissed. Tenderly. We looked at each other with sheepish grins. We kissed again. Passionately.

We spent the rest of the afternoon together. Walking, talking, holding hands, acting silly. It felt good being back in her life. But more important, I felt for the first time that Ellie was glad to be part of mine.

For the next three weeks, Ellie and I were inseparable. We were in love and I felt it was the right time to ask *the* question.

I thought of all the possible scenarios. Should I first go to her father and ask for her hand? Should I get down on one knee to propose? What should my knee rest on? The floor? A pillow? If a pillow, what size? What colour? Where should I ask her? In my apartment? At her place? Outside?

I finally chose the park with the white bridge. I still wasn't sure how to approach the subject but I was fairly confident that Ellie would help me out.

It wasn't that easy. The park was large and I couldn't figure out exactly where I wanted us to be when I asked her the question.

"Rudy, why do you keep moving around?"

"No reason, Ellie. I'm just looking around."

"You seem nervous. Is something on your mind?"

"My mind? No... well, maybe."

"What is it?"

Marry me. Marry me. Marry me.

"Rudy?"

"Yes?"

"Are you going to tell me?"

I cleared my throat and reached for a cigarette.

"Here's a bench," I said. "Let's sit."

I took a long puff, let out the smoke slowly and put out the cigarette.

"You're beautiful, Ellie. Ellie... marry me. I need you. I love you."

"So that's why you've been so restless."

A large smile began to form on her face.

"I love you, Ellie. You're everything I've always wanted in a girl. Looks, charm, a sense of humour, intelligence, good looks... did I mention that already?"

"Yes."

"Well, it bears repeating. Look, I'm going over to the pond. I'll give you five minutes. Think about it."

"I don't need five minutes."

"You don't?"

"No. I just need to ask you one question."

"Ask."

"I want three kids. How about you?"

Chapter 29

My parents were delighted. Ecstatic.

"She'll make a 'mensch' out of you, Rudy. You'll see. She'll make you into a person."

"Ma, I think I'm already a person."

"Not in my book. A person is a 'mensch'. Someone who has a good job, a wife, children, a house. Someone who can walk down the street and hold his head up high."

"And you mean I can't do that?"

"How? Tell me. Do you have a job? A house? Children?"

"Give me time, will you? Let me start off with a wife. The rest will come."

"I know. I know. I'm just worried about your future. You have no job, you're getting married and soon you'll have children. Why couldn't they give you back your classes?"

"How many times do I have to tell you? There are too many teachers. Only the ones with tenure are left. And one year of teaching didn't give me tenure. How many times do I have to tell you?"

"Politics. Feh! I don't believe a word of it. Something fishy is going on."

"Maybe. Who knows? And who cares. I'll get another job. Don't worry so much."

"Thank God Ellie has a good job. Thank God."

Somewhere in between the euphoria and the chastising she insisted on making a special Friday night supper and decided to invite every member of the family, including Ellie's and Leon's parents. It was such a large party that she had half the meal catered. The chicken soup she would make herself, as well as the chopped liver. She had rented six bridge tables with chairs and had set them up in the basement. With twenty-one people coming, we needed lots of space.

My mother, in a crushed velvet fuchsia jacket and matching skirt, was everywhere: fluttering up and down the stairs; from one part of the house to the other overseeing the family and hired help like a Supreme Commander. My father, in his customary white shirt and grey flannels, had to play the part of a two-star General: taking one order after another from Ma. Julie was designated Chief of Staff; her title contrasting sharply with her slinky red satin dress.

"If there's any complaints," my mother told her, "you take care of them. If you feel it's not important, don't bother me. But, if you feel that it calls for my attention, then come right over and let me know. I don't want anyone to badmouth my party when they leave."

"Give me a for-instance, Mom," Julie said.

"A for-instance she needs. All right. I'll give you one. For instance, if you're eating and you hear someone, especially from Ellie's side of the family, complain that the soup isn't very hot or is too hot, then that you can handle by yourself. I don't need to be bothered for that."

"What should I do?"

"You'll grab their soup plate, come upstairs and either heat it up or cool it off."

"Are you serious, Mom?"

"You want they should leave my home and talk?"

"No, Mom."

"Now, if you hear someone complaining that the food doesn't taste good or maybe that someone starts to look green around the gills, then I'd like to be notified right away. Understand?"

"Won't you be at the table?"

"At the table! Doing what?"

"Eating, Mom. Won't you be eating with us?"

"Who can eat? I'll be too busy. You think it's a picnic catering a sit-down supper? Who'll have time to sit down and eat? You think I can enjoy myself when so many people are in the house, staring at everything, wondering why there's still dust on the lampshade?"

"Mom, nobody's going to be staring at the lampshades."

"Maybe not on our side of the family. But who can be sure of Ellie's or Leon's side? Just do as I tell you."

"Yes, Mom."

The two women who delivered the catered food remained to act as waitresses. They were assigned the rank of Private. My mother made their lives miserable that night. All in all, the party was a success. Everyone appreciated the good food, the fine wine, and Ellie's rich desserts — trifle and a chocolate rum cake. Ma had also made her standard sponge cake, apple cake and cheese cake. She had been smart enough not to send my father out to buy chocolates since she knew that at least two or three of the guests would bring some as presents. However, she was taken aback when Leon's parents, both dressed in peach-coloured polyester outfits and platform shoes, showed up with a rather odd-shaped package. My mother instinctively knew, from the way the package didn't have neat corners, that this was not a box of chocolates.

"I wonder what it could be?" my mother said to Leon's mother as she ordered my father to take their coats.

"If you opened it up, Esther, you would know," Gertie said.

"Now why didn't I think of that," Ma replied.

When my mother opened it up and found an orange plastic container the size of an apple juice can and a little plastic shovel, hoe and rake, my mother politely smiled and thanked Gertie and Frank for their generous gift.

"Morris, take a look. See what Gertie and Frank brought us."

"Very nice," my father said. "Very, very nice. May I ask what it is?"

"Morris, for goodness sakes. Gertie, you'll have to excuse my husband. When it comes to kitchen equipment, he doesn't know his eye from his ear."

"Esther, it isn't kitchen equipment. It's for the garden."

"Really? Go know..."

There was also a minor incident with Leon, who had decided to wear his polo helmet in case I became violent again. Not that it was his fault but, unfortunately, he was seated beside his mother at the dinner table and, when reaching for his straw (his jaw was still wired up from my punch), he accidentally knocked his mother's bowl of chicken soup into her lap.

Julie panicked. She had absolutely no idea what kind of a for-instance this instance was. Should Ma be notified or should she assert her authority as Chief of Staff? As luck would have it, Leon took over. He grabbed his mother by the arm, rushed her upstairs to the bathroom and, after a two-minute conference with the Supreme Commander, they plotted out their course of action. Leon would go downstairs and act as if nothing had happened and Ma handed Gertie an old and ratty housecoat to put on while she threw Gertie's stained dress in the wash.

Ellie and I were the last to leave. There were tears of joy in my father's eyes and sparks of anger in my mother's. She was upset with the Zadulka's – Ellie's parents. I only found this out the next day when she called me.

"Can we talk?"

"What do you mean, Ma?"

"I mean, are you alone?"

"Yes."

"Ellie's not there?"

"No."

"They're cheap."

"What?"

"Your future in-laws. They're cheap. They have the money but they're cheap."

"What are you talking about?"

"Didn't you even notice that I was upset last night?"

"I noticed. So did Ellie."

"What did you tell her?"

"Nothing. I didn't know why you were upset."

"Well, when I tell you, don't tell Ellie."

"What happened, Ma?"

"We were discussing the wedding plans last night. Ellie's

parents, your father, and me. I know we're only marrying a son and so we don't have much to say, but at least I would like my friends and family to be well-received. I even offered to pay for the flowers and liquor. And..."

"And?"

"And your future in-laws want a very simple affair. A luncheon. One or two flowers. No wine. I offered to pay for it and do you know what they said?"

"What?"

"'Don't be silly.' Is this a thing to say to a woman who wants only the best for her only son? And that's not all. They said we could invite twenty couples and they would invite twenty couples. I told them that twenty couples from our side would only cover A to L, but that I would be willing to pay for all additional couples."

"What did they say?"

"They said no. Did you ever?"

"Look, Ma, it's not important. So it'll be a small wedding. What's the difference?"

"To you, nothing. You won't even realise what's happening. But how will I live this down? What will the Morochovskys say when they're not invited?"

"What do you want me to do?"

"Talk to someone."

"I'll speak to Ellie."

"What will you say?"

"I'll say, how come the Morochovskys can't come to my wedding?"

I spoke to Ellie and Ellie spoke to her parents. They compromised. The Morochovskys could come.

We were to be married in October. That would give me a full two months to find a job. Schoolboards weren't hiring anyone. There was now a surplus of tenured teachers. I wasn't worried. After all, ex-schoolteachers have a lot going for them: conversational skills, patience, stamina, a healthy appearance and, most of all, guts.

With one week left before our wedding date, I had still not

found anything suitable. Seems nobody was interested in all my wonderful qualities. Seems ex-schoolteachers were only qualified to do two things: tutoring and selling insurance.

"Rudy, there's only three days left," Ellie said as we walked hand-in-hand around the park. "Maybe selling insurance will open up a whole new world for you."

"Ellie, what the hell do I know about selling? I couldn't care less if someone bought insurance from me or not. Besides, I'm not a salesman. I'm not pushy enough."

"How do you know if you don't try?"

"Some things in life you just know."

"That's a defeatist attitude."

"Ellie, I wouldn't make a good salesman."

"I think you'd be wonderful. Besides, how could anyone not buy a policy from you, what with that sexy smile of yours?"

"You think so?"

"I'm positive. Look, give it a try. If it doesn't work out, what have you lost? Nothing. And besides, they said they'll pay you a training allowance and a commission after that. And if you don't like it, you can always look for something else. But at least you'll be working and have a salary."

"Maybe you're right."

"I think you'll be terrific."

"You think so?"

"Rudy, look at that house. The Spanish-looking one. Isn't it beautiful?"

"Yeah. I love it. It's my favourite house."

"How much do you think it would be?"

"Somewhere around $200,000, I guess."

"When you become a famous writer, we'll buy it."

"For sure. And we'll add on a swimming pool and a four-car garage and an indoor gym and sauna and whirlpool. You know, Ellie, I'm glad you like this district as much as I do."

"You feel good here, don't you?"

"Yeah, I grew up here and every time we walk in this park I can see myself as a kid playing on the swings or losing my yo-yo in the pond. My mother would take Julie and me here every afternoon in the summer. And in the winter, my father would take us skating. I had a terrific childhood. Lots of fresh air."

"Rudy Petinsky, I love you."

"Mrs. Soon-to-be-Petinsky, so do I."

Chapter 30

Our wedding was nothing special. Synagogue food, circular tables with tired-looking yellow tablecloths, the traditional *chala* cut by the traditional Rabbi who blessed us with a traditional *brocha*. One hundred guests danced to music that was too loud. Ellie looked beautiful in her white, pearl-studded wedding gown but I looked like a mannequin in a "Rent a Tux" shop. My frilly blue tuxedo shirt was too starched, my cumberbund too tight and the soles of my black patent leather shoes too slippery.

After the reception, Ellie and I retired to our brand-new, high-rise apartment.

That night, we fooled around so much I was sure in nine months we'd have quintuplets. And maybe because of all the fooling around, in the wee hours of the morning I woke up trembling and in a sweat. I had had a nightmare. I had dreamt that I was wall-to-wall carpeting. One minute I was an attractive beige, blending comfortably into the background, my wool neatly aligned. The next minute people were walking all over me. Someone holding a banana daiquiri threw up. It was repulsive. Once awake, I had to go to the bathroom, but I was afraid of who I might meet along the way. A new apartment can be so frightening at night. If this were happening to me when I was ten years old, I'd have reached for my Davy Crockett coonskin hat and my Wild Bill Hickock rifle and easily conquered the bathroom. Hell, I would have overpowered every damn room in the house. But I didn't have those trusty friends anymore.

I finally relieved myself (physically, not mentally), crept back under the covers and touched my wife. Maybe she'd be in the mood.

"Ellie."

"Huh."

"Ellie, wake up."

"What time is it?"

"5:30. C'mon, wake up, you've slept enough."

"5:30, are you crazy?"

"Wanna fool around?"

"Rudy, go back to sleep."

"I can't. I just had a nightmare."

"Aw, poor baby. Tell me about it."

"I'd rather forget about it."

"Okay, let's go back to sleep."

"I'm not tired. Want to have a good time?"

"You may not be tired, but I am."

"Ellie, you won't have to do anything. I'll be in before you know it. In and out. Then you can go back to sleep."

"Rudy, cut it out."

"Am I in yet?"

"Rudy, you're in between my knees."

"I thought it was going too easy."

CHAPTER 31

Leon's book come out two weeks after our wedding. His name was in the papers, he was interviewed on radio and T.V., and copies began selling. Slowly at first, but each time he gave an interview, sales went up, and with each sale I became sicker. After eight weeks, everyone was talking about *Psychosexual Infantilism — The Beast In Us*. It was considered an important work to have on your bookshelf. Ten weeks after publication, "Time" magazine did a review of the book. A full page devoted to my brother-in-law. Three columns with a photo of Leon sitting behind his desk, smoking a pipe. The article was entitled "The New Rajah of the Mind." The following issue of "Time" had Leon's book in the number ten slot on their best-seller list. "Newsweek" followed. Then "People" magazine came out with a three-page spread on Leon: Leon photographed in his office, at home, by his lake in the Catskills, beside his Jaguar, with Julie. "Psychology Today" had Leon on their cover. He was being touted as "psychiatrist of the decade."

I was getting sicker by the day. I developed a rash. Sales were now over the 200,000 mark. I developed a boil. Johnny Carson wanted Leon on his show. The boil burst. Leon did the Carson show. I got an abscess on my molar. Leon was a hit on the show and was asked to come back the following night. My tooth was so infected that it had to be removed. Leon came back from Hollywood with wonderful news. "Beast" was now at the 300,000 mark. I had to be hospitalised. I had developed a cyst under the eye and it had to be scraped away.

Exactly six months to the day of its first printing, "Beast" had sold 600,000 copies hardcover. Paperback rights had still to be negotiated. Foreign rights had still to be negotiated. Plaster and Leon were being inundated by offers. A Broadway producer had expressed interest in buying the rights and it was rumoured that none other than Woody Allen wanted to buy the rights to the film. With all this new-found fame and fortune, Leon had become, if possible, more obnoxious. He honestly believed he was going to win the Nobel Prize. He believed it to the point of taking a week off from his busy schedule and visiting Stockholm. He wanted to tell the President of the committee, upon receiving his prize, that this was not his first time in Stockholm. That he had been there several times and that Stockholm was his favourite spot in the whole wide world. When he bought his plane ticket, he was flabbergasted to find out that Stockholm was not in Iceland.

Four copies of Leon's book were in my parents' home. One lay in their bedroom. On my mother's night table. It was the last thing that she wanted to look at before she shut her eyes and went to sleep and the first thing she wanted to see in the morning. Another was in the den, on the bookshelf, standing upright and placed strategically between "The Rise and Fall of the Third Reich" and "The Indestructible Jews." The third copy adorned the coffee table in the living room. I had told my mother that only "art" books were left lying around coffee tables, but she wouldn't listen to me.

"First a writer, now an interior decorator," she said, rolling her eyes. "What's next for you, Rudy, an astronaut? Besides, the colours on the jacket fit in well with the red couch."

The fourth copy was in the linen cupboard, behind the towels, wrapped in cellophane and protected by a brown paper bag.

"Just in case the other books get yellow with age, and they will," she said, "I'll still have a brand new one."

CHAPTER 32

While Leon had rapidly become "The Mark Twain of Psychology," I was struggling to make a living. The day before my wedding, I had reluctantly accepted a job selling insurance on the advice of my new bride.

I remember my first day at Inwards Counselling. They had given me my own pen, coloured in black and orange with white writing: Inwards Counselling, Rudy Petinsky — Investment Counsellor. I had my own desk with a dull black phone squashed in between two telephone books.

That first morning I was supposed to listen to supersalesman Eliot Yankee's tapes on selling. What the hell, they were paying me a training allowance and I needed the money. So I listened. I listened all morning. The tape would finish, rewind itself and start again. I kept listening. Every once in a while, Mr. Rye, my manager, came in to see how I was getting along. I told him "super" and he left. He didn't really seem to care how I was doing. He just kept saying the same thing: "Keep listening to Yankee. A brilliant man. Keep listening."

After lunch, I decided to place a few calls to inactive clients. Maybe I could get an appointment. I wrote down a few notes: interest rates, tax-saving investments, term insurance rates, inflation fighters. I dialled.

Depression set in that very first day. Six calls and no leads. What the hell was going on? Why did it work for Yankee and not for me? Was my voice not chipper enough? Was my diction not clear? Maybe I sounded too Jewish? Maybe not Jewish enough? Jesus, if I couldn't get an appointment, how would I be able to sell an investment and support myself in the style to which I would have liked to become accustomed?

I left the office and sluggishly made my way home.

"Hi, Rudy. How'd your first day go?"

"No leads."

"Is that salesman talk?"

"Yeah, salesman talk," I answered despondently.

"Rudy, what's wrong?"

"Nothing, Ellie. How was your day?"

"The same. Must have seen over thirty kids today. And, as usual, Barry saw maybe four or five. The rest of the time he just sat in his office reading the newspaper, took a two-hour lunch break and left half an hour early. God, he's so lazy."

Ellie was working at Lincoln College, advising the students on what courses they would need to complete their diploma, and counselling them about personal problems. Fantastic pay.

"Maybe he doesn't like his job."

"What's there not to like?"

"Maybe he's depressed. Maybe he'd rather be doing something else."

"Rudy, what is it? Why are you so down? Did something happen at work?"

"No. Nothing happened."

"Then what?"

"Well... Ellie... it's just not for me."

"After one day you can tell?"

"Yes."

"Rudy, you've got to give it time. The first day on a new job is always rough. But you can't quit after one day. That's being childish."

"Yeah," I sighed.

"Rudy, don't get yourself depressed. You'll never sell anything that way. You'll see, tomorrow will be better. C'mon, snap out of it. Help me with supper. How about peeling some potatoes?"

"Fine," I said lethargically, as I slumped my way to the kitchen.

"Hey, after supper, why don't we go to a movie? Would you like that?"

"I suppose so."

"Sure, it'll do you good to get out."

"I phoned six people today. No one bought. No one was interested. Nobody seemed to care."

"Well, Rudy, it was only your first day. Give it time."

"Yeah, maybe you're right."

"Of course I am. Why don't we open up a bottle of wine? Okay?"

"Okay."

"Sure. It'll make you feel better. By the way, I found out that there's a creative writing course starting in three weeks. Why don't you apply?"

"Where?"

"At N.Y.U. An undergraduate course."

"I'll think about it."

I no longer spent my afternoons in the office. I would either go to the movies or read in the park. My existence had become dull. I was doing very little with my life — accomplishing nothing. I had dropped out of the creative writing course after the fourth session. I just couldn't sit down and write. Plaster's words still affected me and, no matter what Ellie said or tried to do, nothing worked. I would have to wait it out or come to grips with the fact that I didn't have what it takes. In any case, something would have to give.

Something did.

"Good morning, Mr. Rye. You wanted to see me?"

"Yes, Rudy. Please have a seat."

I had a feeling why he wanted to see me. It was my sales record. After being at Inwards for two months, I only had two buyers: my mother and Ellie.

"Well, Rudy, how do you like being at Inwards?"

"Fine, Mr. Rye. I'm enjoying it very much."

"That's good. But we seem to have a problem. How long have you been with us now?"

"Two months."

"Two months. I see. Well, Rudy, I've just had a look at your sales record and it seems that you only have two sales in two months and all those sales came in your first week with us. Is everything all right at home?"

"'At home?' What do you mean?"

"Well, Rudy, usually when a salesman can't make a sale it sometimes has to do with internal pressure. Family, that sort of thing."

"No sir, nothing wrong at home."

"How about finances? Do you have debts you haven't told us about?"

"No sir, no debts."

"Well then, I simply can't understand why you're not selling. What seems to be the problem?"

"I'm not sure. I'm doing all the things that Yankee suggested."

"Fine. Fine."

"And I'm mailing leaflets and going canvassing, but nothing seems to happen."

"Have you tried shopping centres?"

"Shopping centres? No. I..."

"Well, Rudy, why don't you try the shopping mall down the street? It even has an office tower attached to it. Lots of people to make contact with."

"All right. I'll try it."

"Fine. Because frankly, Rudy, if business doesn't pick up, we just might have to let you go. I wouldn't like that to happen, but we do run a business here."

"I understand, Mr. Rye. I'll start on it right away."

I left Rye's office convinced that time was running out. It was a "do or die" situation. Somehow I had to drum up whatever cheerleading qualities I had inside of me. On the way to the mall I gave myself a pep talk. After all, this was combat. I had to get myself in a fighting mood.

As I entered the main entrance, walking briskly, attaché case in my left hand, I tried to look confident. I walked towards the elevator doors and scanned the directory for possible clients. I could feel my adrenaline pumping. I could feel a sale. I knew it was going to happen. The elevator doors silently opened. I entered and pushed button number four. As the doors closed, however, I could feel my exuberance slipping away. I tried to fight it. I tried to hang in. But it was no use. I became agitated and perturbed. Here I was, dressed in a tie and jacket, going to sell a stranger an insurance policy when all I wanted was to sit behind a desk writing best-sellers. Yet it was my bastard brother-in-law who was living my dream. I became depressed. Discouraged. Dismayed. I walked out of the elevator, uptight and anxious. My body felt hot and clammy.

Directly in front of me was a heavy glass door, leading to Painter Realties. A receptionist was sitting behind a desk, talking on the phone. I walked up to her, waiting a minute or two for her to finish. She wouldn't acknowledge me. She was too busy chewing her gum as she typed away with her impossibly long, blood red, fingernails. On my right, I noticed a dark brown door. On it was a gold plate: J.S. Painter, President. I stared at the plate, hesitating whether I should bypass his secretary and just knock on his door. As I was about to make a decision, the door opened and out bustled an impossibly flushed, incredibly rotund man, holding a manila folder.

"Are you Mr. Painter?" I asked, assertively.

"Yes," he answered, breathing heavily.

"How do you do, Mr. Painter. My name is Rudy Petinsky and I'm with Inwards Counselling. May I take a few minutes of your time and tell you a bit about our company and how we may be of service to you?"

"Mr... I'm sorry, what was your name again?"

"Rudy. Rudy Petinsky."

"Mr. Petinsky, I'm very busy now. Perhaps in a few weeks."

"Well fine, I can certainly understand that, Mr. Painter, but if I could show you a way of protecting yourself against inflation, wouldn't you be interested in spending several minutes with me?"

"Perhaps at a future date. I've got tons of people to see. Here's my card. Give me a call."

"Well fine, Mr. Painter. I can appreciate your hectic schedule, but five minutes of your time may possibly result in an earlier retirement for you. Do you think we could step inside your office for a moment or would this evening at your home be better?"

"I'm sorry, Mr. Petinsky. I'm not interested."

"Well fine, Mr. Painter. I can understand that. If you had been interested, you would have called me, that's why I gave you the courtesy of coming to see you. Do you think we could step inside your office?"

"Mr. Petinsky, good-bye. Miss Trent will see you out."

"Well, that's great, Mr. Painter. Perhaps I could pass by later on in the afternoon or would tomorrow morning be better for you?"

"Mr. Petinsky, are you hard of hearing?"

"Well fine, Mr. Painter. I can certainly appreciate that. Tomorrow morning, you say, is best for you?"

"Mr. Petinsky, please get out of here before I call Security."

"Well, Mr. Painter, now you've hit the hammer right on the nail. That's exactly what I'm talking about. Security! That's right, Security. With a capital S that stands for Success. And that's why I came to see you. To spell out to you the word 'success' and show you, if you don't already know, the way to that pot at the end of the rainbow."

"Who did you say you were associated with?"

"Mr. Painter, I'm with the largest investment firm in Manhattan. Inwards Counselling."

"Well, Mr. Petinsky, I had no idea. In that case, perhaps you'd like to give me their phone number so I can call them up and tell them what kind of a raving idiot they have representing their company."

"Well, fine, Mr. Painter. That's just terrific and my company, as well as I, can certainly appreciate your concern. Maybe tomorrow afternoon would really be best for you?"

"God Almighty! Don't you ever stop?"

"I believe I've made you angry. If that's the case, I would like to apologise. It was never my intention to make you feel uncomfortable. Please accept my apologies. Perhaps Wednesday morning would really be more convenient. Let's say around 9:00?"

I was grabbed by the arm. Painter wanted to hustle me out the door as quickly as possible. I resisted. I struggled. I twisted and turned towards him.

"Hey! Hey!" I shouted. "What do you think you're doing!"

"I've been trying to get rid of you for the last five minutes but you just won't leave. You're like a pesky fly."

"Take your hand off me. Right now!"

"Sorry. You had your chance."

"Right now! Release me!"

Painter had a firm grip and I could feel that he was not about to let go anytime soon so I placed my free hand on the corner of the receptionist's desk and tried my hardest to pull myself free. Painter must have anticipated this move because he was now pulling me right to the glass door. Once again, I placed my free hand on the knob and furiously began to twist and then to bend and then to rotate and finally I gave a tremendous yank on the doorknob and Painter, with all this momentum I was creating, flew through the glass door, shattering the door in what seemed like a hundred million pieces.

The next day, Mr. Rye called me into his office and fired me.

"Rudy, I think it's in everyone's best interest if you look for another career."

I emptied out my briefcase on Mr. Rye's desk, giving him back everything he had given me: memo pad, engraved pens, business cards, and walked out of the mutual fund business for good.

I later explained the whole story to Ellie. How I had met Mr. Painter, how I had left Mr. Painter, and how, after I had left him, Mr. Painter had phoned the company and told Mr. Rye that he had hired a lunatic.

Ellie tried to comfort me by telling me that everything would be all right. I, myself, didn't know whether to be upset or happy. I felt relieved that I was no longer a salesman. On the other hand, I had just lost a job that was paying me $300 a week.

Now I would have to go back on the job market. Shit.

Chapter 33

My mother took my dismissal very hard.

"How will you two survive? On Ellie's salary?"

"Ma, I'll get another job. There's lots of jobs out there."

"What kind, Rudy? Driving a taxi? Collecting garbage?"

"I'll get a job."

"You're ruining your life, Rudy. You had it all. You had a profession and you threw it away. And by the by, how am I going to explain to all my friends, as well as our family, that you threw someone out of a window?"

My in-laws thought the world was coming to an end. No one in their family had ever been fired. I told Ellie to have a word with her parents. Try to calm them down. Hell, I hadn't murdered anybody. I had just been fired.

I applied to the School Boards for the coming semester and went out looking for a job. Two days later I was hired by Schuman's Appliance Store. The hours were longer than at Inwards and the pay was a bit lower, but at least it was a job and, by delivering refrigerators and washing machines, I would get some badly needed exercise. I was thrilled. So was Ellie. We both knew that it was temporary. My mother had a conniption.

"My son, driving a truck and schlepping machines! Rudy, what kind of job is that for a married man? You had such a good one – such a good one. With a tie and a clean shirt and nice slacks and a sportsjacket. Rudy, you looked so handsome. And now – back to jeans. And a jersey! Rudy, what are you doing with your life? What? Tell me!"

Unfortunately for my mother, she said all of this to me in front of Ellie. She just couldn't help herself, I guess. And neither could Ellie. She told my mother, in no uncertain terms, that there was nothing wrong with the work I was doing. That it was an honest day's work and that it was only a temporary job.

"I don't ever want to hear you belittling Rudy. Do you understand? There's nothing wrong with what he's doing and he should be given all the credit in the world for trying to be a salesman. He tried. He gave it his best shot and you should be proud of him. Not berate him for it. It didn't work out — that's all. Period."

My mother had met her match. Life is fair after all.

That weekend, Ellie and I drove off to Lake George. A belated honeymoon. Somewhere between the eating, dancing and making love, we had our first fight.

"Ellie, how come we're married?"

"What do you mean, Rudy?"

"I mean, why did you marry me?"

"'cause of your sense of humour."

"What about it?"

"You're a riot, Rudy. You're so serious most of the time, and from out of nowhere you come up with things like no one else can. You really make me laugh."

"All the time?"

"Not all the time."

"Most of the time?"

"More than most of the time."

"So, it's somewhere between most and more. How about right now?"

"Right now, you're arousing me."

"How come?"

"It usually happens when you twirl my nipple around with your fingers."

"Do you want to know why I married you?"

"I'll never get tired of you telling me."

"So you know, do you?"

"Uh huh."

"Well then, forget it. Let's go back to why you married me."

"C'mon Rudy, tell me. I love hearing it."

"Well, I think it was your legs. And then your ass. And then your breasts and then..."

"You think I have a nice body?"

"Ummmmmmmmmm."

"What else?"

"I love the nailpolish you use."

"Pervert."

"I can't help it. I love the smell of it."

"It turns you on, eh?"

"Yeah. You turn me on."

"Keep going."

"I just knew you were the right girl for me. That we'd make a terrific team."

"How could you tell?"

"I just could. You were so secure, so sure of yourself, so positive in your outlook on life."

"And you weren't sure of yourself?"

"I don't know if I wasn't sure of myself. I guess I was mixed up a bit. Maybe naive."

"Why do you say that?"

"Look at how I went to Hollywood. I thought the studios were waiting for me."

"I liked that in you. I mean, I could never just pick myself up and go like you did. I think it took a lot of guts for you to go to Hollywood. There's not many people that I know who would do something like that. At least you tried. And you went to Europe by yourself."

"So did you."

"No. I went on a tour with a group. But you went alone. I couldn't do that."

"Why not?"

"I guess I'd be afraid. I don't know. Maybe my parents sheltered me too much... you know what else made me love you?"

"What?"

"Your kindness."

"What do you mean?"

"The way you would, out of the blue, bring me flowers. Or when we went to a movie, you'd always bring an apple with you because you knew that I loved apples. You don't do that anymore, Rudy."

"Sure I do."

"Oh sure, you wash it for me, but it's me that has to carry it in my purse."

"I feel silly carrying an apple in my hand."

"You didn't mind then."

"C'mon Ellie, then was then and now is now."

"Is that supposed to be profound?"

"Yes. Ellie, you have a purse. The apple fits in. Granted it's a tight squeeze. God almighty, why do you have so much in your purse?"

"I don't have so much."

"Of course you do."

"No, I don't."

"Ellie, once you get through with it, a bobby pin wouldn't fit into it."

"I just carry the regular things. Brush, comb, lipstick, that sort of stuff."

"Just the regular things? What about the five hundred grocery coupons?"

"I like to be prepared."

"And what about the novel you always carry in it?"

"That's for reading on the bus."

"But they get mangled. Can't you take care of them?"

"Don't be silly."

"I mean it. I take pride in my books. A book shouldn't be carried in a purse. You should take better care of my books."

"They're also my books now."

"Never."

"C'mon, Rudy. They're as much my books as yours."

"Uh uh. Everything else is fifty/fifty but the books. They're all mine. And speaking of books, I wish you wouldn't lend them out. I'm not a library."

"Who do I lend them to?"

"Your parents."

"What's the big deal? You get them back."

"I can't stand to see empty spaces on my bookshelves."

"You're nuts."

"Would you lend out your children?"

"What?!"

"It's the same thing. My books are my children."

"You're nuts."

"I really wish you would stop mangling them. And for God's sake, stop reading in the kitchen while you're cooking. They can't take the heat. Their pages unglue. Jesus Christ, Ellie, I found spaghetti stains in the new novel I just bought. Jesus, I haven't even read it and already it's got spaghetti stains. You've got to start taking better care of them."

"You're serious, aren't you?"

"Damn right."

"Anything else you want to complain about?"

"No. That's all."

"C'mon. You don't have to stop. I can take it."

"No. That's all."

"You're sure?"

"Okay. If you really want to know, I think you're rude."

"Go on."

"You're rude because you're always keeping me waiting. At the last minute you've got to brush your hair, or put on lipstick, or take one last look in the mirror. What gets me mad is that it takes you an hour to find your brush. Everything you own is in your purse and, when you need something, you dump it on the bed and go wading through it. I wish you'd organise your damn purse or get a shopping bag or even a suitcase. That way, maybe, just once, we'd be on time."

I was now shouting. Our innocent and friendly and even flirty conversation was not so friendly anymore. And definitely not flirty. Why I was making such a big deal out of this I don't know. Did Ellie's purse really make me mad? I guess. Was it worth getting angry over? I thought so at the time. But then again, all fights seem so important at the time.

"We're always late because you can't find anything in your purse and why do you always have to do everything at the last minute?"

Ellie didn't answer. Instead she began crying and rushed to the bathroom. I could hear a faint voice inside of me say: "You ogre. You bastard. Why did you have to upset her? You were having such a good time. Why did you have to pick a fight? And for what? Over a purse? A lousy, crummy purse?" But another voice assured me it had nothing to do with the stupid purse.

When Ellie came out of the bathroom, red-eyed, I sheepishly went over to her and apologised. Ellie, being kind-hearted and not one to hold a grudge, forgave me. Yet I still felt like a heel. I shouldn't have yelled just because she made us late once in a while. I could have made my point without raising my voice.

However, I did not feel guilty about yelling at her about the books. She would have to learn to be more respectful towards them and I would have to learn to be more diplomatic in the way I argued.

Having to apologise to your wife after a spat does not make you a winner.

CHAPTER 34

Leon wasn't invited to Stockholm. It truly broke his heart. What broke mine was that his book was finally coming out in paperback. He had negotiated a deal for a quarter of a million dollars. Fuck!

Julie was in seventh heaven. She was now the richest kid on the block. And Leon, being richer than his wildest dreams, now considered himself to be *the* authority on American literature.

"You know what writing is all about, Rudy?" he asked, not waiting for a reply. "Writing is vomiting. If you can't get it out, choose another profession."

"That's very profound, Leon," Ellie said, as she helped my mother serve dinner.

"Did you know that Leon has started another book?" Julie piped in, fingering her new pearl necklace. "It's called *The Do's and Don'ts.*"

"*The Do's and Don'ts,*" Ellie looked at Julie quizzically.

"Yes."

"Of what?" my father asked.

"Of writing. What else?" Leon stated haughtily. "I'm writing a book on how to write a book."

"What do you know about writing?" my father asked.

Leon couldn't believe his ears. "What do you mean?" he said. "I wrote one. It sold over one million copies. I, above all, should know."

"Should know what, Leon?"

"How to write a book! Are you feeling all right?"

"I'm feeling fine," my father answered. "So tell me, Leon, what are you going to write about?"

"I just told you. The do's and don'ts."

"Can you give an example?"

"An example. You want an example. Well, all right." My

mother came in from the kitchen and put a plate of pickles and sour tomatoes on the table. Leon immediately stabbed at a pickle with his fork. He repeated the action and missed again. On his third attempt he viciously stuck his fork into the pickle and severely damaged it. He put it on his plate and began slicing it. "I believe that good writing is like a woman giving birth. Inspired writing is like a man trying to give birth. Yet there are too many writers around today who are still writing with a condom around their penis."

"Who?" I asked.

"Who?"

"Yes. Who?"

"You, for one."

"I'm not writing."

"Smart decision."

"I thought Rudy's book had potential," Ellie said.

"Rudy's book is a fine example of the Don'ts. As a matter of fact, I'm using Rudy's manuscript as an example."

"You're what!"

"Don't worry, Rudy. I'm using no names or sections of your writing. You won't be able to sue."

"If you're not using sections, how can you say anything?"

"Just general observations. What not to do."

"Be specific."

Leon moved back his chair: "You won't overreact, will you?"

"Let's see."

"I need your word."

"Okay. Let's hear it."

"Well, this is strictly off the top of my head, but in essence I say that your manuscript is a prime example of a writer, no, a would-be writer writing in the dark without the least bit of intelligence, know-how or craftsmanship. Your novel moves at a snail's pace. It's flat. It lacks sparkle. It's boring and mundane in the extreme. It's simplistic, childish, and utterly unacceptable. It has no relation to the real world. There isn't one iota of interest in it. It's contrived, clumsy and artificial. The..."

Ma had not heard a word of this. She was in the kitchen. My father's teeth were clenched, as were Ellie's fists. I was in a daze and barely heard Julie scream. I saw Leon rise out of his chair in slow-motion. Julie was on her hands and knees. She whispered something in his ear and Leon became frantic. He whipped up the tablecloth and looked under the table, all the while screaming at the top of his lungs: "Fifty thousand dollars! Those pearls were fifty thousand dollars! And you had to unstring them. What do you have in your head? ROCKS? Fifty thousand dollars!"

"Leon, I was just ad... admiring th... them," Julie said through her sobs. "A... and th... the st... string br... broke."

"BROKE! How can a string of pearls break? HOW?"

Ellie went over to them and started looking for stray pearls. Leon went crazy.

"Don't you dare move one more foot. I just bet you'd love to get your pretty fingers on one of those pearls. Get away, you hear? I know exactly how many pearls were on that string, so thank you very much but I'll round them up myself."

I got out of my chair and pulled Leon up by his shirt collar, ready to slap him silly.

He broke away from me and rushed into the kitchen, scurrying under the kitchen table like a squirrel frantically gathering nuts for the winter. "There's one. And another one. They all rolled into the kitchen. They're all in the fuckin' kitchen." He began sobbing and gathering. We could hear him counting. "Forty-six, forty-seven, forty-eight, forty-nine." And then he stopped. "Where's the fiftieth? I can't find number fifty. Julie, where is it? It's got to be here. It can't have escaped, not by itself." He came running into the dining room and glared at us. He let out a sigh and then darted behind the living room couch. Half an hour later, exhausted from turning the house upside down, he returned to the dining room.

"I know one of you has it. Own up," Leon said loudly.

Ma asked: "Are you accusing one of us of stealing your wife's pearl?"

"Maybe I am and maybe I'm not, if you know what I mean."

"I don't. Either you are or you aren't," Ma said.

"Let's put it this way. It's nowhere to be found. I've turned the house upside down. Therefore, if you don't mind, I'd like to check your pockets."

"Out of the question. Nobody checks my pockets. Now go sit down. My meat is already spoiled."

"Eat! How can I eat? Who has an appetite?"

"I do. I'm starved," Ellie said.

"Me too," my father added.

"What's the matter with all of you? Have you lost your senses? A fortune is lying around here and you want to eat! Fools!" Leon thundered. "Nitwits!"

"That's enough!" my father yelled.

"Honey, relax. We'll find it. It'll show up," Julie said.

"The hell it will. Someone has it and won't give it up. I'm out a thousand bucks."

"You're also out of my house," my father told Leon. "I want you to leave right now."

"But Daddy, Leon..."

"Never mind excuses," my mother butted in. "Julie, take your husband home and put him to bed. Maybe tomorrow he'll come to his senses and apologise to your father."

"Apologise? I'll apologise only when my pearl is returned," Leon snapped as he stomped out of the house.

The pearl was never found. Friday nights were now relatively quiet, with Leon and Julie no longer there. Six months later, to the day, Julie called my mother to tell her that Leon was being sued for plagiarism for the sum of everything he had earned from the publication of *Psychosexual Infantilism — The Beast In Us* as well as an additional five million dollars. And who was charging Leon with plagiarism?

The estate of Sigmund Freud.

CHAPTER 35

I arrived early for court. I positioned myself in the third row, on a forty-five degree angle from where the accused would be sitting. I wanted to hear every word, see every gesture, and I particularly wanted to see Leon's cheek muscle twitch while he was being put through the wringer.

Edwin Plaster and another man entered the courtroom. As I was the only other person in the room, Edwin couldn't help but notice me. He came over.

"Mr. Petinsky, come to see the festivities?"

"Yes."

"I'm afraid you won't get your money's worth. Your brother-in-law is being represented by one of the top lawyers in the publishing field. It's an open-and-shut case."

"Is the man you came in with Leon's lawyer?"

"Yes."

Plaster turned around and beckoned him to join us.

"Mr. Petinsky, Delmar Felsit. Delmar, Rudy Petinsky, Leon's brother-in-law."

"Rudy, how are you?" inquired Delmar, limping towards me. He pumped my hand enthusiastically, with an insincere smile on his face. "Nothing to worry about, Mr. Petinsky. Nothing to worry about at all."

I stared down at Leon's attorney, a slick thirty-five-year-old, who wore a perfectly tailored suit on his five-foot body. This pocket-size lawyer was going to save Leon?

"I'm not worried," I replied.

"Good. That's an excellent attitude to have in a courtroom. The judge always knows a worrier."

"Is this case going to be tried by a jury?" I asked.

"No," Delmar said. "Thank God."

"Why?"

"Better for us. I can bargain with a judge but if I have to start pleasing twelve jurists with their silly ideas of the judicial system, I'm a goner."

Delmar returned to his desk, sat down and stretched out his leg. He rolled up his pants and adjusted a strap. A buckle was loose on his plastic leg. While he was adjusting, Leon walked in. I hadn't seen him since he'd stormed out of my parents' home six months earlier. He had lost weight, but otherwise was in good spirits.

"Rudy, my man. How's it going?"

"Fine, Leon. Just fine. Yourself?"

"Couldn't be better."

"You don't seem to be worried."

"Worried? With Delmar handling the case?"

"An open-and-shut case, eh?"

"You got it, Rudy. Open and shut."

People started filing into the courtroom. Julie walked in wearing a conservative black skirt and jacket, a prim, ruffled white blouse and subdued jewellery. Delmar had obviously told her to tone it down and dress like a schoolmarm. She came over and pecked my cheek, then sat down beside me and held my hand.

"I'm scared, Rudy. I'm really scared."

"Leon says it's an open-and-shut case. Nothing to be worried about."

"Leon's gone flippy. He doesn't know up from down anymore. Look how he's dressed. White pants as if he were going sailing. And that tie! Who wears a bright red tie on a dark blue shirt? Who? We're in a courtroom for God's sake. Where's his sense of style? Whatever happened to good taste? Clothes should say 'Hi, I'm a nice person.' You know what Leon's clothes are saying to us? 'Hi, I'm a tool.' "

As Julie was talking, I noticed my mother walking towards us.

"Julie, Rudy, good morning."

"Morning, Mom," Julie said.

"Julie, put a smile on your face. We're in a courtroom, not a funeral parlour."

"Dad not coming?" I asked.

"He's at the store. What is Leon wearing and who is that little man sitting beside Edwin?"

"That little man is Delmar Felsit," Julie said. "He's Leon's lawyer."

"What kind of a name is Delmar? Felsit, I know. But Delmar?"

"What's in a name, Mom? What does it matter?" Julie said, agitated.

"I'm just curious, Julie." My mother gave me a look and asked how everything was going.

"Fine, Ma, just fine."

"How's Ellie?"

"She's okay. She just got a raise."

"Really? That's nice." She looked around the room and noticed someone she didn't know. "Who is he?"

"Joseph Springer. He's representing Sigmund Freud's estate," Julie said.

On our left, also on a forty-five degree angle to us, was another table. A man was sitting there. He was wearing a dark blue, pin-striped suit and a white shirt. His tie was conservative. He was staring at the judge's bench. His left leg was crossed over his right and his arms lay folded across his stomach.

"He looks all business," I said.

"He's going to wipe Leon's ass all over this room," Julie answered.

Ma looked at me and whispered, "I'm worried about Julie. She seems to be in a daze. She talks like a truck driver."

"She's under pressure, Ma. She's just tired."

What we didn't know was that Julie was completely strung out on Valium.

We were summoned to our feet by the court bailiff as the distinguished, no-nonsense Judge Swanberg entered the room and briskly climbed the three steps leading to his seat. He wasted no time calling both counsellors to approach the bench.

Delmar limped up while Freud's lawyer, Joseph Springer, casually strolled towards the judge's bench.

"Good morning, Delmar," Judge Swanberg said. "It's been a while since we've seen you in court. Everything all right?"

"Just fine, Seymour. How's your golf game?"

"Ten handicap. Mr. Springer, I've heard of your reputation. I will not allow any shenanigans in my courtroom. This is not a political, nor a religious, trial. We are not here to hang the accused. We will only judge if the accused did actually plagiarise and, if he did, then sentence shall be passed and justice served. Is that understood?"

"It is, your honour."

"Good. I understand that the two of you prefer to waive opening statements. Is that correct?"

"It is, your honour," Springer said.

"Yes, Seymour," Delmar added.

"Then let's get on with it."

The counsels took their respective places. Judge Swanberg banged his gavel on his desk and the bailiff announced the case. Joseph Springer rose.

"I would like to call my first witness," he said.

The back doors opened and in walked a conservatively dressed sixty-year-old woman wearing a navy blue dress with white lace frill that she had borrowed, I'm sure, from Whistler's mother. In fact, she and Julie looked like they had shopped at the same clothing store for this court appearance.

I heard Julie stifle a gasp. "Oh my god!" Julie muttered under her breath. "This is too much. How can we both be wearing the same outfit? That goddamn saleslady swore this was an original!"

Joseph Springer escorted the woman to the witness stand. The bailiff placed a bible in front of her as Springer waited impatiently for the ritual to end.

"State your name."

"My name is Mary O'Grady."

"And what is your occupation?"

"I'm a cleaning lady."

"And where is it that you do your work?"

"505 Park Avenue."

"Do you clean the whole building?"

"No. Just the top three floors."

"Is Dr. Leon Carp's office on one of those floors?"

"Yes."

"Do you clean his office?"

"Yes. Every night."

"Is there anything unusual in Dr. Carp's office?"

"Unusual?"

"Yes. Anything out of the ordinary that you might come across in your cleaning."

Delmar called out, "Objection."

"I'm merely trying to establish the contents of Dr. Carp's office," Joseph Springer said.

"Over-ruled. Proceed, Mr. Springer," said Judge Swanberg.

"Mrs. O'Grady, could you tell the court what you found in Dr. Carp's office."

"Well, there's always papers in the garbage pail."

"Besides the papers."

"Well, there's always leftover sandwiches on the table."

"Besides the sandwiches."

"Well, there's always books left lying around the office, which I place back on the bookshelves."

"Besides the books."

"Well, there's always magazines on Dr. Carp's desk which I have to put back in a carton box."

"What kind of magazines, Mrs. O'Grady?"

Mrs. O'Grady began to fidget. She placed her hand in front of her mouth and coughed nervously. Springer repeated his question.

"What kind of magazines, Mrs. O'Grady?"

"Dirty ones," she whispered.

"Could you speak louder, Mrs. O'Grady, so that everyone can hear you."

Mrs. O'Grady cleared her throat.

"Dirty magazines. Filthy, slimy, erotic magazines."

"That goddamn idiot," Julie yelled out. "That stupid goddamn idiot. I knew those magazines would do him in. I just knew it."

Judge Swanberg banged his gavel, yelled out "Order," and asked Julie to stand up.

"Who are you?" he asked.

"I'm that idiot's wife," Julie said, pointing an accusing finger at Leon, who had begun to turn red.

"Your name?" Swanberg asked.

"Julie Carp."

"Mrs. Carp, I realise that you must be under a great deal of strain but, in future, if you use that sort of language in my courtroom, I will have to ask you to leave. Is that understood? This is a court of law."

"Your honour, sir. May I..."

"And you are?"

"I'm this little girl's mother as well as the accused's mother-in-law. Please forgive my daughter's behaviour. I assure you it won't happen again."

Judge Swanberg peered over his glasses at the two women, glared at them, and finally told them to sit down.

"Mr. Springer, any more questions?"

"No, your honour."

"Mr. Felsit, do you wish to cross-examine?"

"No, your honour."

"Mr. Springer, do you have another witness?"

"Yes, your honour. Would Esther Petinsky please take the stand."

"So soon?" my mother said.

"Yes," Springer replied and came over to hold the gate open for her.

As soon as my mother had taken the stand, the bailiff held a bible in front of her.

"Do you swear to tell the whole truth and nothing but the truth, so help you God?"

"I'm not a liar, if that's what you mean."

"Please say *I do*, Mrs. Petinsky," Judge Swanberg said, "and let's get on with it."

"I do."

"Mrs. Petinsky, you are a former patient of Dr. Carp. Is that correct?"

"Yes."

"And the reason that you went to see Dr. Carp on a professional basis was?"

My mother said nothing.

"The reason was that you needed help to cope with a problem. Am I correct?"

Delmar stood up and yelled, "Objection." We all turned to him. "Your honour, Mrs. Petinsky is not the one on trial. This line of questioning has no bearing on the case at hand."

"Mr. Springer?" Judge Swanberg asked.

"Your honour, Mrs. Petinsky is a former patient of Dr. Carp. As such, she can provide invaluable information about Dr. Carp's methods of treatment."

Delmar screamed out, "Dr. Carp's competence is not on trial here!"

"I'm afraid my learned colleague has missed the point entirely. I intend to prove that Dr. Carp is money-hungry, and that rather than being concerned with the welfare of his patients, he is more concerned with the size of his bank account. A man like this, a man with no conscience, is entirely capable of plagiarism."

"Objection overruled," said Judge Swanberg.

My mother, now that Swanberg had allowed Springer to proceed with his line of questioning, was pursued relentlessly about every aspect of Leon's practice.

"Did you find Dr. Carp to be helpful?" Springer asked.

"No."

"Why?"

"Because I found out I never had a psychiatric problem. It was simply a case of getting new hormones in my body."

"And may I ask how you discovered that fact?"

"By seeing our family doctor."

"And what did he say?"

"He told me the pills Dr. Carp prescribed were sugar pills."

"Sugar pills?"

"Yes. Little blue ones."

"So you're saying that Dr. Carp knew there was nothing wrong with you. He knew you didn't have a psychiatric disorder. Yet he continued to take your money."

"I guess so."

"Please answer yes or no."

"It's not as simple as that."

"Yes he did or no he didn't?"

"The first one."

"I have no further questions, your honour."

Delmar rose to cross-examine.

"Mrs. Petinsky, how long have you known Dr. Carp?"

"Thirteen years."

"And, in all the time you have known Dr. Carp, have you ever known him to be anything less than a pillar of society?"

"What do you mean by less?"

"Let me rephrase my question. How well do you know your son-in-law?"

"Very well."

"Would you say that he's a good doctor?"

"He makes a lot of money."

"Would it be safe to say, then, that you think Dr. Carp has a successful practice?"

"Yes. It would be safe to say so."

"And if we both agree that Dr. Carp has a successful practice, then we could assume that he is a good doctor."

"Not necessarily."

"I beg your pardon?"

"I said not necessarily. I said that he makes a lot of money. I don't know if all that money comes from being a good doctor or from being a shrewd investor."

"I see. Thank you, Mrs. Petinsky. No further questions."

"You may step down, Mrs. Petinsky," Judge Swanberg said.

Delmar did not look pleased as he walked back to his table. Springer, on the other hand, seemed to be enjoying himself.

Judge Swanberg called a recess for lunch. Julie, my mother and I found ourselves in a small Italian restaurant a block from the courthouse.

"I wish I could treat the two of you," Julie said, "but I'm broke."

"What do you mean you're broke?" my mother asked.

"Well, not broke yet, but after this trial I'll be penniless."

"Maybe you won't, Julie," I said. "Maybe Leon will come through and exonerate himself."

"Leon, for your information, is going to lose everything he has. His practice will be finished. Everything he has, everything we have, we'll lose. The Jaguar, the cottage, the investments, my jewellery, everything. And do you know why I'm going to lose everything?"

"Why?" I asked.

"Because my husband, Dr. Leon Carp, is guilty. I saw him with my own two eyes, the way he wrote the book. He thought I didn't know what was going on. But I knew. He is guilty and he is going to pay. What makes me so angry is that I'm innocent and I'm also going to pay."

"What do you mean you saw him?" I asked.

"I saw him," Julie yelled. "I saw how he did it. How he plagiarised. Tapes. He has tapes and notes and old copies of Freud's books."

"You're kidding!" I said.

"I wish I was," Julie answered.

"Julie," my mother said, "according to you the trial is over. Relax. The only thing that's been established is that your husband is not the best psychiatrist around."

"Wait till this afternoon. They'll crucify him."

"No one's going to be crucified. Don't be silly. You're talking like a shiksa."

"Mom, this afternoon two people are going to be put on the stand. William Cooper and your son."

"I thought my turn was tomorrow. I'm not prepared."

"Rudy, I'm begging you. Don't say anything you'll regret later."

"I have nothing to hide."

"I'm not asking you to hide anything. Just don't go shooting off your mouth. Just answer the questions. 'Yes' or 'no' will do the trick."

"Why William?" my mother asked.

"Because Joseph Springer is a smart lawyer."

"But why William?" she asked again. "What does William have to do with any of this?"

"Because he knows everything, that son-of-a-bitch. He'll put Leon away for a thousand years."

"Why would he do that? He's Leon's best friend," I said.

"Best friend? He's nothing but a jealous leech. He knows everything. I begged him not to tell. I told him we'd be ruined. I even offered myself to him."

"You what?" my mother said, horrified.

"He didn't accept. All he wants is Leon to do time. And why? Because he's jealous that he doesn't make as much money as Leon and because he doesn't have the brains to write a book."

"What did he see?" I asked.

"See! You'll see. You'll see!" Julie said, agitated by the question. She began drumming her fingers on the table. Slowly at first, then picking up speed. "This afternoon," she continued, "this afternoon. Boy oh boy, you can't wait, can you?"

"Julie, I'm curious."

"You're like a vulture, Rudy. Can't you be patient?" she said as her fingers began tapping again. I looked at my mother and raised my eyebrows. She gave me a look that said: "Keep quiet. Don't upset her."

When we got back to the courthouse, I noticed Julie trying to fish something out of her purse. She moved towards the water fountain and quickly swallowed two pills. I waited a minute and then walked over to her.

"Julie, do you have a headache?"

She looked at me with red, glazed eyes.

"What?"

"Do you have a headache?"

"A headache?"

"Julie, are you all right?"

"Fine, fine, fine."

"Let's sit down."

"Some husband I have, eh Rudy? Boy, did I luck out."

Chapter 36

Joseph Springer knew that he was going to win this case. You could see it on his face. Judge Swanberg nodded to him and he stood up. He was smiling as he said, "Your Honour, I would like to call Mr. Rudy Petinsky."

I swallowed hard. I walked over to the gate which separated the spectators and witnesses from the rest of the court. My legs somehow got tangled up and I tripped. I crashed into the gate and fell down on top of it. The gate, with my full weight on it, easily came undone from its hinges. I quickly got up and tried to put the gate back on. Finally, the bailiff came over and forced the gate back into place. I sheepishly walked towards the witness stand.

"Are you all right, Mr. Petinsky?" Judge Swanberg asked.

"I'm sorry, your Honour. Yes, I'm fine."

"Good," Springer said. "Are you ready to answer a few questions?"

"Yes," I answered.

"Good."

The bailiff came over with the bible. I swore to tell the truth and sat down.

"Mr. Petinsky, may I ask your occupation?"

"I'm a truck driver."

"Is that all you do?"

"For a living?"

"Yes."

"That's all."

"Is it true that you have attempted to write a book?"

"Yes."

"But you do not consider yourself a writer?"

"Correct."

"Why?"

"Because I'm not making a living from my writing."

"And your book? Have you tried to get it published?"

"Yes."

"Could you elaborate?"

"I took my manuscript to Kings Publishing, hoping they would publish it."

"And did they?"

"No."

"Why?"

"Edwin Plaster said it wasn't good enough."

"Do you agree?"

"No."

"Then you must feel that Mr. Plaster is not the best judge of your work."

"Correct."

"But Edwin Plaster did publish your brother-in-law's book. Is that correct?"

"Yes."

"Why do you think your brother-in-law's book was published and not yours?"

"Objection," Delmar said.

Springer turned around to look at him.

"Your honour," Delmar continued, "Mr. Springer is asking questions of the witness that are simply not possible for him to answer."

"Sustained," Judge Swanberg said. "Mr. Springer, change your line of questioning."

"Mr. Petinsky, have you read *Psychosexual Infantilism — The Beast In Us*?"

"I have."

"May I have your opinion?"

"Objection," Delmar cried out. "Mr. Petinsky has just stated that he does not consider himself a writer. Therefore he is not qualified to offer a professional judgement on the book — nor is it relevant to this trial that he do so."

"Your Honour, may I ask my learned colleague a question?"

Delmar froze. Judge Swanberg allowed Springer to ask his question.

"Mr. Felsit, why should Mr. Petinsky's opinion concern you? The book has done very well. It's been on the best-seller list. Critics have reviewed it favourably. I don't see what possible harm it would do if Mr. Petinsky answered the question. Do you?"

Delmar hesitated. He was just about to say something, when Leon stood up and said, "Let him answer the question."

Delmar quickly spun around; amazed and speechless and outraged. He scowled at his client. Swanberg intervened.

"Dr. Carp, you are being represented by legal counsel. That means that you may not speak whenever you feel like it. One more time and I will hold you in contempt of court. Is that understood?"

"Yes."

"Mr. Petinsky, please answer the question," Swanberg said.

"Could you please repeat the question?" I asked.

"Mr. Petinsky, what is your opinion of Dr. Carp's book?"

"Not bad."

"Could you elaborate?"

I could see that Delmar looked relieved. I wasn't about to lie. Leon's book was very clever and full of common sense. And I had been very surprised while reading it. His theories were intriguing. The style of writing flowed and was easy to understand. I hated to say it, but *Beast* was good, and it was no wonder that it had sold over one million copies.

Springer's eyes narrowed. "Do you think that Dr. Carp, your brother-in-law, wrote the book?"

"His name is on the cover," I answered.

"Please answer the question."

"I don't know."

"You don't believe Dr. Carp is the author?"

"I said I don't know."

"So you do believe that Dr. Carp is the author?"

"I said I don't know."

"Objection," Delmar called out. "Mr. Springer is harassing the witness."

"Sustained."

"I have no more questions, your honour," Springer said.

"Mr. Felsit, do you wish to cross-examine?" Swanberg asked.

"No, your Honour."

I was allowed to step down.

"Mr. Springer, do you have another witness?"

"Not at this time, your Honour."

"Mr. Felsit?"

"Your Honour, I would like to call upon Edwin Plaster."

Edwin stood up, pulled down his vest, and walked over to the witness stand.

"Do you swear to tell the truth, the whole truth, and nothing but the truth?"

"I do."

Delmar approached the stand.

"Mr. Plaster, please state your occupation."

"President of Kings Publishing."

"Are you responsible for publishing *Psychosexual Infantilism — The Beast In Us?*"

"Yes, I am."

"Could you tell the court how you got hold of this book?"

"Certainly. One day I received a call from Dr. Carp. He introduced himself and said he was Rudy Petinsky's brother-in-law. He mentioned that he had just finished writing a book and would I care to take a look at it. After reading it, I realised that Dr. Carp's manuscript might have a chance on the market. We signed a contract about two weeks later."

"Mr. Plaster, isn't it a bit unusual for an unknown author to call you up and ask for his material to be read?"

"Perhaps it is in other publishing firms, but I have always made myself available."

"Mr. Plaster, when Dr. Carp came to you with his manuscript, had you read it before?"

"Of course not."

"Was there anything familiar about his manuscript?"

"No."

"It was all new material?"

"Yes."

"Did you ask Dr. Carp if all the theories in the book were his own?"

"Yes."

"And what did Dr. Carp say?"

"He told me that the book was one hundred percent his. That he had written the manuscript in longhand and then he typed it up."

"Did the book need a good deal of editing?"

"Surprisingly no."

"And how did you make sure that the book in question was indeed Dr. Carp's revelations and not someone else's?"

"When an eminent psychoanalyst such as Dr. Carp tells you that he has written a book and that the book is wholly his own — in thought, theory and style-one must have faith."

"Is faith enough?"

"Regrettably, no. I had a research team make absolutely sure that Dr. Carp's book was entirely his own writing."

"Then you weren't one hundred percent sure?"

"As sure as I could be, but it is standard practice to make absolutely sure."

"And what did your team of researchers come up with?"

"That *Beast* was entirely written by Dr. Leon Carp."

"No more questions."

"Mr. Springer, do you wish to cross-examine?"

"I do. Mr. Plaster, when you received the manuscript was it ready to be published?"

"No. It needed some editing."

"You have editors on hand at Kings Publishing?"

"We have, as well as freelance."

"Was one of your staff editors called in to handle Dr. Carp's book?"

"No."

"Freelance?"

"No."

"Then who?"

"Myself."

"Would you say a lot of presidents of publishing firms act as editors?"

"I would not know the statistics."

"How many staff editors does Kings Publishing employ?"

"Right now we have one."

"One?"

"Yes."

"And how many freelance editors can you rely on?"

"Three to four."

"Then one might conclude that Kings Publishing is not a very big operation. Is that correct?"

"We are not very big, that is correct."

Springer walked over to his table and took a piece of paper out of his briefcase. He walked back to Plaster, handed him the piece of paper and said, "Mr. Plaster, correct me if I am wrong, but the piece of paper that you hold in your hand is an application for a loan, signed by you. Is that correct?"

"Yes."

"And the amount of the loan?"

"One hundred thousand dollars."

"And the date of the loan?"

"July 6."

"And the date of publication of *The Beast In Us*?"

"October 15."

"You must have felt that *Beast In Us* would be successful enough to warrant a loan?"

"I did."

"And you weren't bothered by the fact that you were already indebted to the bank for another $200,000?"

"No."

"Obviously the bank thought that you were a good risk."

"It's not unusual for publishing firms to get loans from banks. It's done all the time."

"Did you have to put up any collateral for your loan?"

"Yes."

"Is it true that the collateral was fifty per cent of Kings Publishing?"

"Yes."

"And the bank already owned the other fifty per cent of your firm because you could not keep up the interest payments of your first loan, which you have told the court was $200,000?"

"Yes."

"Since the publication of *Beast In Us*, have you been able to repay all loans?"

"Yes."

"You have repaid $300,000 with interest?"

"Yes."

"Then it certainly was a very lucky day for you when Dr. Carp phoned."

"Yes, it certainly was."

"No more questions."

"Mr. Felsit," Judge Swanberg said, "do you have any other witnesses?"

"No, your Honour, not at this time."

"Mr. Springer?"

"I would like to call Dr. William Cooper."

The women in the courtroom, including the court stenographer, whose fingers froze over the keys, stared in awe as the movie-star handsome Dr. Cooper approached the witness stand and was sworn in.

"Dr. Cooper," Springer began, "what branch of medicine are you affiliated with?"

"Psychiatry."

"Clinical or research?"

"Clinical. I work with children."

"I see. How long have you known Dr. Carp?"

"I would say five years."

"And in that time, have you ever known Dr. Carp to be deceitful or dishonest?"

"Mr. Springer, in five years of friendship one sees a great deal of dishonesty, wouldn't you say?"

"Perhaps. Could you elaborate?"

"On what?"

"On Dr. Carp's dishonesty."

"Objection," Delmar yelled.

"Mr. Springer," Judge Swanberg said, "could you be more specific with your line of questioning. And Dr. Cooper, don't reply to questions with questions of your own. Answer counsel's questions."

"Dr. Cooper, you have just told the court that in the five years you have known Dr. Carp, you have known him to be dishonest?"

"Yes."

"Could you give the court an example?"

"Just one?"

"Yes, Dr. Cooper. One example."

"Well, one example has already been given by the cleaning lady."

"Would you be kind enough to reiterate."

"The magazines. The foul magazines, books and movies."

"And where does the dishonesty fit in with all this pornographic material?"

"Where does the dishonesty fit in?"

"Yes. Where?"

"In their marriage. For years, Leon had this motley collection of disgusting paraphernalia and he never said a word of it to Julie."

"Could you give another example?"

"Many."

"Just one."

"He screws people."

"I beg your pardon."

"He takes advantage of people's misfortunes."

"Objection," Delmar exclaimed. "I don't see what this line of questioning has to do with this trial."

"Your Honour," Mr. Springer said, "I am merely trying to establish a pattern. If Dr. Cooper says that Dr. Carp is a deceitful, dishonest person then it would stand to reason that such a man would be capable of stealing another man's words."

"Mr. Springer," Judge Swanberg said, "Dr. Carp's marriage is not on trial here. If you have an example of dishonesty that pertains directly to this case, then let's hear it. If not, then I suggest you get on with it. Mr. Felsit, please sit down."

I looked over towards Leon. His cheek muscle was going into spasms. His face was flushed and perspiring. Plaster also looked uncomfortable.

Springer walked over to his table and retrieved four small pocket books from his briefcase. He held up the copies and said, "Dr. Cooper, these books were written by Sigmund Freud. Have you ever seen them before?"

Dr. Cooper flipped through the pages.

"Not exactly."

"What do you mean by that?"

"Well, I've seen these books but not in this state."

"In what state did you see them?"

"Loose. Unbound."

"Are you saying that Dr. Carp had these four books in his possession?"

"Yes, but not in book form."

"In what form did you see them?"

"Well, some of the pages were photocopies. Some of the pages were scotchtaped on blank pieces of paper. Leon had a binder."

"And how can you be sure that what you saw in Dr. Carp's binder was copied from the books you now have in your possession?"

"I read his binder."

"Does that mean that you read every page or that you leafed through the binder and glanced at a page or two?"

"I read the whole thing, twice."

"Twice?"

"Yes. It was very interesting."

"You found it interesting?"

"Yes."

"In what way did you find it interesting?"

"The way Leon paraphrased."

"Could you give us an example?"

Dr. Cooper quickly glanced through the first book. He knew what he was looking for, and, in a matter of seconds, selected a passage.

"Here's an example. I remember reading this passage several times. It was underlined in red ink, and Leon had written a note to himself in the margin."

"Could you read the passage for us?"

"Our researches have shown that what we call the phenomena or symptoms of a neurosis are the consequences of certain experiences and impressions which, for this very reason, we recognise to be etiologic traumata."

"And what had Dr. Carp written to himself?"

"He wrote 'Change all this to read: We have problems'."

"Do you have other examples of Dr. Carp's paraphrasing?"

"Yes."

Dr. Cooper pointed out six or seven more passages. We were all enthralled. This was it. The smoking gun. The rope to be tied around Leon's neck. When he finished, Springer thanked him and Delmar began his questioning.

"Dr. Cooper, when you say that you read Dr. Carp's notes, where were you at the time?"

"In his den."

"And how did you find yourself in Dr. Carp's den?"

"I went downstairs. I was browsing through the house."

"Do you always browse when you're a guest in someone else's house?"

"No. Not always. Only when I'm left alone."

"And how is it that you were left alone for what must have been, I imagine, several hours, if you had the time to read Dr. Carp's notes? Was it several hours?"

"Oh yes. It was at least three hours."

"You're certain."

"Yes. I arrived at Julie's for lunch at 12:30..."

"Lunch?" Delmar inquired.

"Yes. Julie said that she wanted to talk to me about something."

"I see. Please continue."

"At 12:45, Julie received a phone call and told me that she had to do an errand. It would take no more than half an hour. Not too long after she left, maybe twenty minutes, the phone rang. It was Julie. She told me that her car had broken down – the radiator, I think she said – and she'd be back as soon as she could."

"And you decided to wait for her?"

"Yes."

"I see."

Delmar cleared his throat, stalling for time. He seemed afraid to go on with this line of questioning, but he didn't know a way out. He continued.

"Dr. Cooper, when did Mrs. Carp return?"

"Around five o'clock."

"And all that time you were busy in Dr. Carp's den?"

"Yes."

"I see."

Delmar bit his lower lip and ran his fingers through his hair.

"Dr. Cooper, you say that you've known the Carps for five years. Is that correct?"

"Yes."

"And in all that time, have you known Dr. Carp to be a good provider?"

"Yes."

"Has Mrs. Carp lacked anything?"

"Not that I know of."

Swanberg intervened. "Mr. Felsit, this line of questioning is a waste of the court's time and deliberately trying to divert attention away from what the witness has just said. We are not here to judge whether Dr. Carp was or is a good provider."

Delmar, feeling frustrated, asked Cooper a few more irrelevant questions and quickly dismissed him. Delmar knew, as everyone in the room now knew, that Leon was guilty.

CHAPTER 37

My father had not been to the courthouse. He kept saying, "I'm not interested in gossip. Just let me know when it's Leon's turn."

When that moment arrived, my parents and I drove down to the courthouse, picking up Julie on the way. She was a mess. She wasn't wearing make-up. Her hair was wet and stringy and she had on an old, ratty-looking housecoat. She looked as if she had just walked through a car wash. My mother flew into a rage, dragged her by the arm back inside the house and tried to re-assemble her daughter. There just wasn't enough time. And even if there had been enough time, Julie was being difficult. It was as if Julie had reverted to childhood and was acting out the "terrible twos". She was cranky, irritable and stubborn. When they both came back to the car, my mother was ranting and Julie looked more strung-out than ever. My father and I said nothing.

I know why.

My father said nothing because he was the type that kept everything bottled up and this is why, at an early age, he got an ulcer. I said nothing because I didn't want to upset him any more than he was already upset – having to look at his daughter in this tangled up, disarrayed, discombobulated state – and I certainly didn't want my mother knowing what had been going on with Julie and Ellie.

Ellie and I had now been married for eight months and were already fantasizing about our three kids playing in the park in their scrumptious "OshKosh B'Gosh" overalls, but the time wasn't quite yet right to do anything serious about it. Little did we know that we would receive an adult version of a twisted and demented toddler who enjoyed swallowing tranquilizers with a whisky chaser.

My sister, Julie, fueled by Valium, visited us at all times of the day. In the wee hours of the morning, watching us get ready for the day, she would sip her Chivas Regal as we brushed our teeth. In the late afternoon, when we returned from work we would find Julie, asleep on our doorstep, clutching her whiskey glass. And she would remain with us throughout dinner – never eating, always sipping – and finally we had to tuck in our "child" on the couch only to find, in the morning, Julie even more strung out than ever.

"Get me some more of this, won't you," she slurred, holding out her empty bottle. "I'm done. Need more. Lots more."

"I think you've had enough, Julie," Ellie answered her. "Why don't I make a pot of coffee."

"I'll take some pot. That'll be good. Real groovy. Rudy, give me some pot. That'll tide me over."

I wasn't about to give my sister marijuana to mix with alcohol and Valiums. She was already over the edge as is. Pot would only make her want to go to the roof and pretend she was Mary Poppins.

"C'MON, RUDY. MORE ALCOHOL. MORE CHIVAS REGAL STUFF. GO… GO… GO… DO IT… DO IT… DO IT!" She screamed. "Ellie, tell my goddamn brother to go the store and retrieve two of their finest. GO… GO… GO!"

I knew I had to go. Otherwise she'd go alone and, not being able to stand erect, she'd end up crawling on hands and knees. If I allowed that to happen my mother would never let me have another peaceful day. So what could I do? I felt bad that I would be leaving Ellie with Julie but we couldn't take a chance on leaving her alone. She would end up trashing our apartment and probably throwing everything and anything she could get her hands on out the window just because she didn't appreciate our taste in furniture (as she had once tactlessly told Ellie). So I left Ellie and Julie on their own and raced to the liquor store to get my crazed sister a bottle of her favourite brown liquid. When I got back I could hear Julie's wailing as I got off the elevator. The wailing got louder and louder as I quickly walked down the hallway and burst open our apartment door.

"THEY LIVE IN THE OCEAN... AT THE BOTTOM... DOING NOTHING..." Julie hollered at the top of her lungs, "DOING FUCK ALL!"

She noticed me, grabbed the Chivas Regal out of my hand and immediately poured herself a shot.

"Anyone?" she asked as she offered the bottle up to us.

"Why are you screaming?" I asked.

"Because your wife knows nothing about seahorses and I find that frightfully appalling."

I looked at Ellie. She looked frazzled. The kind of frazzle that I'm sure one feels when one's child has had a major tantrum and needs to be strapped down and muzzled.

Julie continued: "I was merely expressing to your very uptight wife that seahorses live at the bottom of the sea and do absolutely nothing with their time. NOTHING! DO YOU HEAR ME! NOTHING! THOSE L'IL FUCKERS DO SQUAT ALL!"

We sat there and listened to her maniacal ravings and tried to help her come back to the land of the living, but nothing worked.

"Did you guys know that seahorses have the most elegant way of getting rid of their excrement than any other creature on this planet?"

Ellie and I looked at each other, startled.

"Messy. Very messy. And so much toilet paper wasted but seahorses... they do a 360 degree turn around a horizontal axis... just like a dancer. Just like a fucking tiny dancer. Around a horizontal axis. You know, they pirouette while they poop."

I must say that I found this fascinating.

"What's a horizontal axis?" I asked. No sooner had I said that when Ellie shot me a "are you insane, too – don't get her started again" look.

I knew perfectly well what I was doing. Even though my sister was strung out, I couldn't help goading her. I loved it. I got my kicks that way. I loved egging her on, not as much as Leon, but she was a great second. And all the time I was goading her I kept thinking: how can I get her home? I'd like some quiet time with my wife.

"Never mind. It's not important," Julie blurted out. "What is important is that they shit so elegantly. They also make great pets. Much better than cats. I bought two of them for our aquarium and I'm learning so much. Did you know that seahorses get on each other's nerves because they're always hanging onto each other?"

"Really. Hanging onto each other," Ellie said, shooting me another look.

"Am I getting on your nerves because all of a sudden I've decided to hang out with you guys? Rudy, are you sure you don't have any pot?

"Don't you think you'd be better off at home," Ellie quietly asked Julie.

"Dear sweet brand-new sister-in-law. Let me tell you something very important. A seahorse has the ability to hide. That's how it survives. It's called camouflage and that's what I'm doing. Hiding. Hiding behind this bottle, hiding behind these pills and hiding inside your apartment. And I'll keep hiding until this horrific and embarrassing episode of my life is over. Until this fucking humiliating and mortifying instalment of my married life is over with that guy... what's his name?... the guy who's getting sued... the guy who married me... what's his name?"

And as she almost managed to retrieve her husband's name in her ranting repertoire, she finally passed out.

Eventually, Ellie and I stopped caring about my delinquent sister. We couldn't figure out how not to let her into our apartment, considering we had to stumble over her deteriorating body as we tried to let ourselves in. We would help her to the couch and then lock ourselves in our bedroom. We had, by this time, removed the TV from the living room so we could relax in privacy and, when we got hungry, we would sneak into the kitchen, trying hard to slip by our houseguest as she sat on our couch, sipping, swallowing and lamenting.

It took my mother, the formidable Esther Petinsky, to resolve this messy situation. She came over one afternoon, while Julie was hallucinating about her seahorses and decided enough was enough.

"THOSE FUCKERS! THOSE L'IL FUCKING SEAHORSES. THEY BEGAN THIS WORLD AND NOW THEY'RE GOING TO END IT."

"Rudy, help me get your sister home."

"Whose home?"

"Mine. My home. She can't be left alone."

And so Julie moved in with my parents, and, between large quantities of matzohball soup, baby aspirins, and no-nonsense guidance from my mother, she began to sober up and metamorphose back into her greedy, status-hungry self.

Chapter 38

As we approached the front steps of the courthouse, we were faced with a barrage of cameras and microphones. My father just climbed up the stairs, refusing to stop for the reporters' questions. My mother, who would have loved an interview, decided that Julie was not up to it. We followed my father, practically carrying Julie inside, and hurried down the hall. As we took our seats in the courtroom, we heard Joseph Springer say, "I would like to call Dr. Leon Carp."

Leon smiled nervously and rose. The final inning was about to begin.

"Dr. Carp, in the last three days we have heard testimony from many people. There has been hearsay, innuendo, and a bit of gossip, but one witness has, beyond any shadow of a doubt, incriminated you."

"Really?"

"Yes, Dr. Carp. Really."

"And may I ask who that person is?"

"Indeed. The person who has told this court that you are guilty is Dr. William Cooper."

"He's a junkie. Ask any doctor."

"I have."

"You have?"

"Of course. But having an addiction does not disqualify a person from being a witness."

"You're kidding?"

"I'm afraid not. Dr. Carp, you have stated that you and you alone wrote *Psychosexual Infantilism — The Beast In Us*. Is that correct?"

"With a bit of help from Edwin Plaster."

"You mean to say that Mr. Plaster edited your manuscript."

"Yes."

"Can you explain to the court why Dr. Cooper would say that you didn't?"

"Because he's sick?"

"An answer, Dr. Carp. I need an answer, not a question."

"Well, I don't know. Why don't you tell me? You seem to have all the answers."

"The only reason I can think of is that he tells the truth. He's an honest person."

"And I'm not?"

"Well, how can you explain Dr. Cooper's allegations? He has told the court that he saw Sigmund Freud's original work and saw how you plagiarised. He has told the court that he read your blatant rewording of Freud's original thoughts and read your blatant rewording of Freud's original theories. Dr. Carp, could you or do you have an explanation?"

"It's his word against mine."

"At this moment in time it certainly is, but I assure you that in five minutes your word will be worth as much as a three-dollar bill."

"Objection!" Delmar screamed.

"Mr. Springer," Judge Swanberg said, "leave the circus talk out of this courtroom."

"Thank you, your Honour," Leon said.

Joseph Springer walked over to his desk and from his briefcase retrieved a small tape recorder and one tape. He offered both pieces of equipment as exhibits and then placed the recorder on top of Judge Swanberg's desk. He asked for complete silence and then pushed the play button. We waited a few seconds and then, unmistakably, we heard Leon's voice:

"May 22. How can I finish off this book? I need a firecracker. Something explosive. The perfect ending. I need to find something else out of all this mish-mash. One more chapter or even a lengthy epilogue to put it all together. But from where? I've used up all of my resources. The jerk hasn't written anything else..."

Springer stopped the tape. Leon's complexion changed from pink to beige to white. He looked stunned. Springer anticipated what Leon was thinking.

"For the record, your honour, these tapes were retrieved from Dr. Carp's garbage."

"Animal. Filthy animal," Leon muttered to himself.

"Dr. Carp, who are you referring to when you say 'the jerk?'"

"Myself?"

"Are you referring to yourself in the third person when you're talking to the tape?"

"Is that the way you interpret it?"

"Dr. Carp, please answer the question."

"Yes."

"Yes you are or yes you are not?"

"Yes, I am."

"Then you are the jerk. Is that correct?"

"Yes."

Springer pushed the play button again.

"... maybe I can use somebody else. Who do I know who's obscure?"

Springer stopped the tape.

"Dr. Carp, could you tell the court what you meant by the words: 'Who do I know who is obscure?'"

"A figure of speech."

"I'm afraid that's not an appropriate answer."

"Then you figure it out, because that is my only answer."

"Dr. Carp, did you or did you not plagiarise Dr. Sigmund Freud's works?"

"When you say 'you', do you mean 'you' singular or 'you' plural?"

"I mean 'you' singular. You as in you."

"You should say 'you' plural."

"And why is that?"

"Because there are two people involved."

"Really?"

"Yes."

"And may I ask who is the other guilty party?"

"That would be squealing."

"I see. What if I simply ask you who it is. All you would have to say is yes or no. And may I remind you that you are still under oath."

"I suppose that would be fair."

"Is it Edwin Plaster?"

CHAPTER 39

Springer was becoming annoyed. He couldn't get a simple "yes" from Leon. He kept pressing but Leon wouldn't crack. I could see Springer beginning to lose his composure. Beads of perspiration began to accumulate on his forehead. He would take out his white handkerchief every few minutes and gently dab his brow. He changed his tactics and began flattering Leon. Leon softened up but never said the magic word. When Springer realised that flattery was not working, he changed his strategy. He started to make fun of Leon. He goaded him. He insulted him. Nothing worked.

We were all becoming impatient. And when Julie lost her newly acquired self-control and screamed out, "Tell them, Leon. For God's sake, tell them already so I can go home and take a bath," Judge Swanberg finally intervened. He, too, had had enough. He banged his gavel on the dock. When there was complete silence, he told the bailiff to escort Julie from the room. Then he looked at Springer and told him to sit down. Finally, he looked down at Leon and said, "Dr. Carp, etiquette allows a defendant a minute or two to answer a question. You may think that this courtroom has nothing better to do than wait for your response. By not answering, I can only assume one thing."

"What's that, your Honour?" Leon asked.

"That you are guilty."

"Beyond any shadow of a doubt?"

"Even beyond that."

"Can I appeal?"

"To what?"

"To a higher court."

"What for?"

"To prove my innocence. Your Honour, I know my rights. I call for an appeal."

"You may not appeal. Only your lawyer, through proper legal channels, may ask for an appeal."

"Delmar," Leon said, "come here and ask the judge for an appeal."

"Delmar," Swanberg bellowed, "stay seated. I've had quite enough of this. There will be a ten-minute recess. When I return I will deliver the verdict. While I am gone, Dr. Carp, you will return to your seat and Mr. Felsit will explain to you, as well as to Mr. Plaster, the legal ramifications if you still persist with your childish attitude."

Ten minutes went by. Judge Swanberg had still not returned. During his absence, I could see Delmar trying to explain to his clients what would happen if they did not admit their guilt. Leon and Edwin kept shaking their heads. Delmar finally gave up.

Swanberg entered the courtroom. He quickly climbed the three stairs, sat down, banged his gavel and told Delmar, Edwin, and Leon to stand up.

"Excuse me, your Honour," Leon said.

"You wish to address the court, Dr. Carp?"

"I do."

Swanberg sighed and allowed Leon to proceed.

"Your Honour, I'm not completely happy with the way things have turned out. Now that I know how a courtroom works, I realise that I've been shafted. If I had been represented by good counsel, the stature of Mr. Springer, then I certainly think that circumstances would have changed drastically. Knowing this, I would like to call for a mistrial."

Swanberg was silent. He looked at Leon stonily. His nostrils flared. He clutched his gavel so tightly that it seemed in danger of breaking in two.

"Dr. Carp," he snapped, "I have spent the last thirty-five years as a lawyer and then as a judge, and in all that time I have seen many examples of irrational behaviour in a courtroom, but never one as..."

"How dare you!" Leon shrieked. "How dare you call *me* irrational! I am a psychoanalyst. Renowned and revered. I have a thriving practice. I have degrees on my wall. Been on the cover of "Psychology Today". I am a member of the most exclusive golf club in this city. Do you realise what an honour it is to be admitted to Stonybrook Country Club? Don't you know that I am the only Jew to have ever held membership in Stonybrook? Don't..."

"Dr. Carp, I am holding you in contempt of court," Judge Swanberg screamed over Leon's rantings. "Bailiff, remove this man from my courtroom."

The bailiff quickly moved over towards Leon and grabbed his arm. Leon twisted away. The bailiff took out his handcuffs, deftly manoeuvred one cuff onto Leon's wrist, then placed the other cuff on his own wrist. Leon tried to release himself, but just couldn't manage. He ended up on the floor and, in this manner, the bailiff dragged Leon out of the courtroom. With quiet restored, Judge Swanberg asked Plaster if he would like to address the court. Edwin asked if he could have a few minutes with Delmar. Swanberg granted the time. Then Delmar approached the bench. We heard Swanberg call Joseph Springer to join them. They conferred for a minute or two and then Delmar returned to his table. Springer remained standing next to the witness stand. When Delmar sat down he whispered a few words to Edwin. Edwin got up and walked over to the witness stand, seating himself on the chair. Springer reminded him that he was still under oath and asked Plaster if Dr. Carp had plagiarised Dr. Sigmund Freud's works. Plaster said "yes" and then went on to tell the court how he had been part of the hoax.

"I had no choice," Plaster said. "I was about to lose my company. I simply had no other way out."

Edwin was dismissed and Judge Swanberg found the defendants guilty. Edwin and Leon (who was now behind bars) were instructed to pay back every cent they had earned from *Beast*, including a combined penalty of $20,000 and all court costs.

When Swanberg finished, Delmar and Springer simultaneously thanked the court for the decision and started to pack up their papers. My parents and I left the courtroom and searched for Julie. We found her in Leon's jail cell, staring blankly at her husband. Leon was pacing back and forth. Both were silent.

When we told them what the verdict was, Leon said, "That's it? Just pay back everything I earned plus half the court costs plus $10,000? That's it?"

"Yes," I said.

"Are you sure, Rudy?"

"That's it."

"God bless America."

"Of course, Leon," I said, "you still have to spend three days in this jail cell."

"Three days? No big deal."

CHAPTER 40

While Leon was in jail, he received few visitors. Not once did my mother go and see him. From the moment that Swanberg declared Leon guilty, she went into a state of semi-shock. She closed herself in, pulled down the blinds and would not leave the house, fearing that a neighbour would bring up the subject of the trial. She was bewildered by Leon's loss of eminence and embarrassed that she was now a jailbird's mother-in-law.

I had returned to work at Schuman's and was looking forward to the Labour Day weekend coming up. Ellie and I were driving down to Atlantic City after Friday night supper.

We had asked my parents if they wanted to join us, but my mother was still not ready to face the world. She was afraid that someone would recognise her and yell out: "There's Esther Petinsky, the plagiarist's mother-in-law."

The first thing I noticed as we turned into my parents' crescent was the Jaguar.

"Isn't that Leon's?" I said.

"I think so," Ellie answered.

"What's he doing here? How can he still afford the Jag?"

We rang the doorbell. Leon opened the door for us and welcomed us in. He kissed Ellie and shook my hand. Then Julie kissed us. We all entered the living room.

"Rudy, go get your father," my mother said. "He's in the den."

My father was stretched out on the couch, watching the six o'clock news.

"Hi, Dad. What gives?"

"Leon?"

"Yes. How come he's here?"

"He passed by the store today and apologised."

"You're kidding. What did he say?"

"Just that he was sorry about the pearl incident. That he had been under a great deal of strain and the pressure had gotten to him."

"So he's back."

"Yes. Between you and me, I liked it better when he was locked up. For three days I felt the city was safer."

I laughed. It wasn't often my father cracked a joke.

As I sat down and watched Dan Rather tell us about the latest Middle East confrontation, Ellie came in and told us supper was ready.

"So, Rudy," Julie said, "back at Schuman's?"

"Yes, back at work. And you? How's life treating you?"

"Great. We're going to the cottage tomorrow for a few days. Would you like to join us?"

Ellie and I looked at each other. We were shocked.

"No thanks, we're off to Atlantic City for the weekend."

"Oh. Well, maybe next weekend."

My mother, who was still not herself and who had said very little up till then, sat down and stared at Julie. Julie immediately looked uncomfortable. My mother kept staring. Julie tried to look away. Then she began eating her soup. My mother kept staring. Finally, after her third spoonful, she could no longer bear it.

"Mom," Julie said, as she put down her spoon, "what's wrong?"

"Julie, is that a new necklace?"

Julie's face lit up.

"Yes. Leon gave it to me this morning."

"And you're going to the cottage this weekend?"

"Yes. Would you and Daddy like to join us?"

"Leon, what car are you driving?"

"My Jaguar."

"I don't understand. I just don't understand."

"What don't you understand, Mom?" Julie asked.

"I don't understand how the two of you can still drive an expensive car and buy jewellery."

"Oh," Julie said.

"Maybe I should explain," Leon said.

"Yes, please do," my mother said.

"Well, it's this way. Even though I have to pay back a great deal of money, I still managed to... uh... let's just say that some of the money that I made from the book was not exactly declared. Sort of under-the-table money."

"And no one knows about it?"

"Correct. And don't forget that prior to the book I had made quite a few shrewd investments."

"I see. Then you're not destitute or impoverished."

Leon laughed.

"No, Mom," Julie said. "We're not impoverished. As a matter of fact, we're better off now than we've ever been."

"Really! But Julie, you were so scared."

"I know. I didn't find out till a few days ago that Leon had this stash of black money."

"And Edwin?"

"He's wiped out," Leon said.

"Wiped out?" my mother asked.

"Yes. He declared bankruptcy two days ago. He doesn't have a cent."

"Doesn't he have a stash of black money?" Ma asked.

"No," Leon said as he polished off the last of his soup.

"How come he doesn't and you do?" I asked.

"Because we have different accountants."

"And your accountant is sharper than his," I said.

"Correct. Quite a bit, I'd say."

"That's awful," Ellie said.

"Why?" Leon asked.

"Why!" Ellie said, astounded that Leon could even ask such a question.

"Yes, why is that awful?"

"Because he's penniless. He did the same thing you did. Yet you still have everything and he has nothing."

"Don't worry about Edwin. He's a survivor. He'll bounce back."

With the exception of Julie, we were all offended by Leon's

callousness. Ma finally got up and, with Ellie's help, cleared the soup dishes. Julie tried, unsuccessfully, to make small talk. When Ellie and my mother returned with the brisket and vegetables, Ma sat down and said quietly to Leon: "I'm ashamed of you, Leon. Thoroughly ashamed that you're my son-in-law. I must have been blind all these years."

"What are you talking about, Mom?" Julie said. "Nothing's changed. Everything's the same. Leon still has his practice. We lost nothing. On the contrary, we made some money."

"That's all the two of you think about. Money. Did you ever stop and think about the word 'decency'? I can't believe it. Have I been so stupid and so blind?"

"Yes," my father answered her.

"Don't be so quick to judge, Morris. Are you so perfect?"

"I'm just answering your question, Esther."

"It was a rhetorical question. It wasn't meant for anyone to answer."

"If someone asks me a question, I answer it."

"For your information, Morris, the question was not directed at you."

"At who was it directed?" my father asked.

"Morris, stop it. Just stop it. Please. My own daughter. My own daughter doesn't seem to care that a man just lost his business. What matters to her is that she still has enough money to buy more jewellery."

"It's important to me, Mom. I need to buy."

"So buy war bonds!" my mother shrieked.

"Mom," Julie said, "the war ended over thirty years ago."

"Esther," my father said, "control yourself. Some things just don't change."

"Shame on you, Julie. Shame on you. And as for you, Leon," Leon looked up at my mother and abruptly swallowed whatever he had been chewing, "I used to be so proud of you. My son-in-law, Dr. Leon Carp, the psychiatrist. You know what you are, Leon?"

"What?"

"I'll tell you. You're a no-good-for-nothing *nudnick*. You're a weasel. A *goniff*. How dare you call yourself a doctor? You're supposed to treat sick people and most important of all you're supposed to feel something for these sick people. The only thing that you care about are their bank accounts. Shame on you."

"Esther, I don't tell you how to run your life, so don't tell me how to run mine."

"I came to you for help. I trusted you. It's true that you gave me a discount..."

"A twenty percent discount. I didn't have to, you know. I usually give ten percent discounts to family."

"Lucky me. Twenty percent discount on worthless therapy."

"At the time, you thanked me."

"At the time, I didn't know any better. Now I know there was nothing wrong with my head. But you always knew I didn't have a psychiatric problem."

"I'm sorry, Esther, but psychiatry doesn't work like that."

"How does it work, Leon?"

"By probing."

"Probing?"

"Yes, Esther. And deducing."

"Probing and deducing?"

"Yes."

"I see."

"No, I don't think you do."

"I see very clearly now. You probe by asking questions and then you deduce by asking more questions. And when you're satisfied that you have all the answers, you figure out how much the patient can afford and how much of a sucker the patient is. Leon, I know very little about psychiatry, but I do know one thing – you're a disgrace to the profession. You should be disbarred."

"That's for lawyers," Leon said, smugly.

"Mom," Julie cried out, "stop it." She was silently sobbing.

"Why, Julie? It's the truth. Can't you face it?"

"Not now."

"Julie, you're married to a fool. Plain and simple. And I'm a fool's mother-in-law. I didn't know it before, but now I do. America didn't know it before, but now it does."

"America, for your information, is a very healthy country," Leon said, "and will persevere. I'm not so sure about you."

"What do you mean by that?"

"I think you're on the verge of a breakdown."

"Two minutes ago I called you a fool. I was wrong. You're not a fool. You're an idiot fool."

"Mom, stop it! I will not allow you to call my husband names."

"And as for you, my one and only daughter, you're an idiot fool's wife. It's my fault. I should have seen this thirteen years ago. I should have prevented the marriage. You can blame me."

"Your breakdown is becoming more acute, Esther. Now you're becoming unfriendly. A common symptom."

"Save your symptoms for your idiot patients, you quack. I'm not interested any more."

My mother, furious with rage, began to cry. She could not control herself. Was she crying because she could no longer hold her head up in society, knowing that everyone in America knew about her son-in-law's fraud, or because she really had seen the light and was ashamed of herself? I wasn't sure. She left the room. Then the phone rang. Ma answered it.

"Rudy, it's for you."

I got up and went into the kitchen. My mother handed me the receiver and returned to the dining room.

"Hello," I said.

It was Edwin Plaster. He wanted to know if I had any plans for the weekend. I told him that Ellie and I were on our way to Atlantic City. He told me what he had in mind and asked if I could cancel the trip. I called Ellie to the kitchen and explained what Edwin wanted. She said two words: "Do it." We returned to the dining room.

"Leon, you were right," I said.

"About what?" Leon asked, giving me a puzzled look.

"About Edwin."

"What do you mean?" he asked, tightly.

"You said that Edwin is a survivor. That he'll bounce back. Well, guess what? He's bouncing."

"Rudy, once and for all, stop talking in metaphors and tell us exactly why Edwin called you," Julie said.

"Edwin asked me to meet him at his office in one hour. He wants to write a book about you, Leon."

"About me?"

"Yes. Your life story."

"That's very flattering," Julie said as she smiled at Leon.

Leon gave her a menacing glare.

"Flattering! Have you lost your marbles? Don't you see what he's up to?"

"Tell us, Leon," my father said.

"He wants to capitalise on my unfortunate incident."

"And which incident is that?" my father asked.

"Sometimes I wonder where part of your brain is. The part that allows a person to follow, in chronological order, events that happen from day to day."

"My brain, Leon, is in fine shape."

"Then why can't you understand what's going on?"

"Why don't you explain it to me?"

"To me too, Leon," Julie added.

"And me," Ellie said.

"All of you? You all don't understand?"

"No," we all said, provoking him.

Leon's pupils dilated. He shrugged his shoulders and let out a sigh.

"Edwin, because of all the publicity generated from my trial, wants to get out a book as fast as possible. There will be things in the book that did not come out in the trial."

"What kind of things?" I asked.

"Things. Just things."

"Will you be embarrassed by these things?" I asked.

"Embarrassed? Let's put it this way. I don't need more hostile publicity, if you catch my drift. I have to rebuild my practice. Confidence has been lost. I must try to convince old patients that I'm as good as I ever was and I must try to attract new customers."

"Leon, you're a survivor," my father said. "You'll bounce back. By hook or by crook."

"Most likely by crook," I couldn't resist adding.

CHAPTER 41

The first thing I noticed upon entering Kings Publishing were the stacks of boxes scattered around the reception area. The secretary's desk was no longer there, nor were the couch, chairs and end tables. I walked down the small corridor towards Edwin's office. He was sitting on a chair, his back to me. He was busy sifting through papers. In front of him lay a tape recorder.

"Hello, Mr. Plaster," I said.

Edwin turned around. He was wearing a pair of light cotton pants, a dark green jersey, and expensive-looking loafers.

"Rudy, how are you?"

He stood up and shook my hand.

"Rudy," Edwin continued, "you'll have to excuse the office decor. We're in the midst of moving. Please make yourself as comfortable as possible."

I sat down on a carton which was packed with books. I took out my cigarettes and lit one.

"Rudy," Edwin said, "let me explain what's going on. I've been given a chance to re-establish myself. Two days ago someone approached me with an interesting offer. To put out a book about your brother-in-law. Naturally, I accepted. My backer is going to take care of all expenses, including yours, and the two of us will, within five days, have a completed manuscript ready to be published. If you accept, you will be given a $2,000 advance plus ten per cent of all paperback sales. The book will not be published in hardcover. It is imperative that the book be shipped out to book stores in fifteen days. No longer than that. We want to capitalise on the sensational publicity generated by the trial. You will do the writing and I will edit and oversee the operation. We will stay here over the long weekend and by Monday night we will have a first draft."

"We'll stay here for three days?"

"Yes. In the next room are two cots. There's plenty of coffee and we'll order in sandwiches. Are you ready to sign a contract?"

"You say that I will do all of the writing?"

"Correct."

"You will only edit?"

"Correct."

"Why me?"

"Because I feel that you know Leon better than anyone, with the exception of his wife."

"Why didn't you ask Julie?"

"I thought about it, but, between the two of us, your sister has not fully recovered from the trial and this hectic pace might... let's just say that I don't feel she could handle the pressure."

"I see."

"Ask all your questions now, Rudy. I'm eager to begin."

"Have you chosen a title?"

"Yes. *Freudian Slip: The Life and Times of Leon Carp.*"

"Is there any danger of being sued?"

Edwin cleared his throat and smiled.

"None," he said. "This is perfectly legal. Anyone is allowed to write a book about someone else, providing that the facts are accurate and that there are no slanderous accusations. I assure you that we are only going to write the truth."

"Leon told me that there are things that did not come out in the trial."

"Correct."

"What sort of things?"

"Black money. Hidden profits. A few other points."

"Will Leon be affected by this book?"

"Affected? How do you mean?"

"I mean will his practice suffer? Can he be re-prosecuted because of under-the-table money?"

"I'm not sure. Possibly."

"If I don't accept, what will you do?"

"Rudy, this book will be in the stores in fifteen days, with or without your help. If you decide to do it, the book will be a more honest one."

"Can I see the contract?"

I looked over the contract. It was four pages. I didn't understand half of it. Did I have time to call a lawyer? Would Edwin wait? Edwin seemed to understand what was going on in my head. He told me that normal practice would be for me to get a lawyer and read the contract carefully, but, in the interest of time, he would gladly answer any questions I might have. He also told me that it was a standard contract for services rendered. I didn't know if I should trust him. I certainly didn't trust his judgement when it came to my writing – or did I? – and his character was certainly flawed, as was proven in the trial. Yet here was an opportunity staring me right in the face. A published book with my name on it. A book that might actually sell and be read – by real people who weren't my relatives. Wasn't this, all along, what I'd wanted? Not exactly, but it certainly was better than nothing.

"Rudy," Edwin said, "this could be an extraordinary career move for you. We predict that the book will sell anywhere from 500,000 to 700,000 copies. That means that approximately 600,000 people will see your name on a book. There will be newspaper coverage, radio interviews and we're hoping for syndicated talk shows."

"If all you say is true, how much would I earn?"

"Somewhere in the area of $150,000."

"I see." I could feel my heart flutter. I thought back to that cute Spanish house Ellie and I constantly dreamed of owning.

"Well, Rudy, what do you say? Clock's ticking away."

I didn't say anything. I put the contract on the floor and walked to the window, staring down at the traffic. I turned around, picked up the contract, and signed my name.

Chapter 42

Freudian Slip: The Life and Times of Leon Carp, was an instant success. Everyone was reading it. On buses, in subways, in parks, during coffee breaks. Before breakfast, after supper, and before going to bed. Two days after publication, the evening news did a forty-five-second segment on the book. True to Plaster's word, we were invited to speak on radio, and two local T.V. stations asked us to appear on their broadcasts. I was now a celebrity. Strangers recognised me on the street. Acquaintances asked for their copies to be autographed. Friends wanted to know what my next book would be about. Ellie beamed. My parents were proud. Julie sulked. Leon was furious. And my mother, now that I was famous, made my life miserable. Friends of hers phoned, wanting to congratulate me. *That* I could live with. When her butcher phoned to let me know that he was now reserving the choicest cuts of his cow for me, I became annoyed. When her hairdresser called, asking me if I would like to come in, at my convenience, for a styling, I became angry. But when someone from her B'nai B'rith chapter called to let me know that my speaking engagement was scheduled for the following Thursday afternoon, I banged down the phone, called the operator, and asked for an unlisted number.

"This is what you wanted, Rudy," my mother said when I confronted her.

"This is not what I wanted," I yelled. "I did not want your butcher to call me. I do not need Kosher meat. I am very happy with supermarket meat."

"It's not as healthy. Besides, now you can afford it."

"That's not the point. And don't tell me what I can afford. It may come as a surprise to you but I have not yet made enough money to retire. I'm still working at Schuman's."

"You should quit. Someone with your talent should not be

driving a truck. You should get a loan from the bank and start a new book."

"When I'm ready."

"Good. In the meantime, would it be too much to ask if you didn't pass by the house with your truck? The neighbours can't understand that you're famous and still have to drive a truck. They're mixed up. I'm tired of explaining to them about profits and sales and royalties."

I stopped dropping by when I was in the neighbourhood. It was the easiest way out.

Mr. Schuman was thrilled about my success. Business had improved. People came in wanting to see me. Once they were in, Mr. Schuman managed to get them to buy something. He now kept a Polaroid camera beside his cash register, and with the purchase of any item, the customer was entitled to a free photo with me. If they didn't buy, they were asked if they would like their picture taken with a famous author — at three dollars a photo. I protested. Mr. Schuman looked at me, smiled and said, "Rudy, what's the harm? They get a thrill, I make a buck and you become a household word." I dropped the subject.

I'm pretty certain that the first person to buy a copy of *Freudian Slip: The Life and Times of Leon Carp* was Leon Carp himself. The book came out on a Monday. Monday night I received a call from him. He wanted to have a meeting. I told him the next time I was in the neighbourhood I would drop by. Three weeks later, I parked in front of his office and took the elevator up to the fifteenth floor. His receptionist was eating a sandwich. I told her who I was and she gave me a dirty look. She then pressed the button on her intercom and told Leon that I wanted to see him. Leon came out, shook my hand and held onto it as he dragged me into his office. Once inside, he let go of my hand, closed the door and indicated which chair I should sit in.

"Satisfied?"

"Yes," I answered.

"Do you have any idea what this book is doing to business?"

"I can imagine."

"Can you?"

"Yes."

"How can you live with yourself?"

I didn't answer him.

"Do you know that I've been sitting in this office all morning without a client? If I have to sit all afternoon like this, then I can only assume that tomorrow will be no better. As it turns out, my appointment book is empty. It wasn't empty three weeks ago. Three weeks ago, my appointment book was full. Since publication, I have had nothing but cancellations. I am now free until the middle of November. That is two goddamn months from now and on November fourteenth, at ten a.m., a man will come to see me. I will not ask him any questions. Do you know why? Because he will not be a client. No! The man who will sit where you are now sitting will be asking me questions and, if he doesn't like my answers, he will push a few more buttons on his fucking calculator, which, I am sure, is by now overworked. Do you understand what I am saying? Do you have any idea what might happen? Do you?"

"Leon, get hold of yourself. You're starting to spit while you speak. Who is this guy?"

"This guy's name is Robert Souris. Would you like to know why Mr. Souris is coming to see me?"

"Okay."

"Robert is employed by the IRS."

"I see."

"You see nothing, you little fart! How long do you think I can survive if I have to pay back taxes on $200,000, including interest and penalties? And that, may I remind you, is only for last year. Once he starts, don't you think he'll begin an investigation? He's entitled by law to go back five years. Do you have any idea what that will do to my finances?"

"You've got plenty of money invested. Sell something."

"SELL! Sell? Sell what? My stock in IBM? Never. It's still going up. Apple? I'd rather die first. Chrysler? I can still make a fortune there. Gold. No way. I just bought. I have to wait a few more years before selling. I simply cannot liquidate. I could, if the IRS was patient. But between you and me, the IRS is not a benevolent institution. They're greedy. They want their pound of flesh now."

"Leon, did you call me in just to tell me your troubles?"

"Not exactly. I have a plan. Listen, maybe I can stall the IRS for a couple of months. If I can, by that time you will probably be a rich man. Considering how you've made your small fortune, I feel I'm entitled to some of it. Let's face it, without me, you'd still be dreaming of getting published. However, I am not asking for a handout. What I need is a loan – interest-free, of course. If you lend me what I need, I might be able to swing things. What do you say?"

I got up and started to make my way toward the door. I couldn't believe his gall. When I reached it, I turned around.

"Leon, there's another way out."

"No, there isn't. Believe me, Rudy, I've figured out all the angles. This is the only way."

"You forgot one thing."

"Impossible. I triple-checked."

"Check again."

"Rudy, for God's sake, I don't need this extra pressure. What's your plan?"

"Sell your Jaguar."

I let myself out and walked to the elevator. As the elevator door opened, I noticed, out of the corner of my eye, Leon running towards me. He was screaming out my name. The people inside the elevator were staring at Leon as he grabbed my arm and started pleading with me.

"Please, Rudy, I'm begging you. I can't drive a Chevy. What would people say?"

CHAPTER 43

Leon was shrewder than I thought. To avoid the IRS he closed down his practice and had himself committed to a mental hospital in New Jersey.

Just before he entered the front gate of the nut house, Leon stepped out of the Jaguar, handed Julie the keys as well as his identification, and told her that under no circumstances was she to contact him. He kissed her goodbye and said that he would be in touch. She drove immediately to my parents' house, where we were all waiting for her.

"So, Julie," my mother asked, "what will you do in the meantime?"

"I'm going to Hawaii."

"Hawaii?" my mother said.

"Yes. Hawaii."

"What if Leon needs you?" Ellie asked.

"He won't and, as long as he's inside, I might as well get a tan."

"That's what I call standing by your man," I said.

"You think I'm being selfish, don't you? Do you have any idea what the last thirteen years have been like? Of course you don't. Our marriage is like no other marriage in this world, unless you include Kuwait and those other countries. I have no say in anything. No money of my own. Everything I need I must ask for. I just want to get away. I need to unwind. I need to think."

"Think about what?" my mother asked.

"My future."

"Your future?" she echoed, faintly.

"Yes."

"Exactly which part of your future?"

"That part which concerns Leon and me."

"Your marriage?"

"Yes. My marriage."

"You have to think about your marriage?"

"That's right, Mom. I want to decide whether I continue living this senseless life or whether I make a clean break."

"Break?!" my mother exclaimed.

"Divorce," Julie answered.

"Divorce!" my mother thundered.

"Yes. Divorce," Julie stated with authority.

"No one gets a divorce in this family," my mother boomed.

"I might. I just might do it."

"You don't love him any more?" my father asked.

"Love? I'm not sure if I ever really loved him. I think I was in love with only one thing — his potential to earn money. Well, I think that that's finished for quite a while."

"You married him only for money?" my father said.

"You never loved him?" my mother wanted to know.

"I'm not sure. I just need to get away and think."

"A divorce settlement will make you super rich, right?" I said.

"Yes. Very. At least I think."

"How do you think Leon will take this?" my father asked.

"He'd burn his own mother at the stake rather than give away half of his investments."

"So you'll have quite a fight on your hands," I said.

"I won't. My lawyer will."

"That's right. I forgot. You'll be in Hawaii getting a suntan," I said.

My mother, by this time, had left the room. I knew exactly where she was, even though I couldn't see her. On the couch in the living room, lying on her back, her eyes closed and a damp washcloth on her forehead. Silently moaning.

"Julie, your husband is in a nut house," my father said. "At least wait until he's out before you make a final decision."

"Daddy, I can't figure you out. You never liked Leon and now you're standing up for him."

"Julie, you don't kick a dog when he's down."

"That's the only way I can do it, Daddy. If he was still standing, I wouldn't have a prayer."

CHAPTER 44

When Julie's postcard arrived from Hawaii telling us that she was going through with the divorce, we all felt disappointed in her, as well as sorry for Leon. Sure, he was nuts and a lunatic and aggressive and arrogant and a pain in the rear end and selfish and snooty and even at times repulsive, but he was ours.

Who would we talk about? Who would we make fun of? Who would my father have to belittle? The only person in his life that he had an unkind word for — and now this was to be taken away from him. Who would Ellie laugh at? Her colleagues at work looked forward to hearing Leon stories with their coffee. And my mother? Would she be able to overcome the humiliation of a divorce in the family? Knowing her, she would hide out in the basement, in darkness, wearing black for six months.

I had known for a long time that my sister was a spineless fool, not interested in anything or anyone but herself – or, more exactly, her standard of living – but when she called my mother long distance to tell her that she had retained a lawyer to start the proceedings, I finally realised that my sister was not only an idiot, but she also would have the fight of a lifetime on her hands. If she thought that Leon would lie down and roll over while she split up his portfolio, she was more of an imbecile than I gave her credit for. And if Julie seriously believed that Leon would stay locked up — tax write-off or not — if he knew that someone was tampering with his money, not even the power of the government could hold him down.

I hadn't intended to visit Leon at the mental hospital, but when the urge came over me I didn't fight it. I was informed at the reception desk that Leon was tending the gardens in the back.

I found Leon in a crouch position in the middle of some rose bushes.

"Hi, Leon, how's it going?"

"What the hell are you doing here? You want to spoil everything?"

"I have news for you."

"What's that? The IRS is dropping all charges? They want to make me an honorary boy scout?"

"Not quite. Do you know where Julie is?"

"Honolulu."

"I... I... how do you know?"

"Why shouldn't I know? I told her to go."

"You told her to go?"

"Of course. What else should she do while I'm tending roses?"

"Then you know?"

"Know what?"

"About her plans."

"What plans?"

"Leon, Julie plans to leave you."

"Oh, that."

"So you do know."

"Yes. I call my lawyer every few days."

"You don't seem very annoyed by the news."

"I've mellowed. I think it's the roses and the fresh air and the endless mindgames I have to play with the moron shrinks here. Tires you out."

"What about Julie?"

"What about her?"

"Divorce, Leon. For chrissake, your wife is divorcing you. Don't you care?"

"Not particularly. Should I?"

"I don't know. I thought you loved her."

"Love? My, my, you truly are a fool. Here, have a rose, you romantic shmuck."

"You know, I came all the way out here to warn you. Why? Because in some bizarre, peculiar way I enjoy your company. Whatever anger I have bottled inside, you have a knack of letting it come out. There are times when I become nauseous just at the sight of you, but I am absolutely certain that if you weren't around any more I would be more miserable."

"You have a serious complex, Rudy. I could help you but psychiatry for me is finished. I'm officially retired from the profession. And, as for being a foil for you and for your family, that too is over. Get used to it."

He plucked another rose from his garden and handed it to me.

"In my own way, I enjoyed our talks, even though there was never much depth to any of your arguments, and I enjoyed your mother's gloating over my success and the lack of pride she had in you. It was all great fun. But who cares now? An era has come to an end."

"What are your plans?"

"No plans for the immediate future. What about you? Are you still driving your cute little truck?"

"No, I quit three weeks ago."

"If you're looking for a job, they need an attendant here."

"Not interested."

"So what are you going to do?"

"Write."

"Write what?"

"A book."

"Dreams die hard, eh?"

"I guess."

"You're still the fool, Rudy. You spoke into a tape recorder for three days and now you think you can write the Great American Novel."

"I can try."

"You can try till you're eighty. And then what?"

"What if I make it?"

"What if you don't?"

"Won't know until I try. I've already got one success under my belt."

"And Ellie is backing you up?"

"Yes. She believes in me."

"How long do you think that will last?"

"I like to think forever."

"What happens five years from now?"

"Five years is a long time away."

"So you think. I'll tell you what happens. Your marriage becomes dull, routine. You need money. You have children. You need more money. You become older. You need more money. Your wife becomes older. You need still more money. Just how long do you think $150,000 will last? Taxes have to be paid, so cut that figure in half. Divide by five years, that leaves you with $25,000 a year. Can you support a family on three hundred dollars a week?"

"Right now, I have no children."

"Right now, right now. Idiot! Can't you ever plan for the future? What happens if Ellie gets pregnant?"

"She's on the Pill."

"Accidents happen."

"Then I'll become a father."

"How will you be able to look at your infant and tell him or her that Daddy has no job and no likely prospects of getting one unless he drives a little truck? Do you think your child will be very proud of you? And when he or she begins school and the teacher asks, 'What does Daddy do?', you know what little Herman or Eunice will say? 'My Daddy drives a little blue truck and he would like to write a book.' And the teacher will say, 'That's nice.' But behind Herman's or Eunice's back, the teacher will snicker and think you're a fool. And so will all of Herman's or Eunice's friends. Are you prepared to put your child through that kind of humiliation? I'm surprised that Ellie would let you. I thought she had more sense than that."

"Obviously she's as much of a fool as I am. I guess that's why I married her."

"I know why you married her, but for the life of me I can't understand how she could marry you. She seems so sensible."

"She is."

"And practical."

"She is."

"And a realist."

"She is."

"Then what the hell is she doing with you?"

"Opposites attract."

"I should have married my opposite."

"You shouldn't have married anyone."

"What do you mean by that?"

"You screw people up. My sister was not such a bad person before she met you. After thirteen years, she's become greedier than you."

"That's not possible."

"Hard to believe, but it's true. She's even dreaming of cashing in on your life insurance policy, should you croak."

"You're sick."

"Not me."

"Are you serious?"

"Yes."

"Did she say so?"

"Yes."

"I can't believe it. She could actually live happily knowing that I was six feet under? I, Leon the lion – who gave her so much?!"

"Happily? She'd be delirious."

"Monster!"

"You created her."

Leon bent down. He carefully removed half a dozen roses from the bush and lovingly snipped off the thorns.

"For Ellie," he said suddenly as he handed me the bouquet.

"That's very nice of you, Leon."

"I do have feelings, you know. I'm not quite as heartless as I appear to be."

"Maybe you should show your feelings more often. It would allow we humans to relate to you better."

"Let's take one step at a time."

"You know, Leon, I think this place has done wonders for you."

"Let's not get sappy and preposterous. Right now I have to think. Tell me, does your mother still hate me?"

"She doesn't want a divorce in the family."

Leon smiled, then asked: "And your father?"

"He only wants what's best for Julie."

"Fair enough. Listen, meet me out front in twenty minutes."

Leon was prompt. He tossed his suitcases into my car and we headed back home.

"This is going to cost me a bundle."

"A divorce is going to rip you in half. What's better?"

"Getting Julie back is far more sensible."

"And cheaper."

"Absolutely."

"You'll never change."

"If you're looking for miracles, go see a shrink."

"I thought you had mellowed."

"I did. In there. But now I'm back in the real world. Vacation time is over."

"What are you going to do?"

"Liquidate a few things. Get the IRS off my back and then catch a flight to Hawaii."

"What are you going to say to Julie?"

"What do you think I should say?"

"Tell her you love her. That you're sorry. That you're willing to start over."

"Why should I have to apologise? She's the one who's divorcing me."

"Only because of what you did to her."

"Maybe you're right. In any case, whatever I've done I can undo."

"I wish you luck. She's become pretty headstrong."

"I know her weak points. It's just a matter of pushing the right buttons."

Leon turned on the radio. A Beatles tune was playing and Leon began singing along with it. When the song had ended, he lowered the volume and said, "Why did you do it?"

"Wouldn't you have?"

"Yes, but I thought you had scruples. At the very least, a conscience."

"I do. And I feel guilty about it, but I saw an opportunity. Finally, a chance to get ahead. My name, Rudy Petinsky, on a book."

"At my expense."

"Plaster would have written the book with or without me."

"That justifies it?"

"What do you want me to say? I guess I'm no better than anyone else."

I turned up the volume. I didn't want to talk. Yes, I had sold him down the river. True, Edwin would have brought out the book with or without me, but I could have said no. I could have said, "Sorry. Not this way."

I was just like everybody else. Selfish. Eager to get ahead. Me, little Rudy Petinsky, wide-eyed, idealistic, and naive, had turned into the kind of person I least admired – a grown-up.

Shit.